Evernight Publishing

www.evernightpublishing.com

LEGALLY BOUND

DEDICATION

AJ—Please don't kill anyone. Thanks for being everything I needed. This book wouldn't have gotten here without your insight.

Mistress Patty—for always letting me pick your brain when I need new kinky ideas, and everything else you do, daily.

The man—for understanding my crazy obsession, and for supporting me even though it takes countless hours of time away from you.

Jen—Thank you for telling me when shit sucks.

Lili—Thank you for helping me find the perfect faces.

Melissa—Thank you for letting me pick your brain on legal jargon.

Evernight Publishing—Thank you for giving me a chance.

LEGALLY BOUND

LEGALLY BOUND

Bound, 1

J.R. Gray

Copyright © 2014

Chapter One

Daniel Caplin, hazel eyes bloodshot, shuffled into the stuffy courtroom his usual twenty-five minutes early. Just under six feet tall, he really did nothing to maintain his current build. He knew his dark brown hair looked more disheveled than trendy this morning. At some point his partner, Jesse, would call him out about the thrown-together state of his clothes.

The room was worn from years of use as well as the hundreds of people moving in and out of the public building. Budget cuts always prevented things like the restoration of these overused facilities, but he was comfortable here. It smelled like fresh floor wax, the usual for a Monday. By the end of the week, it would change to convict sweat and cologne. He unbuttoned his suit jacket before he sat in the straight-backed chair. His intern had a stack of arraignment files piled at his bench, waiting. He groaned. It felt like every time he walked into work his caseload grew.

Jesse mouthed "Happy Monday" and faked tossing up a handful of confetti as he slipped behind their desk. In his mid-thirties, he was the older of the two of them. With his blond hair and blue eyes, in Daniel's opinion, Jesse was better dressed than any straight guy should be.

Their intern handed them each the new morning files. He skimmed the top one in his pile: a drug charge. As a city public defender, he saw hundreds of these a year. At least the work wasn't going to be hard, because he was too hung over to function like the adult he should be.

Looking over his partner's shoulder, he muttered, "What do you have?" If the man's cases were more interesting, he would beg, shamelessly if he had to, until Jesse traded with him.

Jesse snapped the file closed, almost mashing Daniel's nose. "No, you may not take this. It's the first good one I've gotten in six months." He held up his hand, cutting off the younger man's retort playfully. "I don't want to hear about how you have no life, or a boyfriend, and that you'll have more time for it than I will."

Daniel glared at him. "You just want to add to your workload so you have an excuse not to be home."

"Do you have a point or…" Jesse sipped his courtroom-contraband coffee that only his charm allowed him to have in a room that banned food and drinks. It was his usual iced coffee all year round, which was strange considering the current weather outside.

"You're lucky you pick out all my clothes, and I need you as a best friend," Daniel said, grumbling. "But still, to this day, I don't know how a straight man has better taste than I do."

"I have to make myself irreplaceable somehow." His partner flashed his perfect teeth in a grin.

"Will you at least tell me what it is so I can be jealous and live vicariously through you as I defend another boring drug case?" He laid his forehead on his stack of case files, hoping Jesse would feel bad for him.

"Alleged Grand Larceny." Jesse dangled the file in front of Daniel, his eyes glinting.

"I hate your smug guts." He raised his head and narrowed his eyes, about to utter another comeback when he heard the familiar shuffling of detainees being ushered into the courtroom. Daniel scanned them, looking for anything interesting to lift the dreary Monday, and his eyes went wide when they landed on the face of the man whose bed he had been in last night. "Oh shit," he said too loudly, drawing the attention of the bailiff. He waved her off, muttering, "Nothing."

"What?" Jesse hissed.

"I fucked one of our cases last night," Daniel admitted, knowing he would get it out of him one way or another. There was no point fighting his partner's excellent extraction skills.

"Which one?" Jesse asked, looking over his shoulder, way too amused.

He tried to nod subtly to one of the prisoners.

"You have to give me more than that." Jesse stood up and blatantly turned around to study the men sitting in the rows behind them.

Stiffening in his seat, Daniel tried to keep his back to the man he had seen every naked inch of, as well as had his tongue buried inside of, till the early hours of the morning.

"Dark hair, six feet plus, green eyes." He tried to speak out of the corner of his mouth so no one could read his lips.

"The one with the sleeve tattoo and the huge arms?" Jesse asked.

"Yeah," he answered in a low, sheepish voice.

"I knew it was that one. You so have a type." Jesse flipped back around to take his seat once more. He instantly went for the files, lifting up folders and setting the large stack right in front of him.

"What are you doing?" Daniel kept looking over his shoulder to see if the guy showed any signs of recognition.

"What's his name?" He didn't look up from the stack of files as he spoke.

"Rafael," he whispered as his face flushed just saying his name. "What are you doing?"

"Figuring out what your lay did," Jesse said, positively glowing by now.

"I really hate you," he responded, pulling at his tie and trying to loosen it.

"You'll thank me later." Jesse hummed, plucking out the file and flipping it open. "Oh, hot damn, you picked a good one."

Daniel snatched the file out of his partner's hands, his eyes going wide. Life just got a little more interesting.

All through the arraignment hearing, he found it hard to keep his mind off the previous night spent at Rafael's apartment. They'd had an instant connection. He groaned to himself as it became increasingly hard to focus.

"Do you think he did it?"

"Who knows, but how many innocent men do we represent?" Daniel's stomach knotted. He didn't want the allegations to be true.

"Good point."

They both stood as the Judge came in, his flowing, black robes having fit him better twenty pounds ago. Taking their seats again, they started going through the mass of new cases they had. When Rafael's name was called, Daniel winced but stood up before his partner could take lead on the case. Led to the seat next to them, their defendant and Jesse exchanged a few words.

"The charges are intent for solicitation, attempt to solicit, and violation of parole."

As the clerk read the charges, Rafael's eyes flashed to Daniel, making him unsure of his feelings that were someplace between dirty, turned on, and a hair disappointed in his own judgment.

Jesse explained that they were his public defenders. Rafael looked a little hostile and on edge, but Daniel gave him the benefit of the doubt, knowing he would feel the same under the circumstances. But he wanted to urge him not to piss Jesse off. He was a man to have on your side, not against you.

Daniel remained standing while the Judge read over the file. He glanced over at the opposing table and was taken aback when he saw the District Attorney, Arthur Brunswick, himself standing there instead of one of the Assistant District Attorneys.

"Objections to bail?" the Judge asked, clearing his gravelly voice.

"Sir, Mister Argon has proven he is a repeat offender, and once released, he will be back to his old tricks." The D.A.'s tone was almost bored.

No one laughed at his thinly-veiled joke, but the point he'd made, even if in jest, would work on the Judge. Out of law school for only three years, Daniel was already the partner of the most senior, and well respected, public defender in their jurisdiction. But Brunswick had at least twenty years experience on him.

"My client has been meeting his probation requirements, and he has glowing reports from his parole officer. He has also never been convicted of solicitation," Daniel said smoothly, noting that the previous two charges had been pled down to disorderly conduct and public indecency.

"I see that." The Judge nodded, tapping his pen into the file for a moment, then looking up at the D.A.

"The fact remains," Arthur started, not even looking over at their bench, "that this man has proven twice in the last six months that he can't be a functioning, productive part of society. I think he should be remanded until his plea or until after discovery. I will be pushing for mandatory jail time in this case."

Daniel glanced back at his partner, who looked up as the D.A. made his statement. Knowing the expression on Jesse's face, it was clear he was thinking the same thing—Brunswick had a bug up his ass about this case.

"Sir, he's not accused of murder." Daniel took a breath, searching for the words he wanted to use. "He's not a flight risk. He has a perfect record of being present at all his hearings, and I think it's excessive to hold the man when his crimes are still alleged." He held back his smile, even as Jesse grinned at him.

"I agree with the defense. Bail is set." The Judge struck the gavel and quickly moved to the next case on the docket.

Chapter Two

Daniel pulled open the door to the detention center's small conference room. Tiny, with no windows, it was the epitome of depressing—the fluorescent lights giving everything a sickly color. The once white-washed, cinder block walls were yellowed and chipped. A rickety table with four chairs sat askew in the center of the room. Large, industrial tiles covered the floor and held bits of caked dirt in the corners, clearly pushed there by janitors who were too lazy to take the time to clean the room.

"Oh shit." Rafael's mutter was far too loud, and his eyes went wide when the two lawyers entered. He wondered why Rafael was so surprised. It wasn't like he wouldn't accompany his partner. Daniel wasn't the kind to shy away from things for convenience.

Jesse moved to take the seat across from Rafael, whose fingers were threaded together as he seemingly fought to get his reaction under control. Daniel took a spot in the corner, staying as close to the door as possible. They usually did interviews together, but he was riding a fine line and would have to take himself off the case if he wasn't careful. He knew that if things came to light about his relationship with the defendant, he would have to step aside because of the conflict of interest. There was no reason to taint the case until he knew for sure.

"Well, Mr...." Jesse looked down at the case file, "Argon. My name is Jesse Goldmen. This is my partner Mr. Caplin, whom you already seem to be acquainted with."

Daniel sneered at Jesse's back, the jest in his partner's voice clear.

"We're the city-appointed attorneys you requested." Jesse tapped his finger on the table, then went on, "While they're getting the paperwork for your bail ready, let's talk about your case. As your attorneys, Mr. Caplin and I are sworn to keep everything you say confidential. Do you understand what that means?"

"This is not my first time around the block," Rafael replied in his smooth, articulate voice, a hint of a South American accent matching his Latin coloring. It's what had drawn Daniel to him in the first place. He'd seemed like a businessman, not…. He shuddered, unable to even say it in his head.

"Well then." Jesse took out a pad of lab paper. Every other lawyer in Chicago used a yellow note pad, but not his partner. Jesse's OCD made him use graph paper, on which he wrote a letter in each box. "Let's talk about what you're being charged with."

Rafael shifted uncomfortably, like a caged animal. He turned his gaze to Daniel for the first time since they had entered the room. The glance was brief. Then Raf shook his head and tore his eyes away, making Daniel feel like he was the one on trial.

Jesse obviously took notice of the exchange, prompting him to add, "Would you be more comfortable if my partner left the room?" He looked between them.

"Of course, I'm sorry." Daniel kicked himself for not thinking of it first, but didn't really know if he should laugh or be embarrassed. Maybe he was preventing Rafael from being more open.

"No, the last thing I am is shy, gentlemen." Raf's face held a hint of a smile, curling over the corners of his lips as he looked over again. Daniel sat, more curious than anything else.

"Then tell us about what happened last night, please." Jesse had a sheen of sweat on the back of his neck, and he tapped his foot under the desk.

"I slept with your friend. I was quite sated, and it seemed he was as well. My compliments to him." Rafael answered with a grin. "Then, I went to work, and on my way home, I got picked up by the black and blue, handsome."

Jesse coughed before speaking. "For solicitation?" He shot Daniel an apologetic look as he said the words.

"Ding ding ding!" Raf cocked his head to the side, his accent thicker with his sarcasm. Daniel could only stare. This was a whole different side of this man that he hadn't experienced last night. He'd been all gentlemanly then.

"I have to ask." Jesse swallowed. "Sorry in advance, Dan, if it's out of line, but was Rafael picked up after you solicited him?" He visibly winced when he glanced back at Daniel again.

"No," both men chorused together.

Daniel glared at his partner. "I can't believe you think I would proposition a hooker." The words came out before he could stop them. Everything about this situation had him flustered and acting like he was green, when he was, in fact, one of the best public defenders in the city. After he got himself in check—again—he put on a professional face, determined to stick with it.

Jesse shrugged. "Some people get off on that. I'm not judging." He shifted, not making eye contact and looked back at the case file, muttering to himself.

"No offense to your public salaries, but you two combined couldn't afford me," Rafael added.

Daniel blinked, staring at the man that had bent him over the foot of a bed the night before, fucking him till he had forgotten his name. "We make pretty good money."

"My clients are at the top of their professions. Most of them are fortune-five-hundred earners, CEOs, and…oh…a prince." Rafael offered a smile, displaying his perfect teeth.

His expression remaining tactfully neutral, Daniel could feel the familiar arousal stirring in his gut. Through all this, the seriousness and awkwardness of the situation, somehow the notion that Raf was a high-priced escort…turned him on.

"Well, now that we have that cleared up, let's move on, shall we?" Jesse looked more uncomfortable by the minute as he tugged on the knot of his designer tie.

"You look much better when you're smiling, boy." Rafael dropped his tenor, changing to the voice Daniel imagined he used with clients.

That one word from him filled Daniel's mind with images—demanding images, feelings, and tastes—of the night before. His arousal stirred even more. It was disconcerting. He'd never had someone affect him like this. The room was hot, as it always was, but his face grew flushed. He had been the top in every other relationship he had been in, but with Rafael, it had been different. He shifted in his place against the wall, crossing one foot over the other to try and disguise his now-apparent hard-on behind the thin slacks he wore.

"I really don't want to know, do I?" Jesse rubbed his eyes with the heels of his hands.

"You don't." Daniel reached up to hide his grin behind his hand, then scrubbed it down his chin.

So much for professionalism. He felt like a school girl or…something. He didn't know.

Raf was watching him closely with his piercing jade eyes.

"Topic, please." Jesse tapped his pen on the notebook, returning everyone's attention back to the business at hand. "When you say you went to work, is it safe to assume you were soliciting?"

"I don't sleep with people for money," he snapped.

"You just said we couldn't afford you." Jesse raised one brow, stopping his pen's motion.

"I'm a paid Dominant." Rafael wore his smirk proudly, looking over and meeting Daniel's eyes to say the rest. "It's not illegal to beat people at their request."

Jesse looked over at him as well, and this time, a sly grin tugged on his lips. "Danny boy…"

Daniel held up his hands. "Whoa. It's not what you think, either. I didn't pay him for that. I didn't pay him for anything."

"Is someone going to explain this to me, because I feel like I'm missing out being married to Susie Homemaker," Jesse huffed, tossing down his pen in a dramatic tantrum that was not unusual for him.

"Do you want to fill him in, or shall I?" The words rolled off Raf's talented tongue.

"Look, I don't know anything about that side of things," Daniel mumbled.

Rafael licked his lips over. "Could have fooled me last night," he said playfully.

The shifts in Rafael's attitude were giving him whiplash. He kept seeing flashes of the man he'd been with last night as opposed to the pompous ass sitting in front of them.

"This is going to be a long case, isn't it?" Jesse pinched the bridge of his nose and sat back. "I can feel a headache coming on already."

Daniel's lips curled up. "Don't act like you don't love to hear about what goes on in my bedroom." The tension in the room seemed to bleed out. Their conversation, unprofessional or not, had him relieved.

"Don't make fun of a sexually-starved man. It's bad karma." Jesse pointed at him as he spoke.

He repressed any further comments that would embarrass his friend.

"Since you don't seem to be volunteering, let me explain." Rafael's intense stare gave Daniel the distinct impression that he was being undressed with each passing second. "I'm a paid Dominant. That means I'm paid to dominate clients…not to have sex with them."

"Does sex ever happen?" Jesse wrung his hands together.

"Does that matter?" Rafael shot back.

"Should it? Maybe not. But to a judge, it's going to look bad if you do end up sleeping with clients who pay you for your…services," Jesse explained, then exhaled slowly.

"I have slept with some of them." Rafael said the words with no remorse. It surprised Daniel, and it made him cringe. It was starting to become more clear, he'd slept with a prostitute. Even though he found something hot about the act of soliciting, in an erotic spank-bank fantasy in his mind, something about sleeping with someone who did that for a living turned his insides into knots.

"Is that what happened last night, Mr. Argon?" Jesse went directly back into lawyer mode.

Daniel knew his partner was masking his feelings about the situation and pegged him with a stare when the man straightened in his seat and stacked his papers.

"It's Rafael, and no, last night was strictly professional." His eyes shifted to the left as he spoke.

"This is the third time in six months you've been picked up for solicitation, Mr…. Rafael." Jesse consulted the file again just to make sure.

Daniel's eyes flashed wider. In his mind, three times in six months made their client guilty.

"Can we plead it out? I'll write a check for the court fees and see about having the public service faked." Raf sat back, putting his hands behind his head.

Daniel didn't like the type of people who tried to buy their way out of everything. He crossed and uncrossed his arms.

"I don't think you understand how serious this is...wait," Jesse stopped, putting the pieces together fast. "Why are you using public defenders if you can write a check for the fines?"

"I pissed off a cop, okay? Cop problems mean less business, less business means less cash in my pocket, and less cash in my pocket means my normal lawyer who charges six hundred an hour is a bit out of my price range." Rafael ran his fingers through his disheveled hair. He looked like a wreck from his night in lockup.

"Is this cop singling you out?" Daniel asked, finally moving across the room to take the seat next to his partner. He couldn't decide if Rafael was telling him the truth. The side of him that had felt that intense connection with Raf the night before wanted to believe him, but his analytical side was skeptical. It was easy to make up excuses and blame a cop—they saw it all the time. But hearing that struck a chord. It made the situation different, more about the job than his fucked-up feelings. It was something he could hold on to. After all, he'd really gotten into law to help innocent people. He felt for them. And right now, he wanted to believe Rafael.

"Yes, but there's nothing I can do about it. Can we just get this thing rolling?"

"If a cop is harassing you, we may be able to get all the charges dropped." Daniel took over the conversation. The situation seemed plausible, and Raf really hadn't seemed the type to him last night or even now as he sat in front of them.

"I like you, Daniel, and you would make a smoking-hot sub." Rafael leaned across the table, resting on his forearms. "I would like to see you again, but just because we had sex doesn't mean you can fix all my problems. I can handle it."

Daniel brought a hand up to his mouth. Rafael's words had struck too close to home, bringing out his helpful nature. After last night, Daniel realized that his submissive side was something he wanted to explore. Looking at the situation now, though, he had to consider that maybe, for Raf, it had only been about the sex. Could he be reading more than he should into the connection he thought he felt?

"My partner is right." Jesse pushed his way back into the conversation, ignoring the sexual remarks Daniel knew he'd have to explain later. "If all these pick-ups are because the arresting officer has issues with you, then we have a real defense here."

"He's never the arresting officer." Rafael blew out a breath, sitting back heavily. "It's not worth a fight."

"Then how do you know it's him?" He pursed his lips, and Daniel could tell by his friend's body language that he was not impressed.

Rafael looked between both of them. "Because when I told him I wouldn't be his Dominant anymore, he told me he was going to make my life hell."

Daniel just barely repressed his "Oh shit."

"Could this be an overreaction on your part?" Jesse asked.

"Right, overreacting. What other plausible reason can you think of for the constant arrests…unless I'm really guilty of hooking, which I'm not."

"I'm not convinced you're not," Jesse snapped.

"Hey. Back to the point," Daniel quipped, trying to cut the tension. "Do you have evidence of this?"

"No. It was a face-to-face conversation." Rafael's intense stare was on him now.

He felt like he was on a rollercoaster of emotions this morning. He'd gone from excited at the prospect of meeting someone new last night, to shocked, to turned on, to repulsed, to sympathetic, and now, he had come full circle. Maybe he was losing it. *I can't be the only one feeling this, can I?* There had been a connection between the two of them last night, he was sure of it. Raf was the first guy in a long time he'd felt that with, and he hoped he wasn't developing a thing for bad boys. He was at the point in life where he wanted something more.

"You're on probation for these two other charges, which is a miracle. A third is a ticket straight to the penitentiary." Jesse looked up, crossing his arms over his chest. "We can't help you if you're lying to us."

"I'm not lying. I pled to the other two because my lawyer assured me it was the only way I would get out of them with an officer up my ass." Rafael clenched and unclenched his fists. "With the evidence, there was no way to get around it. What would you have advised me to do?"

Jesse held his stare as he shuffled the papers in the file, then placed them all back together. "We clearly need a lot more than the hour we have set aside for council. But, Mr. Argon, let me be clear, you're facing jail time if you're found guilty."

"Fuck." Raf scrubbed a hand over his face. "But my other lawyer got me probation the last two times."

"But now, with two under your belt, that's not going to happen." Daniel tried to be nice about it, but the truth was harsh. "It shows a pattern."

"You have the D.A. on the case, and you can bet he won't let you plead it out. We got your bail set, if you can afford it. Let's get you out of here, and then we can set up a time to discuss your case." Jesse shifted in his seat and waited for the answer. Most of their clients couldn't afford their bail.

"I think I can manage it. I'm going to call my boss."

Chapter Three

"I'm going to add sleeping with a prostitute to my bucket list just so I can cross it off." Daniel sipped his Guinness, side eyeing his partner. It was better if he made the joke instead of letting Jesse get the first jab in. He'd fucked up, and he would handle the consequences. It's how he was about everything—move past it and get on with life.

"You're making light of this way too easily." Jesse pressed his face into the counter of their favorite bar.

"What else can I do?" He shouldered his friend playfully. "No regrets."

"I don't know." Jesse loosened his tie without picking up his head. "But the more pressing question is, you bottom? Since when?"

Daniel's cheeks flushed, and he looked away. "Just for him. It was kind of…" He didn't know how to explain it.

"My mind is blown." Jesse turned his head and stared at him. "Kind of?"

"Shut up, curious fucker." Daniel refused to make eye contact, keeping his eyes on the rows of bottles along the back wall. "Why do I share details of my sex life with you?"

"Because I'm your best friend."

"I need new friends." He sipped his beer, not looking forward to the rest of the week. As if today hadn't been awkward enough. Rafael had struck a chord with him—hit on an irrational part of him that took away all common sense. He was going to have to find a way to put his attraction, and that spark, out of his mind so he could focus on the case and seem less like a blundering idiot.

"Now, tell me. I love Priscilla, but you see more action in a weekend than I get all month. Indulge your best friend." Jesse gave him puppy dog eyes.

"I will never understand why a happily married man wants to know about my gay exploits." Daniel took another drink of his beer, trying to ignore the pleading face.

"Because hearing about any sex is better than going home to my wife who's decided that sweatpants are better than regular clothes, and that charity events, where anorexic trophy-wives show off by spending their husband's money, are more important than anything else."

Daniel chuckled at the excuse. Jesse had a different one every day of the week. "Do you realize how pathetic you look?" he asked as he ordered a second round, since both their beers were getting low.

"Good. Maybe it's working then."

Daniel checked his watch. "You're going to miss dinner."

"I'm stuck in court, like I am at least three nights a week. Damn budget cuts, bigger caseloads, and overworked judges. Chicago is terrible."

"I like Chicago, and this time of year is pretty." The crisp fall weather had just set in, and it meant he'd no longer swelter in his suit. "If you were as honest with her as you were with me—"

Jesse interrupted with the wag of a finger, not lifting his head. "I don't fuck you, so I don't have to lie to you."

"Good thing gay marriage isn't legal here. If that's the way it works, I never want to get married." Daniel shoved him.

"Stop stalling. You know I'll get it out of you." Jesse never sat up. Instead, he kept his head down, running his hands over his dirty blond hair and messing up the style it had held all day.

"Next time I go out, I'm making you come with me." He joked as their beers arrived.

"Priscilla would kill me if I came home smelling like those gay clubs you frequent." Jesse tried to sip his beer with his head still down. "I wonder if I could get a straw over here."

When the bartender came over with a bendy straw, Daniel pinched the bridge of his nose. "Don't indulge him. He's like a puppy, and now you'll never get him to leave."

"I think it's too late for me. Plus, he's cute. I can't help it," the girl laughed. She saw them at least three times a week, and his partner's antics were nothing new.

Jesse held up his ring finger like he was flicking Daniel off. "Cute but with a tiny shackle."

"All the good ones are married. Let me know if you need anything else." She walked off to fill other drinks.

"I don't know how you do that." He looked between Jesse and the cute bartender.

"What's that?" Jesse stuck the straw into the side of his mouth to slurp his beer.

"You get every single girl to check you out, ask you out, and then you turn them down."

Jesse had a close-cropped goatee and always had a light dusting of scruff on his jaw. He was ruggedly handsome and very well dressed, and his five-year-old behavior seemed to draw in women by the dozens.

"It's the hair. Now spill."

Daniel let out a soft groan, starting to recant the previous night's events.

"But you're a top?" his friend interrupted.

"How many times do we need to clarify that point?" He twirled his empty beer bottle around, not meeting the other man's gaze.

"I thought you hated giving up control?"

"I did."

"Carry on."

Daniel finally finished describing everything in perfect detail.

"He walked you home?" Jesse perked up.

"He wasn't so…" He searched for a word.

"Sir Douchey?" his partner offered.

"Standoffish. He was charming. We had a pleasant conversation, and his accent…" Daniel shrugged one shoulder. "I saw glimpses of that today, but it seemed like he had walls up that weren't there yesterday."

"If that cop bit is true, he has reason not to trust us, Dan. We're part of the system that's fucking him right now." His blond hair obstructed his eyes a little.

"But we're on his side." Daniel rubbed a hand over the back of his neck, knowing his partner was right.

"Cops should be on his side too, but it looks like he's taking it up the ass from 'em, and not in a good way." Jesse mumbled his words a little.

"Well, this sucks. He's the first promising guy I've met in awhile." He sighed, realizing it was true as he said it. "I hope he didn't get picked up after he walked me home."

"Well, shit. A guy can't be romantic anymore without getting his balls busted." Jesse flagged the bartender over. "Another round?"

"Sure. You make me sound like the woman in this situation." Daniel set aside his empty bottle.

"In this instance, you are the woman." Jesse slapped a twenty down on the bar.

"That's the last time I tell you about my fun," he said as he begrudgingly grabbed his next beer.

"No, that will last me all week with the wife. Don't take away the only action I get." Jesse gave him a pouty lip.

Daniel blinked a few times. "Disturbing, by the way, and that may work on your wife, but I think you look stupid." He downed half his beer in one draw.

"I have no other unmarried friends. I need something," he grumbled.

"You don't think it's a little strange you use a gay man's trysts to fantasize about while fucking your wife?" Daniel gave him a pointed look.

"I change the gender in my head." Jesse flashed a huge grin and made a jacking-off motion with his hand under the bar counter. "Who said I use it with her."

"I'm going home to forget this day ever happened."

"See you bright and early for your hooker's first council meeting."

Later that night after his partner had gone home, Daniel began the short walk from the bar toward the conjoined courthouse/holding facility where he had left his car that morning. Since he had done most of the work on them, he knew Rafael's papers would be processed any minute now. Stalling outside the building, he hoped to run into Rafael. His breath caught in his throat when he saw the man in question walk out of the place. Crossing the street before he could stop himself, he pulled his trench coat closely around him as he darted through the rush hour traffic. Horns blared, drawing Rafael's attention to him as he made himself look like an idiot crossing the street in the middle of traffic.

"Only a lawyer would bolt across a busy street in front of a police station and not worry about a jaywalking ticket."

Daniel looked around sheepishly. "They like me too much to arrest me. I've gotten them more guilty pleas than their scare tactics."

"You advise your clients to plead guilty?"

He looked dingy from his night in jail, but the attraction was still there on Daniel's part. "If they're guilty and I can get them time off for a plea or lesser charges." He shrugged one shoulder.

Rafael stared at him for a moment as if he saw right through him. "Enough of the small talk. Why are you here, boy?"

He swallowed back the lump in his throat. He liked when Raf called him that. "I just got off work and saw you." He felt bad about lying, but coming out and saying he wanted to hook up again would be considered misconduct. He couldn't risk his career for his heart.

Rafael eyes dilated as he stalked closer. "Don't lie to me."

"How do you do that?" Daniel held his ground. He wanted to see the man he had gone home with. Wanting to experience that same feeling he'd had last night, the more he and Rafael went toe-to-toe, the more he worried that maybe it was only a fleeting memory.

"What do you really want?" Rafael's voice was a harsh whisper as he leaned close.

"Do you need a ride home?" he forced out.

"There are cabs for that. What do you want?" Raf demanded, his eyes dark and intense as he leaned closer still.

"Do I have to say it?" Daniel's shoulders slouched forward, and he dropped his overwhelmed gaze.

"Yes." The word was icy, and he could still feel Rafael's intense stare.

Due to the late hour, the area around the government building had mostly cleared. Plus, the cold stopped people from lingering outdoors.

"I want you to fuck me again. I want to be tied up. I want…" To be controlled.

Raf inched closer to bite the exposed skin under his ear. "And I want to flog your pretty skin and leave my marks on you."

Excitement grew, and Daniel began to think that maybe there was a chance of getting some part of last night back.

"But as my track record suggests, I shouldn't trust people who are in a position to fuck me." The flash of the man Daniel had been with was gone, and the wall was back in place.

"Where is the guy I went home with?" He had to know.

"You don't think as a paid Dominant that I can't be charming when I want to be, do you?" He reached out, signaling a cab.

"I think this is an act to protect yourself." He stalled as Raf turned to head toward the cab that had pulled into the No Parking zone.

"I've learned to have many faces to protect myself." Rafael slid into the back seat and slammed the door.

Daniel cursed himself for even trying.

****

Rafael looked back at Daniel as the cab pulled away. Regret hit him hard in the chest, but he kept quiet. He had a bad habit of trusting people he shouldn't, and this time, it might cost him his freedom. He had to stop focusing on relationships and start focusing on work and the only person who had ever given him a fair shot: George Siris. Ironically, that was the very person he was currently disappointing with this mess as he missed night after night of work. He gave the cabbie the address of Amenti, the BDSM club that George owned.

A no-show last night, without explanation, he would be lucky if all he got was a tanned ass for it. George was a sadist, but he was the only man who had ever been kind to him after leaving the foster homes he'd grown up in.

The last thing he wanted to do was face George sober after a night in jail, and the prescription bottle that sat on his counter at home came to mind. It would have been easy to nip home and grab it before he went to the club, but it would take him half an hour or more out of his way. With city traffic, it was time that couldn't be spared, especially if he hoped to see clients tonight. Plus, his boss had an uncanny way of knowing when he was strung out. He clenched and unclenched his jittery hands. The tragedy in all of this was that he had really liked Daniel. He was like a breath of fresh air in the darkness he was used to. He was smart, sexy, and a natural submissive, even if he didn't know it.

But he kept seeing the same scene play out in his head all day. He knew lawyers and cops were chummy—he watched enough Law and Order to see how they scratched each other's backs. All it would take was a favor like all those cops had done for Detective Lance McCoy, and then his legal team would turn against him. If he told them too much, or got too close, it would just bite him in the ass like it had with the cop.

Running his fingers through his messy, dark hair, he couldn't wait to be able to shower in his private room at the club. Positive he smelled like vomit and sweat from the cell he had sat in all night long, he cringed even remembering it. By nature, he was a neat freak, and the holding cell, nicely put, was a breeding ground for the cesspool that was Chicago.

The cab pulled up at the nondescript warehouse that was out of place on the north side of the Boystown area, but the exclusive cliental knew what it housed. The rest of the city figured it was a zoning mistake. One thing Chicago had going for it was that people minded their own business. With the city's rich history of shady businesses, they'd learned to look the other way. He tossed some cash at the cabbie and climbed out into the breezy night. It wouldn't be long before snow covered everything in sight. The leaves were already falling off the trees and clogging the spaces between cars parked on the street.

He scrubbed a hand over his face, half hoping George wouldn't be in yet, and walked through the side door. Making it all the way down the hall and to the much-needed shower, it wasn't until he was standing under the hot spray before he heard the door to his private bathroom open. The shower doors were clear, but he didn't bother getting out or trying to cover up. Neither of them had any shame, and they'd both seen the other naked in one aspect or another.

"I see you choose to show up to work when it's convenient for you." George didn't have to raise his voice. He was scary enough at a normal volume. He stood in his usual custom-made, Victorian era suit with knee-high military boots. The cut of the suit fit his perfectly-muscled body like a glove. It displayed all of his best qualities, from his piercing blue eyes to the dusting of gray in his hair and close-cut beard. He was stunning for a man half his age, let alone one in his early forties.

"McCoy got me again. Well, one of his lackeys did." Rafael rinsed his hair and flipped the water off. When he stepped out, George handed him a towel. "Thank you, Sir." He ducked his head in a slight bow, a gesture of respect for the most senior Dominant in the city.

"I thought that had all been worked out three months ago." There was a hint of growl to the man's voice.

Raf kept his eyes downcast as he dried himself. "Apparently not, but my new attorneys show some promise," he lied. He knew he was screwed, but his drained bank account made it impossible to do better.

"It's time to bring charges against McCoy. If you don't, I will."

Rafael bit his tongue, trying not to interrupt. "I did, Sir. I told the lawyers this time. I need a letter from you, please. I think it would help them believe me."

"It's been sitting in your desk drawer since the last time you were arrested." George turned to go, then cast a dark glance over his shoulder. "There is nothing more to this? He's still after you because I kicked him out of the club, correct?" Raf could tell his mentor hated himself for causing this issue, but he couldn't tell him the truth. George was big on trust but not so big on forgiveness.

"Yes, Sir, it seems he's taken it on himself to try and get to you through me." It was a half-truth, but he really thought he could get away with it. He would succeed if his public defenders didn't turn on him, and well, if they did, he would be in jail anyway.

"Use the letter and get this taken care of, or I'll step in." He walked from the room, his boots clicking on the hardwood floor as he moved down the hall.

It seemed that George had always had a soft spot for him. He was the best friend Rafael had ever had, and it was killing him to keep lying to him. He felt as if he was barely keeping his head above water, all because of one stupid mistake. Trust had always been hard for him, and after putting that trust in someone other than his boss and having it backfire so badly, it made him never want to do it again. It was looking like that instant of trust was going to cost him his job, his freedom, and his best friend and mentor.

He left his bathroom, and went into his adjoining private playroom. Pulling clean clothes from the closet, he dressed quickly in his usual leather pants and tight black tank top. Once done, he went to the large desk off to the side of the room. With the letter in hand, he called down to the girl that worked in the club's office. He had her send the letter, along with the cell phone records he had printed and a note, by courier to Daniel's address. Then Raf put on a face and went to work.

LEGALLY BOUND

Chapter Four

Back at the county offices a few days later, they had half an hour to talk before court.

"Did you get the letter I sent you?" Rafael could almost feel the dark circles under his eyes. It had been almost three days since he had slept. Usually, after a night of work at the club, he would sleep all morning. This court thing and spending time in lock up was making that impossible, and he couldn't stop working. He needed the money. George had already advanced him the amount to cover bail.

"I did, and I have an idea." He wore a wicked grin, but when Raf raised a questioning brow, Daniel said nothing.

Jesse sat reading a thick stalk of papers, and he kept glancing at the open books spread around him. Not acknowledging, of their presence, he sipped coffee, something Rafael considered unusual in a room that had large "No Food or Drink" signs posted all over it.

"He always like that?" he asked in a whisper, jabbing his thumb toward Jesse.

"He's reading precedents." Daniel took another glance at the file in his hand and shifted. He seemed uncomfortable, which, in his opinion, wasn't good for a lawyer. "Plus he doesn't like to talk till he's had his contraband coffee."

He raised a brow. "Contraband?"

"One of the bailiffs wants in his pants, so she brings it to him every morning."

"Isn't he married?" He thought vanilla people were better about keeping cheating under wraps.

"That's the odd thing about it. He is, tells everyone, but women still fawn all over him. In the three years I've known him, I haven't been able to figure it out." Daniel shrugged and checked his watch.

"I can hear you two nitwits," Jesse grumbled.

That shut them both up, and Rafael straightened his suit, ready to sit through another boring motion hearing that he was sure would result in nothing. His public defenders had said they were trying to get more time for discovery, but he didn't see it happening. With his past, he knew no one would give him the benefit of the doubt. The two men talked in a hushed whisper now, but he couldn't make out their words. That was fine because he was waiting for McCoy to get to them and turn them against him anyway. No one was as nice as Daniel seemed on the outside.

Zoned out by the time the Judge came into the courtroom, Rafael was half a beat behind everyone as they stood. He sighed, putting that down as another blunder that was going to discolor the man's opinion of him. When he sat down, though, he sat up a little straighter, trying to give off his best air of sincerity and turning off the domineering aspect of his personality the best he could. Submissives enjoyed being talked down to, and many of his clients were high-powered public officials. But they only enjoyed such treatment behind closed doors, not with witnesses.

Daniel took the lead again starting up opposite the D.A. He looked calmer than he had at the first hearing, and Raf only half-watched as his lawyer entered in a "not guilty" plea. Thinking he'd heard the D.A. scoff, he stiffened, pushing down the hot flash of anger that ran through his veins. He was tired of being judged before any of the evidence was even presented. The truth was, that even if he'd done it before, he wouldn't sell himself now. Without a doubt, he was worth more than that to himself.

"Your Honor, can we meet in chambers to discuss a motion of a sensitive nature?" Daniel asked when the judge questioned if there were any housekeeping matters before he set a date for the trial.

A sensitive nature? Curious about what his lawyers had up their sleeves, a flash of panic hit Rafael. Were they trying to have him declared insane? Or were they withdrawing themselves from the case because of the one fling he had with the guy? Jesse had said it didn't matter what had happened between them, and hell, the man had tried to take him home again a few days ago. Was Daniel quitting because he hadn't put out? That thought made him feel cheap. It made him feel like McCoy did, like he wasn't worth more than what he could offer in bed. Anger twisted in the pit of his gut as the Judge agreed. When Daniel and the D.A. stepped forward to follow the Judge into chambers, he moved to get up and go with them.

Jesse grabbed his sleeve, preventing him from moving without making a scene. "Trust him," he muttered, and Rafael felt the command behind his tone.

****

Daniel was nervous as he took a seat next to the Arthur Brunswick in the Judge's chambers. Of those in the room with him, they probably had a combined fifty or more years experience in trials to his three. Jesse had insisted he argue the point since it was his idea, but that didn't make it any less nerve racking. He tugged at his cuffs, waiting for the Judge to speak.

"What was so important you dragged me in here?" Judge Stenson asked in his gruff tone.

Daniel knew it was an act the man put on to keep things short and to the point. A way to cut through the normal bullshit most judges had to put up with daily. He had always found Stenson to be on the side of justice, which he was glad about now that he was on such an important case for them.

Brunswick stared smugly, but he pushed it out of his mind, choosing his words carefully. "We have reason to suspect that our client is being unjustly harassed by officers of the 19th Police District and some of the 23rd." The D.A. and the Judge gasped, but he went on. "I have a motion here for a cease and desist while my partner and I come up with sufficient proof for our case."

"That is a pretty strong accusation, son," Stenson barked.

"I agree, but my client has a standing history of being harassed that we think we can prove." He could feel Brunswick's eyes boring into him.

"I think this is nothing but a pathetic grasping at straws of a man who has long had trouble following the laws of the city. Now he's trying to slander the good names of the men and women who serve to protect us from the likes of lawbreakers like him." The D.A. had an edge of anger to his tone, but Daniel was sure it was planned. He wanted to look outraged that anyone could even suggest a thing. But it wasn't something new. All the residents of the city knew the cops and everyone else could be, and were, bought on a daily basis by the gangs and the mafia. It wasn't called the Windy City because of the winter weather, but for the swaying officials who could be blown from side to side with enough cash.

Judge Stenson studied him hard. "And you think you have the means to prove this?"

"I am confident that the past six months of harassment my client has received will be brought to light by corroborating witness testimony." He was praying he could get said testimony, now. It wouldn't be easy. The first battle would be to make sure McCoy stayed off Rafael's back to keep him out of jail while he and Jesse did their investigation. This way their client wouldn't have to suffer behind bars for something he was innocent of. Plus, Jesse had an ace up his sleeve.

"I think it's outrageous to drag the 19th's name through the mud while this kid goes on a witch hunt to clear the name of a prostitute," the D.A protested, almost on the verge of yelling.

"I think you both know as well as I do," he said, "the corruption that has run rampant in this city, and is it really that far out of bounds to believe that a cop would abuse his power to make an ex suffer after a bad break up?" They both were staring at him, and Daniel suppressed a grin. Score one for us.

"You have proof that Mr. Argon had a relationship with a police officer?" Judge Stenson asked.

He set a file on Stenson's desk and placed his hand over it when Brunswick reached for it. "I have the statement of a club owner who is an upstanding member of the community as well as my client's cell phone records ready to enter in as evidence."

"It shall be so entered."

As Daniel lifted his hand, the Judge picked up the file and immediately scanned the evidence, then looked up at the D.A. "I'm inclined to side with the defense on this one, Arthur."

"I would also like a gag order put in place so these proceedings are kept confidential till our investigation is complete. My client has good reason to fear retribution from the officer responsible, as well as his supporters, if this gets out," he added hastily, still avoiding the eyes of the D.A.

"I agree. Arthur, you'll keep this under wraps. Not a word to the officers as you prepare for this case as well." Stenson eyed the D.A. "You and I both know more serious charges could come out of this, and you don't want to go down on the wrong side of it."

"I understand, your Honor," the D.A. conceded.

"You both are dismissed. I'll call the Chief of the 19th District myself and have him call his boys off your client by my order."

"Thank you, sir." At this point, Daniel couldn't hide his grin anymore. It was a small victory, but one nonetheless, and he wanted to go shove it down Rafael's non-trusting throat.

****

Rafael couldn't believe his ears as they talked outside the courthouse. "He really can't come near me?"

He was in awe over what Daniel had done for him. It was the first good news he'd had about the whole thing in six months. The feelings he had been trying to hide all hit him in a rush, and he let out a laugh, but stopped it quickly. It felt like a million pounds had been lifted off his back, and he could finally let some of the tension roll off his body. Maybe Daniel was on his side. Maybe there were people he could trust other than George. He wasn't going to blindly believe it, but the possibility was out there, at least.

"No he can't. If you're harassed on your way to work or on the way home, or you see them following you, call me right away, and I'll go to the Judge." Daniel wore a smug grin while he kept his hands tucked into the pockets of his slacks, and Rafael couldn't help himself as his eyes drank in Daniel's form. The man's cocky demeanor was unbelievably sexy. As the stress bled off him, he could focus on some of his other urges—like having this man on his knees in front of him.

"Thank you." He held Jesse's gaze, giving him a smile. "Now, how do we go about getting more proof? I don't think my boss' statement will be enough."

Jesse looked between the two of them and faked a gag. "Can you two wait to flirt till I'm out of earshot?" He shuddered. "In answer to your question, Mr. Argon, no, we need a witness that can substantiate your claims, someone McCoy asked to do his dirty work or someone who overheard him asking his flunkies for the favor. Otherwise, it's just hearsay. We need hard proof that these cops were told to follow you. The jaded lover thing was great to get the order in place, but now we need to back it up to get you off."

"Got you." Rafael bit down on his lip. He knew that wouldn't be an easy feat, and he knew from personal experience. Cops, just like the BDSM community, were very protective of their own, and the chances of getting someone to snitch were going to be nearly impossible. The vise tightened in his chest as the stress crept back in.

"Don't get discouraged. Jesse has an ace up his sleeve." Daniel reached out like he was going to touch him, but then he pulled his hand back.

"I'm off. The old lady is going to kick my ass if I miss our weekly dinner at Daddy's." He rolled his eyes and kicked at a pebble as he turned toward the parking garage.

"I think I was wrong about you," Raf said. He wasn't very good at apologies, but he knew he owed one to Daniel.

"This has nothing to do with what happened between us, and I want you to know that. I care about my job. Besides, Jesse and I believe you," Daniel assured him while rubbing the back of his neck, a look of uneasiness crossing his face at the same time.

Rafael took a step forward, closing some of the space between them and dropping his voice. "I think I believe you. I want to take you up on your offer from last night if you're still interested."

Daniel's eyes widened a little, and he nodded slightly, but then hesitated. "Maybe it's better if we don't…" Daniel let out a breath and chewed his lip, looking into his eyes.

Keeping a neutral face, a skill perfected through years of practice as a Dominant, Raf wasn't used to rejection. "All right then." He thrust a hand into his dark hair. "Have a good night."

Sticking his hands in his pockets, Daniel rocked up on the balls of his feet. "Let me give you a ride home at least." Hesitating, the guy rooted around in his pocket until his hand finally reappeared with a key.

Rafael's quirked his brow. "Don't feel like you need to do that. I'll catch the next cab." He looked up to the traffic-filled streets, headlights shining in every direction. It was going to be hard to find an open cab right now.

"No, I insist. It won't put me out. You're not far from me." Daniel started to cross the street toward the parking garage, but Raf hesitated.

Daniel looked over his shoulder and gave him a slight grin. "Even if you don't trust me, you can, at least, believe I'm not going to kill you."

"All right, but maybe I should call someone after that statement."

Following closely behind him, they crossed the street to a Jeep. "If you feel you need to, handsome." Unlocking the car with his key fob, Daniel let him slide in.

Rafael raised a brow, locking eyes with Daniel as a hand reached toward him, and he was more than a little disappointed when the man only flipped on the seat's heater. The fact that he liked getting busy in public places where the risk of getting caught was a strong possibility had always been part of his problem. It had led to one of his arrests, but he wasn't going to tell Daniel any of that. After the man's hand lingered on the switch between them, he felt fingers brush over his thigh just before they returned to the steering wheel.

"Sorry. I figured it would help you warm up faster." He adjusted his seat and put the car in drive.

Raf lifted his hand to set it on Daniel's thigh, but then thought better of it. The man had told him "no," so how many ways did he need it spelled out? Instead, he flexed his fingers against the cold and tucked his hands under his legs to warm them.

The drive was a little awkward for him. It was odd to sit next to a guy who had turned him down. He was never good at small talk, and he always seemed to come off standoffish when he tried. Finally, the car pulled up in front of his home, yet he remained seated, looking over at Daniel.

"I guess I'll see you in the morning," Daniel said, as Raf finally reached for the door handle.

The mixed signals he was getting from the man were confusing, and here he thought he was pretty good at reading people. "Bright and early with your charming partner." He knew he should just go, but his hand seemed frozen on the door.

Daniel reached out, pretending to pick a piece of lint off Rafael's coat. "Try not to go out of your way to get arrested." There was a sly twinkle in his eyes.

"I figured I'd go seek out a few cops and egg their cars. Nothing out of the ordinary." He leaned into the odd gesture so that their shoulders were touching.

Daniel dropped his gaze to their connected hands before moving to set his palm on Rafael's knee. "I feel like there is something unresolved between us. It's making it hard to focus."

"I agree." He turned in his seat a little, bringing them closer together.

Daniel looked up at him. "Maybe we should try and fix it…" His voice trailed off.

He leaned in so that his hot breath blew across Daniel's cheek. "How do you suggest we do that?"

Daniel swallowed, causing his Adam's apple to bob in his throat. "Let's go inside," he said softly.

Rafael brushed his lips over the other man's, pushing all the thoughts in his mind out. He didn't want to think tonight. He wanted to feel the way the way he had the other night with this guy.

"Do you want that?" There was power behind his lowered voice. Inside, he wasn't even sure he wanted Daniel to say yes, but he had to ask or he wouldn't sleep tonight. He wasn't the type to pass up opportunities. Plus, he had, for the most part, decided that this was a good idea, that this man could be someone he actually trusted.

"Yes." Daniel's voice was hardly more than a groan.

"Yes?" Rafael placed his hand on Daniel's hip.

"Yes, Sir."

His mouth went dry when the response was accompanied with a warm body leaning in even closer. After the way he'd acted before, he hadn't really expected that kind of an answer. "What do you want?" he said playfully.

"You're not going to make me say it, are you?"

"I want to hear it." Raf brushed the scruff of his cheek over Daniel's clean-shaven one.

"I want you to invite me inside." When Daniel turned his head, soft lips skimmed over his skin.

"Is that all?" Pushing for an explanation, he slid his hand further up Daniel's thigh and felt the man shiver.

"Yes...No."

His head was spinning. This man seemed to be just what he needed—someone that took his moods and temper in stride. It was an odd feeling to be wanted this way—for himself—instead of being wanted for the services he provided. He pushed it out of his mind, though, not wanting to jinx things. He tried to convince himself that this was nothing more than a repeat of the other night. It would be something that allowed them both to blow off steam. He knew Daniel was too smart to get involved with someone like him for long term. People like Daniel ended up with other men with the same status. They ended up having pristine houses, dogs, and weekend date nights. Rafael knew he would never fit the bill there. He waited on the next answer.

Daniel pulled back, gazing at him with his hazel eyes. "I want to stay the night."

"Follow me."

LEGALLY BOUND

Chapter Five

Rafael was uneasy as he led Daniel into his place. He wanted to be sure he was making the right choice about trusting him. It was hard for him to let anyone into his life, but it was getting impossible for him to ignore the feelings he had when around this particular male. Once inside, he flipped on the lights while chastising himself for not having more control. Now was not the time to take on and train a new submissive, but there was something about Daniel he couldn't say no to. Hell, the man didn't even really know what he was getting into, yet. For all Raf knew, this was just a phase for this guy— a fling. He'd be gone after he got what he wanted. When he turned back around, he found Daniel hovering by the door.

"How does this work?" He shed his coat, and Rafael moved to take it from him.

"You mean with me being a Dominant?" He considered his answer as he turned away to hang the coat. This wasn't like him, and he hated his own indecision. The man was his lawyer, and he'd be pushing it if he tried to make him more than that. But he wanted to push it.

"Você será minha morte. You will be my death, you know," Raf muttered, earning him a raised brow. "I can, and did, have vanilla—normal—sex with you, handsome." Putting the drama out of his mind, he turned back to the man, wanting another night before he'd have to behave. He was determined to enjoy Daniel now that he was here, for however long he was here, and damn the consequences.

"You can't tell me what we had was…vanilla."

Raf sensed how uncomfortable he'd become. With one brow raised, he felt Daniel's fingers nimbly move over his chest. He liked the man's boldness. Just like his cockiness, it suited him.

"It was 'in-between.' Did it turn you on?" It was hard to focus with Daniel's well-manicured hands on him.

Daniel looked up at him through his dark lashes and nodded.

"Speak," he commanded.

"More than anything I've ever experienced."

The words stirred a primal need deep within Rafael. There was something about training Daniel that hit a chord. He wanted to show him, to teach him. His chest grew tight, and he could almost taste the male's submission.

"Upstairs, on your knees at the foot of my bed."

Daniel dropped his hands from the buttons on Rafael's shirt and headed upstairs.

Unable to control his feelings, Rafael talked himself into his decision to indulge just this one night before all hell broke loose tomorrow. He removed the rest of his outer clothes and took to the stairs to have the "boy" do the rest for him. A soft moan passed between his lips when he saw Daniel sitting, balanced on his heels, with a perfectly straight back. The male's eyes downcast, he didn't lift them when Raf stroked his fingers down his spine.

"Sit up on your knees and undress me." He stood before the kneeling male near the edge of the bed.

Getting up on his knees, Daniel finished what he had started downstairs.

He watched as the man unlaced his leather shoes, then slid them off his feet. His socks were next before those expert fingers moved to his belt. The contact caused

Rafael to start to stiffen beneath his jeans, his hard-on filling his pants making it hard for Daniel to undo the clasp.

Abandoning his work once he had the fly spread open, Daniel buried his face in Raf's groin. He closed his eyes as he unbuttoned his shirt and let his head loll back. Daniel's mouth worked over his cock through the revealing cotton fabric, nipping and biting playfully. By the time he was free of his shirt, his pre-cum had soaked a spot on his briefs. Then, Daniel's fingertips tucked into the back hem of his underwear, dragging them down with his pants.

When the kneeling male licked the inside of his thigh, Rafael knew what he wanted. But he was going to wait. "Stand and let me watch you remove your clothes."

Daniel's hands shook, but he did as he was told, obviously taking his time to expose himself in a slightly dramatic move. He drank in the hard lines of muscle adorning Daniel's abs as well as the deep cuts of his hips where they dipped into his slacks. He'd seen hundreds of men and women naked in his profession, but never had he seen one as perfect as Daniel. He was long and lean with the body of runner. None of the over powering muscle so many men liked, but he wasn't small by any means.

Daniel ran his hand down his own stomach, tip-toeing his fingers across his naked waistline. Rafael was captivated. He exuded top, but his submissive side was so beautiful. Rafael wondered if the male would be able to switch.

"Like what you see, Sir?" The way the words were said felt like a taunt.

"You should watch your tone." Raf curled his large hand around his own base, stroking himself for the man to watch as a sly smirk adorned his lips. "Or maybe you need to be punished." He let his brows bounce.

"Yes, Sir." Daniel lowered his zipper and, in one motion, swept off his slacks and boxers, leaving himself fully exposed.

"I want to watch your pretty lips on me, boy."

"Yes, Sir." The man dropped down in front of him once more. Without hesitation, the man's tongue met his skin, eliciting a groan from Rafael.

Exploring Raf's sac and hilt before flattening his tongue, Daniel stroked up the underside of the shaft. Then he kissed away the clear fluid pooling on the tip before taking him into his mouth. The warmth made his toes curl as his dick was shoved to the back of Daniel's throat. When the male swallowed around his thick head, the amazing talent earned a groan. Energy pulsed through Raf, and he rested his hands on Daniel's shoulders while Rafael's hand wrapped around his girth at the base, stroking into each swallow. The world around him vanished, and the void was filled by pure sensation—wet lips, suction, a hand on his thigh, and a tongue laving over every vein.

He opened his eyes to watch Daniel's lips stretch over him, holding his gaze as he swallowed around the cock filling his throat. Starting to feel the familiar tingle of his release building, Rafael realized he was way too good at this. "Fuck, stop," he ordered.

Daniel groaned as he backed off, disappointment showing on his face. "Sir?"

"I don't want to cum just yet. I want to mark your beautiful skin."

His eyes flashed with something he couldn't read. "Please, Sir."

But as he read more of the emotions that crossed his, Rafael could tell he had never been beaten. "Go stand next to the bedpost."

Daniel moved before he even finished his sentence.

God, he would make a good sub.

He knew he shouldn't want like he did—shouldn't feel this way about a guy he'd just met. But Daniel seemed to be everything he wanted, and more. He walked up and skimmed his fingers over the curve of Daniel's ass before bending at the knee to extract a case from under his bed.

"Hands over your head." Taking a long breath, his senses tingling, Rafael flicked the latches and pushed the case open.

He chose cold, steel cuffs and hooked them onto the ornate rings on the top of the bedposts. He'd bought the bed for this very reason. Securing one hand, then the other, Daniel was now on full display for him.

Daniel's chest expanded with his heavy breathing. Coming up from behind, Rafael wrapped his arms around him, pressing their bodies together—the gesture surprisingly tender. He could feel smooth skin against his. It was hard for him to put into words how he felt about this individual right now without leaving himself open to hurt, so he indulged in this small, innocuous show of intimacy.

"Are you okay?" Rafael whispered.

"Nervous, but it's the good kind," he admitted.

"I love when you're honest with me. It's very important to me, and I require it at all times." Rafael returned to the case, brushing his fingers over the instruments of his profession. "You sure you want this?"

"Yes." Daniel cocked his head as if trying to see what was happening.

He chose a flogger, one with a wide leather head that made a nice sound against the skin. "Say termo if you want me to stop, okay? That will be your safe word."

"Yes, Sir."

"Repeat the word."

"Termo, Sir."

Rafael smiled. Daniel's pronunciation of the Portuguese word was near perfect. The flogger was light, and it twirled in his fingers with ease. Lifting it, he stepped behind the man and saw him flinch.

"Relax." He teased the leather over the male's skin.

He struck lightly, making sure to cover the whole area he planned to hit, warming up and desensitizing the skin. Daniel's back pinked, but he remained quiet.

"Doing okay?" He smacked Daniel's ass hard with an open hand, then pulled back, poised to strike. "Remember your safe word?"

"Yes." There was an edge of annoyance in the response.

"Sir…" Rafael reminded him. He loved the teaching aspect. His voice was stern, but the way Daniel's body reacted was worth the reminding.

"Sir," Daniel repeated with indignation. This time the words were definitely spoken with a taunt.

It wore at his resolve to go slow, and his arm flew forward. The leather hit skin, causing Daniel to cry out. The sound he'd made laced with the thwack of the flogger went right to Rafael's cock. The male's head slumped forward to press into the iron of the bedpost. There was a nice red mark in the center of his back where he'd been hit.

"Doing okay?"

"Mmmhmm." The only reply.

Rafael didn't correct him. Instead, he laid the flogger over his back in quick succession—five, six, seven times. Not hard enough to do any real damage, only to give the man a taste. He grunted and moaned with each hit. Pausing momentarily the light sheen of sweat that had formed over Daniel's skin glistened in the low light. His back was striped with light pink lines from the toy. He took a quick second just to enjoy the sight. Daniel was perfect, from the cut of his muscles on his lean body to the way he held himself, stiffening and settling back before each strike as if he had to remind himself to relax.

"Sir?"

"Doing okay?" He teased the tip of the flogger over the reddened skin.

"Amazing, Sir." His voice was higher and laced with a sigh.

Daniel seemed lost in euphoria, and Rafael knew that tone of voice well. He figured Daniel was getting his first taste of sub space.

Working over him, alternating hard and soft strokes, the boy never uttered his safe word. After another ten minutes, Rafael returned to his case and found a spreader bar and a cock ring. He strapped the bar to Daniel's ankles and snaked his hand around to clamp the ring in place.

"Let's see if we can't make that better." He bit down on the place where the male's neck met his shoulder.

When he pulled back, his cock throbbed at the sight of his teeth marks marring Daniel's skin. The lube was close, and he needed it. He coated two fingers with it, sliding one into the male's tight ring of muscle. The bound man pushed back onto his fingers as much as he could.

"Good boy." Pumping his fingers in and out through the tightness a few times, it took a bit before he could get the second in. Soon the puckered entrance was coated in lube, ready to be taken. "Do you want me inside you?"

"God…please…anything…" Daniel gasped when Rafael scissored his fingers, cutting off his speech. "Please. Inside me. Now."

"That is not the way we ask, boy." He twisted his fingers and leaned in to bite a path along the arch of his willing subject's shoulder.

"Sir, sorry, Sir."

The gasps spilling from the man's lips told him that he was close. With a kiss to Daniel's spine, he withdrew his fingers.

"Maybe I should leave you here awhile to think on it." Rafael made quick work of the condom, tearing open the foil and slipping the latex ring over his straining erection. Daniel whimpered and begged, and it made him move slower, savoring the moment. "Poor boy, so new. I won't punish you any further." As he said the words, he let the male feel his swollen tip press into his entrance.

"Thank you, Sir."

Upending the bottle of lube over himself, he continued to tease the boy with his tip, dipping inside the tightness, then pulling back to massage around the rim. Once they were both glistening with fluid, Rafael started to ease into the opening.

"Such a good boy. You just earned your own release." He rocked his hips, working his cock into Daniel and wishing he could see the parade of expressions cross Daniel's face as he took all of him. Daniel's forehead slammed forward, and a low, animalistic hiss left his lips. Raf winced, knowing the man would have a bruise there from the iron post.

Daniel's ring clenched down around his cock once he'd slipped past the vise squeezing his shaft.

"Goddamn," Rafael moaned, wrapping one arm around the male's waist and his other around his neck.

Bucking hips begged wantonly for more. "God you feel so good…"

Raf could tell Daniel had bit his tongue when he clenched his teeth cutting off his words. He leaned closer to say, "I like hearing you. It's okay." He tightened his arms around his lover and started to drive his hips into him.

Daniel pulled at his cuffs and fought back, writhing against him, asking for more with his body.

"You're going to be sore tomorrow," Rafael grunted after a gasp tore from his lips. He knew they both would have bruises.

"I don't care, Sir," Daniel panted, pressing his ass back to meet Raf's thrusts, stopping only when Rafael's cock was fully seated.

They both stilled for a moment, and he enjoyed the sensations surrounding his dick. Rafael swallowed hard, controlling his impending release. There was something about this man that set him on edge and pushed him too close to the line. Daniel flinched when Raf's chest bumped into the spray of bruises on his back.

"You feel incredible, so tight," he reassured the bound male, flicking his tongue up the male's spine.

Daniel was bent slightly at the waist, hanging from his arms, spreading himself wide open for the taking. The image spurred him on, and Daniel's reactions only fed his need.

"And you feel…God, like I could die happy. I'm so full." The words were punctuated with an enthusiastic backward thrust.

Rafael let himself go, slamming home with everything he had, his balls slapping into Daniel's ass with each pass. He lost himself in Daniel's cries of pleasure.

"God, yes, harder…" was moaned in repeating succession—chanted, almost like a prayer.

"Ask me if you can cum."

His lover's whole body clenched in his arms, his toes curled, and his hands balled into fists. "Can I cum, Sir? Please."

"Yes."

Daniel complied, spilling long ropes of cum that painted the bedpost and floor with his seed. His moans sent fire racing through Rafael's gut, and he pumped into the tight ass three more times, fucking him into the metal post. The way the man's body tightened around him, snagging on each vein of his cock, pushed him over the edge, hurling him into ecstasy. His knees went weak and pleasure licked up his spine as he filled the condom while the tight ring he was buried in milked every last drop from him.

Panting, Raf sagged against the smaller man and laid his cheek against his shoulder blades. He could feel his lover's ass still softly pulsing around his over-sensitive length, and he could hear the pounding of both their hearts. He wanted to stay here, just like this, hiding from the real world. He couldn't get enough of Daniel when they were this close. He knew it was dangerous to get so attached, but it only seemed to get worse as he fought it.

When he was completely spent, he untied Daniel, helping him down onto the bed to stretch out. He went to the mini fridge in his bathroom for ice and came back with it and his aftercare kit, climbing onto the bed to join his man. Reclining out beside him, he kissed him slowly and tenderly, setting the ice over his chafed wrists. Daniel winced away from the cold, but Rafael was persistent in holding it to his red marks.

"Don't fight it. You need it," he urged, whispering into Daniel's lips until he stilled. "You were so perfect up there. Wow."

"I did okay?" The question sounded hesitant.

"More than okay. You're a natural." Raf took another slow, sensual kiss before sitting up. "Roll over to your stomach."

Daniel complied, and he got a look at the damage that had been done to the man's skin. It was dusted with light bruises, and the sight made Rafael hard again. He gently rubbed the aloe over the marks, and then applied a layer of vitamin B cream.

"What's that for?" Daniel's voice sounded like he was still floating as his head dropped to the sheets—his muscles slack and relaxed.

"It will help you heal faster." Raf bent down, kissing the bite marks he had left, then applying the cream to those, too.

Daniel shifted, adjusting the ice pack on his wrists. "I should get home. We have an early morning meeting with Jesse."

"Stay," Rafael whispered, kissing under his lover's ear and pulling back to stare intently into his eyes. He'd betrayed himself with the word, but he didn't care. He wanted to be the Dominant for the night and take care of his submissive, even if he had to give him up in the morning.

"Are you sure?" Daniel sounded unsure.

He knew things could never work between them, that Daniel was just scratching an itch, but he wanted it here and now. "I am. You can drive me to the courthouse in the morning." He pulled Daniel in by the hair for another kiss. After that, they stayed there exploring each other until they were both too tired to keep their eyes open.

****

Morning came way too fast for Daniel. He tried to roll over but was restricted by a set of strong arms holding him in place. His lips curled into a smile. It felt so good to be wanted and cared for. He didn't want to let himself get too attached, though. The bed sheets crinkled as he moved to slip out of Rafael's embrace. He needed a shower and coffee in order to process rational thoughts, or he was going to have a real hard time with his "poker face" in front of Jesse.

He stepped under the hot spray and heard the shower door open. Rafael stood naked before him, with his hair rumpled and sticking out every which way.

"Can I join you?" Rafael raised a brow, and Daniel's eyes dropped to see that the man was ready to go for "round two." Clearly, today was not going to be his day…or was it?

Chapter Six

"Here's the plan. I'm going to go in first, and you're going to come in about five minutes later." Daniel had been plotting the whole way over.

"Why do I feel like I'm back in high school, lying to my mother?" Rafael leaned over to bite his shoulder.

Daniel winced, a mixture of pleasure and pain forcing the memories of last night front and center. "If we walk in together, Jesse will give me the 'I'm very disappointed in your ethics' look and demand a later discussion. You have no idea of the slide shows I've had to sit through." He rubbed his hand over Rafael's thigh. He knew it could never be more than a fling, but his feelings were getting away from him. He wanted more. In fact, because of the seriousness of the case, whatever they were to each other had to stop the minute they walked through the doors. He should have stuck to his guns last night. Temptation was so hard, and he was starting to understand drug addicts a little better.

Rafael gasped, smacking a hand over his chest. "Are you ashamed of me?" He wiggled his brows playfully, and Daniel was almost dreading his return to his standoffish nature in front of his partner. He wanted to know why Raf had built such high walls around himself.

He could tell by Rafael's smile that he was faking the hurt. "Yes, very. It's not good for my image to date BDSM hookers."

Another gasp filled the car. "Paid Dominant. God, you're supposed to spin my image in a good light. You're my lawyer."

A finger ran along this inside of his thigh while Rafael glared at him.

"Because to 'vanilla' people, 'paid Dominant' sounds better?" Daniel shot him a skeptical look as he pulled into a parking space behind the city office building.

"Good point. But I've converted you to the dark side now, so you have to find a positive spin."

He felt Rafael's fingers trace over the outline of his dick. "Stop that. It will be impossible to hide a hard-on from Jesse." The words came out only half-heartedly as he bucked his hips up into the touch.

"After all the down talk, it seems to me you need a punishment." In a flash, Rafael's fist closed around Daniel's length and squeezed.

A mixture of pain laced with arousal shot through him, and he groaned again. "Sorry, Sir," he said, pressing his head back into the seat rest.

"It's too bad I can't train you." Rafael's thumb stroked over his tip, making a wet spot in the material with his pre-cum.

"I know, Sir," was all he could manage.

"Go be a good boy and get me out of this." Raf released him and unbuckled his seatbelt, then got out of the car.

Hitting lock on his key fob, Daniel took a slow, deep breath. "See you inside in a few?"

"Yep." Rafael had a half-smile adorning his lips that he couldn't place. He ignored it and made his way toward the entryway.

Ditching his coat in his office closet, Daniel walked in and sat down at the conference table, only to find Jesse already sitting there. He was leaning back in his leather office chair with his fingers laced behind his head.

"Later than usual," Jesse said curtly.

He shifted uncomfortably under his partner's gaze and checked his watch. "I'm ten minutes early."

"Yes, and you're usually twenty five minutes early." Jesse's eyes never left him as he folded his hands together on the conference table.

"Traffic." Daniel took a copy of the case file and buried his nose in it. "This the new discovery?" he asked, trying to change the subject.

Jesse ignored him. "Have a wardrobe emergency?"

He put the file down and glanced at his tie, shirt, and then his jacket. "Did I spill something on myself at breakfast?" He tried to keep his expression neutral and play it off, but he knew that wouldn't work with his partner.

"Forget what you wore yesterday?" Jesse raised both his blond brows, still looking unamused.

"Did I wear this suit yesterday?" The straight man, of all people, would notice he wore the same suit two days in a row. He cursed himself.

"You did, and that shirt, and that tie." He waved a finger at him.

Daniel just stared, and Jesse stared right back. Seconds ticked by, and their stand-off was only interrupted by Rafael yanking open the door to the conference room like he owned the place. There was a twinkle in Raf's eyes and an amused smile on his lips. "Morning boys. Am I interrupting something?"

"Nothing at all. Have a seat." Jesse looked at their client, then paused, looking between the two of them before returning his gaze back to Daniel.

He shrank back under his partner's intense scrutiny. "What?"

"What is that bruise on your forehead from?"

Daniel lifted a hand to his head and made a garbled sound in the back of his throat, and Rafael burst out laughing.

"I hit my head." He shifted and picked the file back up.

"On what?" The intense, icy-blue glare didn't leave him.

"Um…" When nothing came to him, he started to panic.

Jesse gasped and nearly fell backward. When he righted his chair, he leaned forward and smacked both hands down on to the table. "You two fucked last night, didn't you?"

"No!" Daniel looked around, grasping at straws.

"Your morning-after poker face sucks balls." Jesse shook his head, hitting the table again. "I knew you would never wear the same suit two days in a row. You're gay, for God's sake."

"That face really does suck," Raf agreed, taking a seat. "You need to work on that if you're going to try and pull anything else over on your partner."

"I understand you're a single man needing to stick it in every hole, but come on. Can you leave the defendant alone?" Jesse grinned triumphantly.

"So much for your plan to have us come in ten minutes apart." Rafael gripped himself under the table for Daniel's benefit and rolled his eyes at him. "My balls nearly froze off."

"I give up on life." Daniel dropped his face to his arms and mumbled, "There is not enough coffee in the world for this."

"Speaking of, do you have any coffee? Your ass of a partner wouldn't let me stop. He said it would be," Raf made air quotes with his hands, "'suspicious,' if we both had Starbucks cups."

"More suspicious than his poker face?" Jesse wore a coy smile.

"Nothing is a bigger give away than his poker face. In fact, we should get him to play Strip Poker one day." Rafael shot a glance at Daniel.

"I hate you both," he muttered, still too happy about the night before to let Jesse diminish things. He recalled the look of the bruises in the mirror this morning, and the way his backside burned a little.

"In all reality," Jesse put on his lawyer face, which he hated, and laced his fingers together, "you two need to stop seeing each other. It will only hurt our case if your cop buddy digs and finds out."

"I thought he had to stay away from me." Rafael's face fell, and he didn't make eye contact.

"Do you think that will really happen?"

Raf shook his head.

"I didn't think so. So you two need to be on your guard." Jesse flipped open the file sitting in front of him.

"Okay, I get it. How bad is it?" Rafael's eyes dropped to the file.

Daniel's heart sank into his stomach when he heard the man he'd been with for a second time last night agree. He didn't want to stop seeing the man. Rafael made him feel something he had never experienced before. He was not naive enough to believe in love at first sight, but there'd been an instant connection with Raf. It was possible that he would never find that kind of connection again—so fast and intense—and it was being ruined by circumstances out of his control. He blew out a long breath. Right was right, though, so he let it go.

"Well, we got the prosecution discovery this morning. It looks like Daniel's victory yesterday pissed off District Attorney Brunswick something fierce. He was out for blood before. But now he has a big issue on his hands he needs to disprove quietly before it becomes a media nightmare for him in an election year." Jesse took out his graph paper. "Daniel and I need to study this evidence and try to refute as much of it as possible. I didn't expect it so fast, but I'm guessing they are pushing for a fast trial, which means we need to hear your full story so we can get to work on this."

"Anything I need to do, I'll do." Rafael looked over, pressing his tongue into his cheek, which made him wonder if there was something more behind the words.

"Well, this is your third offense in six months. I found out this morning that the D.A. is pushing for the maximum sentence." Jesse's expression was stone cold, his blue eyes giving it to Raf straight.

"Oh, shit. He can be a real bulldog, and he's trying the case himself," Daniel muttered, feeling horrible for Rafael. Trying to curb his emotions so Rafael wouldn't see them, he didn't allow the sadness he felt to show. It hurt knowing he would have to let the first man he had a connection with go because of something that was out of his control.

"What are we talking about? My other lawyer got me off with fines, community service, and probation last time because of overcrowded jails." Rafael looked between the two of them, a worry line forming in the middle of his brow.

"Frankly, last time you should have had a mandatory forty-five day stay. Your guy worked a miracle and pleaded it down." Jesse tapped his pen on the desk. A sure sign that his partner was annoyed with Raf's entitlement.

"For a second offense?" Rafael looked shocked before muttering, "No wonder he charged me so much."

Daniel nodded. "Because you pled down the first offense, they shouldn't have done that for the second."

"Wait," Jesse put a finger on a line of text in the file he had been skimming. "You were busted at eighteen?"

Raf's eyes widened, and he blew out a breath. "Yes."

Daniel's head snapped around, and he picked up his own copy of their client's file. All his doubts came tumbling back as he read about the man's first offense years ago for soliciting. He was numb. He was usually so good at reading people.

"When were you going to tell us this?" The anger was clear in Jesse's tone. "Now they have had this information days longer than we have." He grabbed the file to read it more closely.

Daniel sighed. Things were beginning to look very bleak.

"Actually then, this is your fourth offense, and the first one wasn't pleaded down?" Jesse sighed. "This previous solicitation works against you, and I bet my life on the fact that Brunswick will use this to prove a pattern with you, which totally screws our police harassment angle." He leaned back in the chair, pinching the bridge of his nose.

"But that was five years ago." Rafael reached up and pulled at his hair.

"You were eighteen. It counts." Daniel resisted the urge to throw the file down, and instead, simply laid it on the table. Even if Raf wasn't lying now and this cop was out to get him, the record still stood.

"The only good news is all the overtime this is going to require." Jesse glanced down at the scattered file and gave into his OCD, putting everything right again.

"Only you would see his freedom in terms of yours." Daniel flipped through the rest of the file, looking for any other possible surprises.

"Getting away from the wife is like a 'get out of jail free' card."

"And drugs?" The words were blurted out as he read the rest of the charges. Why he was so blind to Rafael? He felt like such an idiot for sleeping with him a second time. "The first charge involved drugs? Am I reading this right?" Shock overwhelmed him. He had felt such a connection, and had believed Raf's story so fully that he hadn't suspected there was more to it.

"Well, that would be why it wasn't pled down," Jesse scoffed. "You need to start talking, or I'm going to recommend you take the jail time. Stop wasting my time and effort with your lies," he said, crossing his arms, his usually playful face stoic.

"I used to hook before I found Amenti and George." Rafael slowly let his hands fall from his hair and looked over at them.

"I need more information," Daniel grumbled. "I thought you said it was all the cop who had it out for you?" He hated being misled. To him, it was just the same as lying. A pang of guilt hit him in the gut. Not only could he get himself in trouble with his misconduct with this defendant, but his partner too.

Rafael wrung his hands. "It is this time. I swear to you. I've been keeping my nose clean."

Jesse passed him another file with a side glance, which Daniel knew meant more. He was so angry, and the betrayal he felt cut deep. Resisting the urge to shove the file to the floor and storm out of the room, he would remain a professional and finish the case. He scanned the old charges. "You were brought in for solicitation and drug possession. You served a month because of the amount of meth you had."

Throwing his hands up in the air after reading the charges out loud, Daniel felt like he was trapped in an avalanche. Meth was not something to mess with, and these were serious charges with mandatory minimums in the city's war on drugs. It would go a long way in the D.A.'s favor to show the Judge that Raf was going back to old habits.

"I got into some bad shit when I was younger. My boss, George, helped me out, got me clean, and turned my profession into an honest one." Rafael turned his face to the ceiling, pushing his fists into his eyes. "I'm telling you, I don't sell myself anymore."

"So, you were a prostitute?" Daniel had enough of the back and forth, the play on words. All he wanted was the straight truth. And he wanted it now, even though it made him wince inwardly after saying it. Glad they'd used condoms, he still felt a little dirty and more mad than anything. Yet, somehow, he was turned on at the same time. He had to get his head straight soon, or he was going to lose it.

"Yes." Rafael answered. "Past tense. I used to be." He gritted his teeth and sat up straighter.

Daniel softened, seeing the resolve on Rafael's face. He'd seen a lot of liars, but this man didn't seem like one of them. Torn between anger and the connection he had felt, he drove his nails into his hand, trying to consider Raf's story. It was plausible, which was more of a problem than people would imagine. He could tell many stories about drug addicts using any excuse in the book. Working in his profession this long, his instincts were pretty good. He had learned to trust himself, but it seemed he couldn't now.

"You told us you weren't yesterday. You can't lie to us, past tense or present. We need the honest truth to put together a defense." Jesse took notes on his lab paper.

"I'm not now." Rafael set his jaw, and a glimpse of the Dominant that had been present the night before came back. "My lawyer assured me it wouldn't come up before, and I forgot about it. I was a kid, barely eighteen. That's not who I am anymore."

"Well, someone found it." Jesse shifted, brushing off his paper. "It was purposely kept out, which is why it somehow didn't get brought up at your last two cases."

"But now it's been introduced as a pattern to go against our harassment angle." The wheels in Daniel's head were spinning, and the more he put together, the more agitated he got. "Don't you see? This could really hurt us. Had we known, we would have kept the harassment under wraps and sprung it on them at trial, instead of giving them time to prepare." Kicking himself for that motion now, he hated making mistakes, intentional or not. But he couldn't have known.

He pulled the case file back and began to read, not looking up, while Jesse and Rafael spoke. "And it looks like you were on probation when you got arrested the second time. That causes a big problem."

"Fucking bastard, McCoy! God, I should beat the shit out of him for this, but he'd like it too much." Raf clenched his hands together. "He must have pulled my file and saw this. He started all this, and the motion you filed must have made him really mad. I'm sorry." He looked defeated. Daniel tried to hold on to the anger, because at this point, he couldn't let him get under his skin anymore.

"It's probable, so we need to go after him," Jesse pushed. "Our only out now is proving this, move forward, and make the best case."

"What can I do against a cop?" Rafael's face gave away what he was thinking. "He'll have been careful, too."

"We're going to have to figure something out," Daniel said. "He's got to have enemies in the district that want him out. Maybe someone overheard him asking for favors, since he was never the arresting officer?"

Raf shook his head. "No, he was never the arresting officer. The detective is too smart for that. It would make it too easy to trace back to him. I always saw him when I was being booked, though. He made sure to gloat a little."

Jesse wrote that down. "That's good. We can pull his time sheets to see why he was in the precinct when you were brought in. It's a start."

Wracking his brain to try to come up with an answer, Daniel just shook his head instead. "It's going to be hard to get a cop to talk about another cop in the same department, but maybe we can find someone in another unit that might have been around."

"I know where they hang out, there's a cop bar close to Wrigley Stadium. We can ask around." He took a new piece of graph paper and started making a list.

"What am I looking at if I'm found guilty?" Rafael directed the question at Jesse, but his fellow attorney hesitated, glancing at him first. "Don't look at him. I can take it."

"The D.A. is pushing for a mandatory six months, and that's if you're not still using." Jesse kept his eyes on the file while speaking. His partner hated delivering bad news.

Daniel wasn't shocked, though. This was the third strike in six months for someone the courts had been lenient with before, and considering Raf's history, it made perfect sense.

"Shit, you're serious?" The shocked Rafael put a hand over his mouth.

Jesse nodded. "I need you to answer some questions, and I need the full truth. The answers don't matter to me, but I need to know so we can come up with a plan."

"Okay." Raf's tone was flat, and he dropped his gaze to the floor.

Daniel couldn't get a read on Rafael's emotions.

"Also, you two have to stop whatever this is." Jesse stared him down, making a hand gesture between him and their client.

"Is it that really that big of a deal?" Rafael asked.

"Yeah, it is," Daniel answered. Had he known what he knew now, last night wouldn't have happened. He was ready to stop. "It makes me lose credibility."

"Daniel is also the best public defender in the state. If he can't work on this case, you have no chance," Jesse added.

Daniel felt his face flush a little as his partner continued.

"Look what he's already done for you by getting the CPD off your back. We can't have your cop buddy dragging down his name. I already have to take the lead because of what happened." The words were spoken pointedly to their client while Jesse continued to write.

"Oh." Rafael kept looking past Jesse to stare directly at him, really studying him.

Daniel shifted under the scrutiny, then shrank back and shrugged. "Sorry, I should have stopped it."

"How could any of us have known all this when I took you home that first time?" Rafael's voice was so low Daniel finally had to look up to meet the man's eyes, a frown crossing his face at the same time.

"Okay, first, are you using now?" Jesse interrupted their moment.

Rafael swallowed hard. "I do on occasion, but it's nothing hard."

Daniel put his forehead on the conference table. He could feel his partner's eyes boring into his back. "I didn't use anything with him."

"That better be true." Jesse glared and pointed. Daniel could feel it without having to look up. "You've put yourself at enough risk sleeping with our client."

Daniel knew his friend was clean as a whistle, and if the man ever found out he was lying about something that serious, it would end their friendship. Drugs had never been his thing. He stuck mostly to kinky hook ups.

"Daniel has never used with me. I just use a bit of weed here and there," Rafael confirmed.

Jesse crossed his arms over his chest with what could be described as the 'father approach' look.

"And an occasional Vicodin after a long night at work to help me sleep," Raf added quietly, slipping a hand into his pocket. "I spent ten years in and out of foster homes, then lived on the street for three, prostitution was the only way I was able to get by. I'm not proud of it, and of course, the drugs I was on at the time were worse, but my head was not in a very good place. Sleeping with grown women that want you for your fifteen-year-old body does something to you. But I'm not making excuses for myself."

"That's…" Jesse started.

Rafael waved off his partner's interruption. "I am explaining myself to Daniel so he doesn't hate me."

He could feel the man's eyes on him, waiting for him to lift his head.

"I was young and dumb. I've let some of my old stupid habits take over again, but I'm not hooking. I have respect for myself now."

When he finally lifted his head, Rafael's gaze held his. Daniel swallowed hard, feeling the truth in the words. Maybe he was stupid for wanting to believe this man, but he did. Grasping at anything, he didn't respond. He just held Raf's stare, grappling with the overwhelming hold the man had on him. What he really wanted was to forget everything—Rafael's past and his mistakes—and just feel what filled him when he looked into Rafael's eyes. But he didn't have that luxury.

"Well, you have a few weeks to get clean and stay clean." Jesse breathed out noisily, breaking them both out of their thoughts as he went back to writing. "That starts now."

"Why do I need to get clean?" A slight flare of his nostrils accompanied Raf's words.

Daniel had seen it many times. It was the defensive druggie behavior coming out. None of the addicts they represented ever thought they had an issue, even if their skin was rotting off their face. The anger suddenly came back to him. He never understood the repetitive behavior of addicts. "Because the first charge was drug related, and you were still on probation when you were brought in the second time. It could very well be relevant. The Judge could order a drug test because staying clean was part of your probation," he said with more bite than he realized.

"I'm going to need to call and talk to George." Rafael pulled out his cell phone.

"Now?" Jesse asked.

"Soon. I'll need a few days off to deal with this and maybe more cash when this is all said and done." Setting the phone on the table, Raf looked up at the Jesse.

"Back to the questions. When can we do your first drug test? If we can show you've been clean when we go back to court, it will help."

Daniel watched - his reaction.

"Well…how long does Vicodin stay in your system?" Their client kept his focus on Jesse.

"Three to eight days depending on height, weight, and fitness level. I'm sure my partner can tell us how good a shape you're in." Jesse glanced over, not even cracking a smile.

"Three days." Images of licking the male's very fit body came to mind as he spoke the words. Unable to get a bead on his emotions, he flushed cold with anger, then hot with arousal, then rocked with…stronger emotions. He feared he was in a little deeper with Rafael than he was comfortable with, and that had to change.

He had resolved to be professional and help as much as he could, and he'd not let his feelings extend past that. Now, he just had to figure out how to turn off said feelings that he knew he had.

"How do you know that off hand?" Rafael ignored his groan.

"Part of the job. These are things we deal with daily." Jesse wrote a few notes on his pad. "Detox and get back to me so we can do an in-house drugstore test, then an official one."

"Why do you have to an in-house first?" The fact that Raf didn't meet his eyes as he spoke made him wonder if the man was ashamed by his earlier admittance.

"Because if there is any record of a real one, and it's positive, the prosecution will find out." Delivering the news made Daniel feel bad. Rafael shouldn't have to deal with all this over a bad cop.

"Is that all?" Rafael asked.

"Nope. You'll need to be here for the rest of the morning answering our questions." Jesse got comfortable in his chair.

"I'm going to go order lunch." Daniel got up. His chest ached more than it should for a client. It was going to be more difficult than he'd imagined to keep his heart out of this case. Wanting to call his contacts to see what else the man was into, he had to know if this was finally the truth. Maybe a healthy dose of the truth would help him see the male for what he really was.

As he gathered his things, he glanced at Rafael. He had used up his chances with Daniel, and now it was time to find out for himself. Fool me once, shame on you, but fool me twice, and shame on me. The words his father had always told him suddenly filled his mind.

"Order me my usual." Jesse flipped a page on his pad.

"Will do."

When they all sat back down half an hour later, Daniel had gotten his head back on straight, and he needed it because Jesse was brutal with his questioning. He had never heard his partner hit a defendant that hard. It was starting to give him a headache listening to details of Rafael's sex life. His partner didn't let up for the next three hours, wanting to know every detail of what was involved with this prick cop and their client.

"So, let me get this straight. Your cop is a 'switch' that likes to sub only for you, which you can't prove. You helped get him kicked out of Amenti because he's a Dom that doesn't respect safe words. Right?" Jesse concluded, looking at his notes.

"That's the basic story." Rafael seemed calmer, which made Daniel relax.

"Why not give him a taste of his own medicine?" He asked, knowing enough about the lifestyle to respect safe words.

"Because I have respect for myself and my play, and I don't think it would work. It would just get me more arrests." Raf sat still, not fiddling or looking away as he kept answering the questions.

Finally, the lawyers were done with Raf and they let him leave, but the interview had left Daniel with more lingering questions.

LEGALLY BOUND

Chapter Seven

Rafael fingered the bottle in his pocket as he walked home. He had no one to call to help him through the hell that stopping the use of the drugs was going to cause his body. George would surely be there for him, but at the same time, he had too much pride to admit to his mentor that he had been using again. Plus, George could have a bad temper and would turn his back in an instant if he thought Raf had betrayed him. It wasn't worth the risk. He would have to weather this alone.

The wind whipped around him, blowing the colorful, falling leaves in every direction. George was going to be upset that he'd have to miss more work. He needed a good excuse. Maybe Daniel would write him a note? He chuckled at the idea that put images of playing doctor with Daniel in his head. He felt guilty about what he had done to the man. He had been so used to shutting everyone out, he had possibly blown a good thing by lying. But honestly, if anyone knew the full truth about him, they wouldn't want him. He knew how people looked at guys with troubled pasts who worked in the sex industry. He was better off alone. Daniel had been a taste of something he knew he could never have, and it was why it was so hard to let go.

George had taken Rafael under his wing five years ago, and he'd made him a lot of promises. King, as most people called him, was the owner of almost all of the BDSM clubs in the Chicago area. His hand was in every pocket in the city, and his contacts were unbelievable. He should have gone to his boss, in the beginning, with the truth about his involvement with McCoy. He hated lying to his mentor, but at the time, he'd thought it would be the easy way out. Never had he thought McCoy would go this far because of a bad break up. Boy, had he been wrong.

The truth was that he was also embarrassed about his drug past coming back. He didn't know anyone who had never used, except for maybe a few straight-lacers. If it wasn't alcohol, it was weed or pills. George tried to keep that stuff out of his clubs as much as possible, but it wasn't that easy.

Raf turned the pill bottle between his fingers. He could take the rest of the pills tonight, then start clean tomorrow. The idea was very appealing, even if it was just to get one more night of numb peace. He waffled with the idea and could almost taste the sleep the pills would bring. It had been hard for him to sleep without them. After the meth, when he had been truly clean, he was lucky to sleep two hours a night. That was why, in the end, he had started on the weed. The Vicodin had come later.

Stopping near a trash can on his walk home, he pulled the bottle from his pocket. Not sure if he could toss it, he hovered there for a long time while attempting to think through the situation.

He looked up to George like a father, and disappointing him would be a low blow. That fact alone kept him from going to the man when all of this came out. Without his boss' knowledge, he'd been seeing clients on the side, off the books. He wanted the extra cash, but knew he shouldn't have done it with McCoy, knowing the detective was bad news. Once George had kicked McCoy out of the club, he shouldn't have continued to see the man. But the guy had offered to pay him triple per session

Squeezing the bottle in his hand again, he reconsidered the idea of going to George. George was his best friend, but if Rafael came clean now, he would lose it.

Although, if he got tossed in jail, he could kiss George's help goodbye. His boss wasn't one to forgive once his trust was broken, and between the drugs and sneaking around with McCoy, he had done more than break that trust. He clenched his teeth together, hating himself for being so weak.

His mind made up, he threw the bottle in the garbage and hurried off before he couldn't resist the urge to retrieve it.

The next morning Rafael's head was pounding when he came to. Thunder hammered in his ears, and he could feel every beat of his heart along with the excruciating pulse of blood through his brain. The throbbing kept up, like someone was banging on the walls of his brain, trying to escape from the inside out. Rolling to his side sent a deep ache through every bone in his body. He didn't think cutting himself off from a few Vicodin a day would feel like this.

"Rafael?" He heard the words, but they were muffled.

When he heard the voice again, the drumming in his head made sense. Someone was at his door. Tumbling out of bed, he stumbled down the stairs as the world tilted and swayed around him. He fell into the front door and had to stand and breathe a minute before he could pull it open. A blurry Daniel came into view.

"What are you doing here? Your partner said we couldn't fuck anymore." Raf lurched, bending at the middle and holding himself up by the door jam.

"You're two hours late for our meeting this morning. My partner sent me to check on you." Daniel pushed past him, entering the apartment. He didn't move till Daniel half-carried him to the couch.

"What time is it?" he asked when he got the urge to vomit under control.

"Ten."

"Shit, I'm sorry. I was up half the night puking. I must have slept through my alarm."

"No wonder. You reek." The dark haired male walked back over to close the door, then took off his coat before he turned back.

"I don't need your pity. Tell Jesse we can go over stuff tomorrow." Raf closed his eyes. Each one of Daniel's words felt like the point of a chisel being hammered into his forehead.

Daniel crossed his arms over his chest. "Your addiction is worse than you said it was."

"It's not worse. I told you I took some Vicodin." He resisted the urge to cover his ears. Their conversation sounded like nails on a chalkboard to his sensitive brain. "Go, I don't want anyone to see me like this, let alone you."

"Maybe I want to help." The words held anger behind them, and he couldn't deal with that right now.

"No one wants to help. You just want me cleaned up for court." Rafael put his hands over his ears. "Can you talk quieter?"

Daniel lowered his voice. "Maybe you say that because that's how everyone has treated you your whole life, but I do want to help. I care." He moved to go, but then hesitated before asking. "What did your boss say?"

"I told him I was sick and needed a few days off." Raf dry-wretched again and put his head between his knees as he felt the couch cushion sink.

"Is that a good idea? You said you needed the money." Daniel ran his fingers down his back.

"I can't see clients like this," he managed after a few minutes. Trying to shrug the man's fingers off of

J.R. GRAY

him, he found it was too much work to expend the energy. He really hated fake pity.

"You need help." Daniel got out his phone and started flipping through his contacts.

"No." he ordered, and heard him shut his phone.

"Why not?" He moved closer as he spoke.

Rafael picked his head up to look Daniel in the eyes. "I can't afford it, and McCoy will find out."

"At this point, you getting clean might be worth the jail time."

He looked up and could only growl.

"Let's at least get you cleaned up and get some coffee in you." Daniel offered a hand. "We need to go see Jesse before he flips."

There it was. The male was only here because of the case. He wondered if Daniel often went this far to win. Maybe he was a 'whatever it takes' guy. It wouldn't be the first time someone had pushed him to do something just to benefit themselves. He was used to it by now. The sad part was that he had thought Daniel actually liked him that first night they'd been together. He let Daniel help him to his feet and limped toward the stairs. They made it to his master bath without incident. Daniel pulled open the door to the massive walk-in shower, and memories of their recent fucking flooded Rafael's mind.

"I don't think I can stand long enough to shower." He hobbled over and sat on the edge of the tub, reaching over to grab his tooth brush. Once it was loaded up with toothpaste, he stuck it in his mouth and continued on. "Sorry I'm sure I look like shit." Leaning over to spit in the sink, he tossed the toothbrush down, then looked back. "Little better?"

He chuckled. "Okay." Stroking a hand down his back, Daniel got the bath water running. "Let's get you undressed."

The gestures were so kind, they threw Raf off. It was nice to be treated like a human when most people would have treated him like the addict he was. The human contact was nice, and he leaned into Daniel, absorbing the comfort. When Rafael looked at him, he spotted the rock-hard erection behind his slacks. It took all his control not lean forward to rub his face against the aroused groin. The kindness being bestowed on him was more of an aphrodisiac than anything he'd ever experienced in kink.

It took some effort to get to his feet with Daniel dragging him up by his armpits. Once standing, Daniel knelt in front of him and stripped him of his sweatpants.

"You know, if you keep acting like my sub, I'm going to try and keep you." Despite his pounding head, his cock was at full attention.

"How am I acting like your sub?" Daniel slid his hands under his shirt, tracing his abs as he lifted it off.

"Undressing me and running me a bath." It was something he had never even dreamed of, nor thought he deserved.

"I thought this was for aftercare?" Daniel didn't step back once Rafael was naked.

"Yes, it can be, but you can also do it as foreplay to your Dom." Too weak to keep standing, he sank back down to the edge of the tub.

"Ah, sorry. I don't know the rules." Daniel felt the water and nodded for him to get in.

Tearing himself away from the man's touch, Raf pivoted and put his feet into the warm water. The broad shouldered male was there helping him into the massive tub. He stopped himself from uttering the words on his lips. He wanted Daniel in front of him, not for sex, but for the calm that filled him when they were close. It would feel much better to have the male's bare skin pressed into his chest, but he didn't ask. Daniel remained, shifting his weight back and forth.

"You should go," Rafael forced out.

"I know, but I don't want to."

"Don't leave." Rafael looked up at him.

****

Daniel's illusion of addicts was shattered. Rafael wasn't one of the drugged-out, pathetic men he dealt with on a daily basis. He was sick, and he needed support. When he'd walked in the door, he had been determined to be there as a friend, to help. But once he'd seen how bad his condition was, something changed. Every rational part of his mind said no, but with the stress of the case and the upheaval this morning, he needed to do this. He wasn't ashamed, either. An hour of carnal pleasure would take their minds off things and ease them both in different ways. He just hoped he wouldn't regret it. The shock of finding out everything he had yesterday still felt like an open wound, but it was hard to deny his feelings here and now. The command had to be obeyed.

It was a snap decision, but more time with Raf wouldn't break the bank, and it might just help them both forget. An hour of bliss would go a long way toward giving him the strength to deal with things, and he would put money on it that the man before him needed the stress release as well. He tried to convince himself that's all it was.

Daniel started on the buttons of his own shirt. In the meantime, Raf sat up, then picked up a lighter next to the candles around the tub and began lighting them.

Smiling to himself, he liked seeing this man's romantic side, even after being sick with withdrawal all night. He set his folded clothes on the counter, then turned to face Rafael.

"Come on in." Rafael flopped back with his eyes closed.

Daniel tested the water with a toe, then stepped in, disturbing the water as little as possible as he eased into the warmth. The heat spread through him, warming the chill in his bones. Raf parted his knees so he could sit between them. He rested his head back on a firm shoulder, and strong arms slid around his chest. He ran his fingers up the full-sleeve tattoo Rafael had on his right arm. It was an intricate design of patches of armor and chainmail. Exquisitely done, it must have taken hours. His other ink was hidden on the inside of his opposite bicep written in what Daniel assumed was Portuguese with an unfamiliar symbol. The stubble on the other man's jaw burned his cheek when he turned on a whim to kiss him.

"You make me calm, steady…" Rafael murmured into his ear, his tongue flicking over the shell.

His body shivered in response to his lover's tongue, grinning as he remembered how subspace felt. Denying that it was anything more than his need to feel good, he knew his thoughts shouldn't be going there. He couldn't allow himself to see Rafael as anything more, nor could he fathom how such simple gestures and words could make him feel this way. "And you set me free."

"It's my job to give you everything you need," Rafael urged.

"You do." Daniel turned again, catching his lover's lips with his. The kiss was languid, but intense, and it lit a fire inside his body.

The connection was undeniable, and he had never felt this way with anyone else. Rafael's hands roamed his chest and abs, dipping lower with each passing stroke, and heating up every patch of skin they touched. Daniel reached back and wrapped his hand around the back of Raf's neck, pushing his long fingers into his hair. It was exhausting denying the spark between them, even for twenty-four hours. He felt like he hadn't had much sleep. With a slight tug, he held their faces together. Rafael's fingers traced the line of his hip. Each beat of his heart hammered in his chest, and he was sure Rafael could hear it. It was a little embarrassing to want him this much when he was sure the feeling wasn't returned.

"We shouldn't be doing this," Rafael hissed into his lips. It felt like a blow to the chest that he didn't see coming. He didn't understand how this male couldn't feel what was happening between them.

For Daniel, it was more. It felt like he was denying a part of himself by staying away. "I know."

It was the middle of the day, and he should be at work deposing their client. But naked sounded so much better at this point. He knew he was smarter than this, but he just wanted this one moment where it was all right to feel—where he didn't have to be professional or in charge.

Rafael's hand splashed out of the water as if he was moving to get out of the tub, and Daniel's stomach dropped. Rafael was going to kick him out of the tub. Instantaneous shock brought him back to the moment when hot pain seared down his chest.

"Fuck." Drops of melted candle wax hit his chest and shoulders.

Rafael had picked up one of the candles and was tipping it over his skin. His chest clenched as he awaited the pain he craved. He loved wearing his lover's marks on his skin like badges. Dark blue wax hit the hollow of his throat and pooled there, drying. It burned deep into his skin, but it was freeing—something he could grasp and hold onto in his mind so he didn't have to think about his growing feelings. No wonder it was so intoxicating. Raf's erection prodded his ass with every groan made. It was very clear that Rafael got off on controlling his pain, and he was happy to oblige. He was starting to love it.

"I want to edge you," Rafael gasped, putting the candle back in its place.

"Okay." He would have sold his soul at that point for some peace of mind. Rolling his ass into Rafael's groin, the water sloshed around them, spilling out of the tub.

"Do you make a usual habit of agreeing to things you don't know the details to, my lawyer friend?" Raf nipped at the curve of his shoulder.

"I don't care what it is. I want to please you." He meant every word. This man's pleasure increased his. He wanted to have his feelings returned, but since that was impossible, he was okay with being an object of pleasure for the time being.

"Are you sure you've never been a submissive before?" Rafael's fingers coiled around Daniel's cock, stroking it from root to tip. "You seem to know all the right things to say to push my buttons." His voice had a raspy edge to it.

He had to get his groans under control before he could speak. "I'm being honest. Fuck, every time you touch me it's like I'm starved for attention."

Rafael chuckled low. "You're not allowed to cum." The words were spoken as a hand squeezed the base of his cock.

"Planning on torturing me for the sins of my partner?" The question earned him another squeeze, and he involuntarily bucked his ass off the bottom of the tub.

"I can't torture him, can I? So, I'll settle for you." Raf bit down hard enough to leave teeth marks under his ear.

"So I get tort—?" His own gasp caught him off guard as Rafael used his free hand to grip his sac. "Fuck. You're making it hard to concentrate. So I get tortured, and then I get 'the interrogation' from Jesse this afternoon. How is that fair?"

"I like the sounds you're making too much to stop." Rafael's fingers brushed his rear entrance, causing a jolt of electricity to shoot up his spine. "I'm going to enjoy you getting another tongue lashing from Jesse later, but you'll be too satisfied to care."

Raf's fingers massaged lightly over the sensitive area causing Daniel's eyes to roll back in his head. "Wait! Did you say satisfied?" he asked between gasps.

"I did. You're too sexy, and I want to hear you crying out my name."

"Sir?"

"Whichever." Rafael abandoned Daniel's rim and took another candle from the ledge.

He braced himself for the burn but quickly relaxed when the speed of the fist on his hard cock increased. Finally, the burn came, heightening the pleasure, pushing him further out of his mind and into floating bliss.

"Don't cum," Raf reminded him in his baritone hum as he resumed his pace with his hand again.

Daniel's breathing grew labored, and it took everything he had to fight the impending release. His body started to spasm, but he bore down, keeping his intense focus till it passed. He was panting when Rafael slowed and let him settle back into manageable pleasure.

"Very good, boy." Rafael's voice seemed far away, background noise to the high he was riding.

When the muscular body cradling him leaned up for a new candle, it forced him to sit in a more upright position. With the fresh candle in hand, Rafael poured the wax down Daniel's back, making his body clench as pain rolled down his skin. The rough hand on his cock brought him back once more. The edge was so near he could taste it. The tension and stress in his body needed the release, but he was forced to hold back.

Draining some of the water out of the large tub, Raf exposed the base of Daniel's sex. The loss of the warm water around his cock helped him keep control.

"Thank you…" he started to say when a molten drop of wax hit his slit and rolled down his length. "Fuck, God damn Raf!" he cried out and threw his head back into the man's shoulder.

"It could have been worse, boy. Be thankful for the hot water." Rafael now drizzled a few drops of wax over the top of his sac, barely showing above the water line.

Most thankful that this more sensitive flesh was not completely out of the draining water, he barely managed to speak. "Raf…" Daniel winced as more wax hit the base of his cock before the candle was finally set aside.

"Do you want to cum now?" Rafael's soothing voice asked.

He almost didn't answer—he was too caught up in his focus. "Please, Sir," he croaked out at last.

"Cum now."

It wasn't a request, it was an order, and Daniel gave in. His body jerked and spasmed, the coil in his gut snapped. It took him to a place of ecstasy he had never been to before, and bliss captivated him. Rafael's hand expertly worked over his length, helping him ride the intense wave that seemed to go on for hours. It might have just been minutes, but he was breathless when it stopped.

Gasping first, he could only speak one word. "Wow."

"Did you enjoy that?" Raf slid his hand up Daniel's abs, pulling him closer into a hug.

"You were right. I don't think work is going to be possible the rest of the day."

Rafael chuckled darkly. "That good? You seemed to cum for a long time."

"Can we call in sick so you can use me for the rest of the day?" He didn't mind the hint of begging in his voice.

"If only. Your partner is going to be curious enough about what kept you so long."

The second the phone started vibrating from his pants where he'd left them on the counter, the words spilled from Daniel's lips. "Speak of the devil."

"We should head over there." Rafael sat up.

"If we have to."

LEGALLY BOUND

Chapter Eight

Daniel was nervous as they all sat down around the large council table.

"Feeling okay?" Jesse asked after he got his grid paper set up.

"Little bit. Your partner had to drag me out of bed. I spent the night puking." Rafael held Jesse's gaze like a pro.

Jealous that Raf could lie so well, it had never been one of his strong suits.

"Sorry it took us so long to get back here. I had to get cleaned up," Rafael said smoothly.

"Don't worry about it. Surprisingly, it's a slow day. We could use it around here." Jesse glanced at him. "I had them push back your appointments till tomorrow.

"Thanks. So, what did the D.A. say?" His voice was cool and collected.

"Really?" He pinched the bridge of his nose. "I cannot believe you two. Next time our client needs to be found, I'm going."

"What did I say?" Daniel threw up his hands.

Rafael just laughed.

"You have an 'I just got laid' face." Jesse rolled his eyes.

"I do not." He needed to look in a mirror and see for himself.

"It's worse with this one. He erases all the lines of stress on your face. It's like you went and got a cum facial or something." Jesse shook his head and went back to his notes.

"It's my magic cum." Rafael said it so matter-of-factly that everyone started laughing and the tension drained from the room.

"What did the D.A. say?" Daniel asked again when they had all caught their breath.

"Not good news. The only deal he will entertain is cutting the jail time to three months." Jesse held up his notes from the call.

Daniel took them, quickly skimming over them himself as his eyes went wide and Raf swore under his breath. "Election year?"

"You got it. So unless you're willing to go hard after the cop, Raf, it's the best deal you're going to get. Something like this, when the D.A. is up for reelection, could get you nine months and fines." Jesse accepted his notes back and put them in the file. "But it could be more if we can't get the evidence we need."

Rafael exhaled slowly and looked between the two men. "Maybe I should take the deal then."

****

The rest of the day dragged on for Daniel, and he was happy when his slave driver closed the last file. "Can I go drink now?"

"As long as it doesn't end with you drunk-dialing our client." Jesse crossed his arms over his chest and narrowed his blue eyes.

"I got nothing, but I won't see him again." He thrust a hand into his hair.

"Stay away from his place, yeah?" He confirmed.

"After I drive him home, I will pretend it's a high radiation zone or something."

"How about it's a zombie quarantine?" Jesse's eyes lit up like a kid on Christmas.

"You and the zombies, man." Daniel grabbed his messenger bag and slung it over his shoulder.

"When you come to my house begging for food and shelter, I'm going to tell you to remember this." Jesse stood up and stretched. "Why are you giving him a ride? We finished up with him an hour ago?"

"Car got impounded with the last arrest. It's evidence."

"Ah, so dropping him off and meeting me at the bar?" He stared him down like a disapproving parent.

"Giving me a time limit so I don't get naked again?"

"That and so I don't have to go home." He grinned.

"You're like an evil father figure."

"Your fantasies better stop there. None of this father-son fetish crap. You're not getting me naked!" Jesse jabbed a finger in his direction.

Daniel dragged his palm down his face, holding in the laughter. "I would never fuck you." He grabbed his coat and turned to leave.

Jesse gasped. "What?"

"You're not my type, and besides, you're straight."

"But if I were gay?" He looked really hurt by his admission.

Daniel shook his head, stifling the laugh that threatened to leave his lips. "Not my type. I like my men dark."

"We're discussing this later. I'm an attractive man," Jesse called after his back as he left the room.

Following Jesse out of the conference room, he spotted Raf sitting on a bench in the hallway. "Ready to go?"

"Yeah, I want to go back to bed."

Once they were outside in the howling wind, Daniel couldn't hold back his question. "Quickie?"

The high Rafael had given him earlier still heavy on his mind, he tried to convince himself that if he got it out of his system, he would be able to move on…or something like that.

Raf groaned. "But what about your partner?"

"Last time?" He waggled his brows for effect.

"Fine, but I want you sprawled out and cuffed to my bed." Rafael had a glint in his eyes that made Daniel's pants tight.

"We don't have time. Jesse is meeting me at the bar," he grumbled as they got in his Jeep and took off toward Raf's place.

"Then we better get started." The demanding male leaned over the center console and nipped at his cock through his slacks.

"Shit," he bellowed, bucking his hips off the seat and swerving to avoid hitting a jaywalker who darted out into the street.

"Focus," Rafael hissed, dragging down Daniel's zipper just enough to lick over the tiny patch of skin it exposed.

Thankful it was a short drive to his place, when they got out of the car, both their bulges were on display. Rafael attacked once they got through the gate, his hands roaming as their lips met in a clash. They stumbled to the door and had to break apart so Raf could open it. They were on each other before the door was shut, forcefully tearing each other's clothes off. At the same time, Daniel told himself this would be the last time.

"Don't rip my buttons off. I need to wear this when I leave," he groaned, sliding his hands into the back of Rafael's pants.

"You said quick." He worked open the tiny buttons on his dress shirt and growled with impatience.

Grabbing Raf's chin, Daniel pulled their mouths back together while they finished stripping. It had only been hours since the last time he came, but Rafael had not been inside him. The craving he felt for him was worse than any addiction. "I need you inside me."

Raf kicked out of his pants and dug around in a nearby drawer for supplies. His eyes darted around the room. "On the couch on all fours," he commanded.

Daniel did as he was told, coiling his fingers around his aching cock as he crossed the room. Rafael came up behind him, then bent to lick over the sensitive flesh of his ass in preparation. The contact made him groan and his body shudder. "I don't need it." he admitted, enjoying that fact.

"My good boy. I should have made you were a plug all day so you could think about how I would fill you later."

Daniel nearly whimpered at the idea of wearing something for Raf all day while working with Jesse. His entire body flushed and got hot.

"You like that idea, don't you?"

All he could do was nod because Rafael's cock had found his entrance, gently rubbing over it.

"I want you to ride me…" Raf backed off and sat on the couch, stroking himself over the condom.

"Yes, Sir." He got up and climbed over Rafael, straddling his hips. Rafael coated himself with more lube as he watched.

"So eager to please. I love it." Placing a hand on Daniel's hip, he urged him down until he was fully impaled.

As the pressure washed through him, Daniel's head fell back. Raf guided him in a rocking motion over his length. Each movement made the tip hit his prostate, sending tendrils of ecstasy licking up his spine. He moved faster, rising up on his knees just to fall back down, fully sheathing Rafael inside him over and over. Sweat covered their bodies as they quickly overheated, slicking their skin and easing their movements.

Raf seemed like he could go on forever, and Daniel thought he knew why. To test the theory, he raised both hands to grip the man's biceps and dragged his nails down his flesh, leaving angry red marks in their wake. It seemed to spur Rafael on, if his cry was anything to go by. He could feel his lover's body tensing as it neared release below him. Leaning forward and sinking his teeth into Raf's shoulder, earned Daniel the reaction he wanted. Rafael shot up, bit down on his exposed neck, and with powerful thrusts came hard. Daniel couldn't hold back as Rafael fucked the release out of him, and he painted both of their chests with his cum.

His mind hazy, he draped himself over Rafael's body, lying in bliss. The male's fingers trailed down the dip of his spine to the cleft of his ass, then back up. It was a simple gesture, but it felt so good. He kissed Raf's chest, then closed his eyes.

"Our relationship will never work, Daniel." Rafael pushed back from him to scrub a hand over his face. They were still naked and breathless, but it seemed reality had set in.

"I know." Daniel got up to grab something to clean himself off. "But if you're going to take the deal we made, shouldn't we talk about it? I won't be your lawyer anymore." He was grasping at straws, and they both knew it.

"It's more than that. I can't get off without kink, without the control or the pain. I've made that pretty evident."

"I want to learn." Daniel sorted through his clothes, hunting for his boxers.

"It's not something you can do for a boyfriend. You'll be unhappy as my sub once we get past the new stage." Rafael looked like he wanted to say more. "Kink is not something you learn. It's a part of who you are."

"You're wrong about me. This whole new side I'm seeing of myself—it's the best of me personally, and it's the best sex has ever been for me." Stuffing his tie into his pocket after he got dressed, he continued. "Do you think it doesn't turn me on because I didn't know it existed until this point in my life?"

"This is a horrible situation." Still naked, Raf got to his feet. The sight of the ink woven into the man's skin, perfectly outlining his muscles made Daniel's cock swell again. "We can't do this right now. I can't train you. I need to try to not go to jail. I just have to figure out how."

Daniel felt his face fall. He'd felt more alive with Rafael than he had ever felt with any other man. "Yeah, you're right. Jesse will kill me if we do anything."

"You don't want a relationship with me anyway. I'm a pay-for-play Dominant. My dominance will never be fully yours. You couldn't handle it."

Raf was full of excuses, and it made his blood boil. "I thought a Dom/sub relationship was all about open and honest communication, not an assumption of what the other's wants or needs are?"

"Have you been reading?"

"I'm a lawyer. Research and setting up a strong defense are my strengths, Sir." Daniel emphasized the last so it almost sounded sarcastic as he locked eyes with Rafael.

A low, baritone growl sounded in the base of Rafael's throat. "You're getting punished for that."

"How can you punish me, Sir?" He knew by the man's tone that he'd found the right button to push. It was not through reason, or argument, but through his sheer defiance and the connection they'd formed that he knew this man so well.

Raf was on him, throwing him back down on the couch and gripping both of his wrists, roughly pushing him flat on his back. "Boy, I don't tolerate cheek from anyone, and certainly not from someone I fuck."

Daniel ground his hips upward, showing what the aggressive action and tone of voice did to him.

"You just spent ten minutes lecturing me on why our relationship wouldn't work. I think I'll keep the cheek till you beat it out of me." He lifted his head off the cushion to bite Rafael's chin, hard.

He muttered something in Portuguese that Daniel could not understand. "If Jesse gets wind of this," he said, gesturing between them, "it won't be good. You said you could only do a quickie. He's waiting for you."

"Good thing there's an ass-load of traffic," he growled, kissing along Rafael's jaw line, left exposed while he was speaking.

Raf pulled back, and Daniel's mouth chased his retreat, but he wasn't fast enough.

"Up," Rafael said in a cool, commanding voice.

His body complied, even before his mind could process the words.

"Go to my room and undress, fold your clothes, and present yourself at the foot of the bed," Rafael demanded as he sat back down.

"U-undress without you watching me?" Daniel stammered.

"Did I give you permission to ask questions? If you want this, you'll submit to me and do as you're told, when you're told." The response was snapped through gritted teeth. Raf had become a different person from the one he'd been in the council room that day. Different from the one he'd been before when they were together on this very couch. He'd become the man Daniel had only seen glimpses of. "Do you want to be trained?"

"Very much," he said, turning around to head for the bedroom.

"Don't you mean, 'Yes, Sir?'"

"Yes, Sir. I'm sorry, Sir." The calm Rafael's controlling side brought out settled over him. Daniel stripped quickly once in the bedroom, folding all his clothes over the back of the chair. His hands shook as he took his place at the foot of the bed just as ordered. Sitting back on his heels like he'd been shown before, he hoped the position was right.

He waited. It seemed like the minutes stretched into hours before Rafael, now fully clothed, appeared in the doorway. Daniel's heart dropped. He had hoped the man would be naked, too. Something he had read about a submissive giving his or her vulnerability to their Dominant by being naked when they were clothed suddenly came to mind.

"Very nice. Such a pretty boy you are." Rafael crossed the distance between them to stroke a finger down the center line of his chest.

The phone, sitting on top of his pile of clothes started to ring with his partner's distinctive ringtone. "Can I answer it, Sir? It's Jesse."

"Make sure he believes your lies this time."

"Hello?" he answered.

"So help me God, if you don't get Raf's dick out of your ass and get over to this bar in the next ten minutes, I am taking both of us off the case," Jesse yelled. He was mad, and that rarely happened.

Daniel hung his head. "On my way." He avoided Rafael's eyes. "Sorry."

"Our relationship wasn't meant to be. I'll keep things professional." Rafael sounded as defeated as he felt.

"Thanks." Daniel was back in his car within minutes, his chest aching, but there was nothing he could do about it.

Chapter Nine

"One would think you could keep your dick in your pants when giving the guy a ride home." Jesse was staring at the door with his arms crossed over his chest when Daniel walked in.

"I'm weak." He sank into the seat next to his best friend. "What was so urgent?"

Jesse's eyes went wide as he gave him a scolding look. "Work is keeping me out of a very important Friday night dinner party my wife's father is throwing."

"Your definition of 'work' is terrible." Daniel ordered himself a draft, hoping to ease the pain. He was going to have to do something to get Rafael off his mind.

"I'm here with my partner, and we're discussing a case." Jesse wiggled his brows and brought the glass to his lips. "If you're not here, I'm lying."

"What case are we discussing?" He took the beer he was brought and took a long, slow pull of the cool liquid. Smacking his lips in satisfaction, he wondered if maybe drinking was the answer to forgetting Raf. "And your definition of not lying is terrible."

"The one you keep trying to fuck up the ass," his friend deadpanned. "I go with avoidance and half-truths."

"To be clear, it was him…" Daniel trailed off and winked.

"If you're going to tease me about your trysts, I'm ending our friendship."

He took another long drink just to annoy his partner before he replied. "Then who would keep you late at work?" His lips broke into a wide smile.

"I need to have an affair with my secretary." Jesse scrubbed a hand over his face.

"Your secretary is a sixty-year-old obese man." He grimaced in disapproval.

"Technicalities." Jesse rolled his eyes and sipped his Blue Moon.

"I think I'm going to try and drink my mood out of the gutter." Daniel squeezed the orange into his beer, then picked it up and drank back half.

"Not a good idea," Jesse warned.

They drank in silence for awhile as they both watched the pre-game match up on the bar's TV. "Daniel, you're my best friend, and you know I love you, man, but what the fuck have you been thinking lately? All jokes aside, why would you risk it for that guy?"

They were a few beers in, and Daniel was not surprised by his friend's turn of the conversation. He had been waiting for it.

"He's the first guy…" he started, but couldn't find the right words. "You know I've been going out and sleeping around, but I swore off that off a few months back."

"Yeah, after that dude passed out while you were going down on him." Jesse smirked.

He winced. "Yeah, that. Anyways, I got tired of all the play with nothing behind it. I decided to dive into work and focus on that, but Rafael happened. He's the first guy I've had a connection with since my college boyfriend." He looked back up at the screen, knowing he sounded like an idiot.

"I know the feeling."

He thought he saw a wave of emotion cross Jesse's usually unreadable face out of the corner of his eye, but he didn't press, he was too wrapped up in what he was feeling for Raf.

"I feel like I'm letting go of something that could make me happy, for my job," Daniel said after a few minutes.

"I guess that's the choice you need to make. You're taking a big risk with a guy who has already misled you, and it could very well ruin the job you love," Jesse said carefully, staring at him. "You need to drop this. Marriage isn't all it's cracked up to be, and in the end, you're not going to find someone who sweeps you off your feet like it happens in books. But this...your job...this is going to last."

Daniel laughed. "Not everyone is as cynical as you are. Some of us do want to have a partner."

"Ball and chain, and no one ends up happily married." Jesse looked back at the pre-game.

"But you're right. It's all risk for little chance of reward. I'm being stupid."

"Have you two talked about any of this?" His partner asked, still watching the game.

"We don't talk..." As he spoke the words, he realized their truth. "We kinda just fuck."

"Well that's not a good way to conduct a relationship." Jesse laughed, then threw back the rest of his beer. "Not that I would know, since I currently can't stand to be in the same room as the Mrs."

A few shots of scotch later, the game was over, and Daniel's mood had tanked. Rafael was heavy on his fuzzy mind, and Jesse had lost interest in him and, instead, had begun flirting with the barmaid. Letting his head rest on the cold, resin-coated bar, he didn't realize he had said the words out loud until his partner replied. "I need to get out of here."

"The Bears are on in twenty minutes." Jesse looked horrified at the idea of leaving.

"I think I'm going to grab a coffee next door and try to sober up before the game." Daniel swayed when he got to his feet. He wondered if his friend would lose all respect for him if he just went home and jacked off in the shower.

"If you ditch me to go jack off in the shower while crying and thinking about your convict, I'm going to film it for X-Tube."

"I hate you," Daniel muttered as he headed for the door. "You know me way too well, and it's stalker creepy."

"I only watch you through your windows when I can't sleep." Jesse wagged his brows in a way that scared him.

Pulling open the door, he was hit with a blast of icy wind. "So most nights." Before he ducked out, he looked over his shoulder to see Jesse shrug.

The coffee shop was three doors down. Daniel pulled his coat tightly around him as he walked, hunching forward to fight the wind that whipped down the streets. The tinkling of a bell sounded when he stepped inside the shop. A large fire burned along one wall, and an alluring armchair beckoned him. He ordered his usual vanilla latte and took it to the seductive seat close to the fire.

"Hey, Dan."

His focus was so intent on the fire that he hadn't noticed anyone had approached until he heard his name. Picking up his head, Daniel turned it toward the voice. "Oh, Ty, sorry. I didn't see you there." Sitting right next to me. He could have kicked himself. He was so wrapped up in Rafael that he had missed his very attractive friend.

"I would say I get that a lot, but I don't." Tyson Gandy shifted in his seat, turning his body a little closer. He had a crooked nose and a strong jaw, but it wasn't his face that got him most of the looks. The Navy officer, with clean shaven hair, was huge, not in height but in stature, with bulging muscles covering his form. His love for tight tees that showed off his ripped body helped as well. They were both tops, so they'd never gone there, but Daniel had found him to be a good wing man.

They chatted a bit while they both drank their coffee. Soon, he was warm enough to take off his overcoat.

"Here, let me help you with that." Ty got to his feet to help him.

When they both sat back down, he could tell there was something on - his mind. "Spit it out, man. If you think too hard, you might kill brain cells. As a sailor, you need all those you can get."

Ty met his eyes and faked a laugh. "Very funny, and this from the lawyer." The black man leaned over to pick a piece of lint off his dress shirt. "You know that guy you went home with from the bar over on Addison Sunday night?"

"Rafael? Yeah, what about him?"

I had to walk into a coffee shop and find one of the only three guys who had seen me go home with Rafael that night? He silently kicked himself.

"Are you into that type of play?" Ty scooted to the edge of his seat, and Daniel's eyes automatically dropped to the spot between his thighs.

"Experimenting a little with it, but I like the idea." Daniel finally brought his gaze up to the other man's.

"I'm a member of Amenti."

It struck him that the other man meant the club his client worked at. "You play?" Daniel's excitement was growing. He wanted to explore the world more, even if Rafael was off limits.

"I'm a Dominant." Ty flashed a grin. "Are you looking for a play partner or training?"

Suddenly uncomfortable, he shifted in his seat. All his gay friends knew him as a top. "Ah, well I was kind of thinking I'd like to be a submissive."

Both of the male's brows shot up. "Really?"

He kept his cool, making sure to not look ashamed. "It's freeing."

"Good for you." Ty gave him the impression that he was looking at him differently now. "Want to meet me there tomorrow night?"

Having no interest in dating him Daniel couldn't refuse this key into the world he wanted access to. Ty was a perfect in. "You know, I think I would."

"Meet me at nine?"

"Sure. Text me the address."

Chapter Ten

The next night, Daniel pulled open the nondescript door at the address Ty had texted him. Moving up a staircase and through another door, he found himself in a parlor-like room. There was a coat check and another door with a bouncer at the end of the dark hall. It seemed these people didn't mess around.

The place was decked out in what he would call a "gothic style," but not with cheap crap like so like many punk clubs used. The wrought iron chandeliers looked like they had real burning candles in them. The girl's uniform at the coat-check fit to the point where he had to wonder if someone had painted it on her. It was a tight corset, done in black and dark reds. Her blonde hair was in pigtails, which made him raise a brow. She had a collar with a name tag hanging from it and wore less than he'd ever seen a woman wear out in public.

"Can I help you, sir?" she asked in a higher tone then he had expected.

"I'm meeting a friend. Tyson Gandy." Daniel shrugged out of his trench coat.

The girl scanned a list. "He hasn't come in yet."

The door at the top of the stairs opened, letting a breeze into the hall along with the man he was there to meet.

"Hey there." Taking off his coat, Ty handed it off to the woman behind the coat check. "Can you put him down as my guest? His name is Daniel Caplin. Tell the King I'm responsible for him."

"Yes, Sir." She dropped her eyes to the floor, not meeting Ty's gaze. Daniel handed over his coat and turned to take in the other man's appearance. He was clad from the hips down in leather pants that hugged and displayed his nice ass, and he wore a tight tank top which showed off his muscular chest. Maybe he wouldn't be opposed to letting Ty top him once or twice.

"You look good." Ty interrupted his size-up, and he had to tear his gaze away from the way the pants hugged his hips.

"Thank you." Not owning even one piece of fetish wear, Daniel had dressed in his usual black slacks and a dark gray button-down shirt. "Is there anything I should know?"

"No. Just stick by me, and you'll get the hang of it. You're not here as a sub or a pet, so you can talk to whoever you want."

"Got it." Daniel followed alongside as they passed by the bouncer and descended into chaos. He couldn't process everything going on. It would've taken hours to figure it all out. There were naked people, semi-naked people, people tied to what he recognized as a St. Andrew's Cross while other people beat them, and collared people sitting on the floor at the feet of others who pretended they didn't exist.

"It's something, ain't it?" Ty chuckled as he led him to the bar.

"It is a lot to take in." Daniel didn't hide his obvious stare. He took a seat at one of the stools at the bar and turned to face the open floor.

"More fun happens in the private rooms, but we'll hit those later." Ty gave him a wink and licked his lips.

"I won't lie. I could sit here all night and stare." He wished Jesse was here to enjoy it with him. A naked girl chained to a cross on stage was being lashed. That had to be up his partner's alley.

"You turned on?" Ty asked, getting closer to him.

"More intrigued," Daniel said, ignoring the man's advance.

"You're such a lawyer, having to study everything from every angle. When you decide what you think, I'll be here." Ty rolled his eyes.

"In my defense, I would be checking your ass out in those leather pants if there wasn't so much other fun stuff to distract me." He took the offered beer but didn't look away from the two guys across the room, making out and fondling each other.

"Had I known leather did this to you, I would have done it long before now. Next time, I'll have to wear the leather in a place you can take it off."

That got Daniel's attention, and he looked over. "Are you flirting with me?"

"I am." Ty tipped his beer to his lips.

"What do you like to watch?" He sat back on his stool and surveyed the room again, feeling a bit uncomfortable.

"I like to watch some of the shows. I also like to scene on the stage and in the private rooms. How do you feel about that?"

Daniel thought for a second while he watched the man on stage caning a naked man chained to the cross. "I'm not opposed."

He tore his eyes away from the men when someone came over to talk to his friend.

"King." Ty stiffened and inclined his head.

"Who's your friend?" a deep, rich voice asked.

Daniel turned and stared, drinking in the man. He wore a Victorian era suit made modern and had his hair pulled back and tied at the nape of his neck. Handsome, the man had an air of authority that set him on edge.

"George, this is Daniel Caplin. Daniel, you need to refer to this man as 'Sir' or 'King.' He is the most well-respected Dominant in the city," Ty instructed.

The name sounded familiar, but he couldn't place it. "Sir, it's a pleasure." He wanted to bow or something, but he wasn't sure of the etiquette.

George inclined his head and Daniel shifted as the large man took him in. He didn't breathe until George looked away.

"Is this your new sub or a Dominant in training?" The man had a booming tone that would have made opera singers jealous.

"No, King, he's not mine." Ty paused, and Daniel thought he heard a "yet" muttered. "He's new to the scene and interested in being trained as a submissive."

"You're an attorney for the city?" George asked.

He shrank back a bit as the neatly-dressed male's gaze landed on him again. "How did you know?" Then quickly added as an afterthought, "Sir."

"There's no need to be nervous." George chuckled, turning back to Ty. "He's a good looking one. He won't last long."

"I agree." Ty had a glint in his eyes.

"Carry on." The King of the underground moved away, and Daniel breathed again.

"Intimidating, huh?" Ty laughed.

"Yeah."

"Even to the Doms, but he's a good guy. He takes care of his people."

Daniel's eyes followed George as he swept through the room with authority. When the man paused again, it was in front of Rafael.

Shit! He tore his eyes away and started plotting excuses for a quick escape.

After his initial shock, he noticed that Raf appeared to be feeling better after his detox. He was still a little pale, though, and his skin was grayed. He watched as Raf and George spoke briefly. The man who'd been on his mind constantly wore black leather with boots, which he wholeheartedly approved of. Boots were a huge turn on for him. But instead of a shirt like Ty wore, Rafael was bare-chested, the perfect dips of his hips on full display for the room.

Daniel knew he must be working, and he was not proud of the fact that he was jealous of the other men and women Raf would be playing with. It wasn't because he had a problem with him beating other people. It was because he wanted the man's attention for himself again. He was ripped away from his scrutiny of George and Rafael when Ty started talking to a group of men and began introducing him.

He felt like fresh meat at a gay bar, and he assumed a new member of the community was similar to a new gay at a club. Since he hadn't come here attached, Daniel gave in and greeted the men and women who came over. He found his groove using his humor to defuse the tension he felt and getting the group to laugh.

"Do you use this to choke your subs?" he asked, tugging on the topless man's tie.

"Or, I let them choke me." The man gave him a wink, leaning in to snap his teeth.

It was oddly arousing, and he was about to comment that he would love to give it a try when he felt a hand on his shoulder. Turning, he found Rafael behind him.

"Can you excuse us for a moment gentlemen?" Raf led him a few feet away, then turned on him. "What are you doing here?"

"My friend, Tyson Gandy, invited me here. I didn't think I'd run into you. I'm sorry," Daniel stated, then looked down at his feet.

"I'm not mad. Surprised is all."

Rafael had a light sheen of sweat covering his chest and back, making him glisten in the low light.

Trying to keep his mind on thoughts of his grandmother, Daniel knew it would be impossible to hide a hard-on in the slacks he wore.

"Yes, I saw two clients earlier, and I have a semi-private scene set up later." Raf tucked his thumbs into his leather pants.

"Semi-private?" He cocked his head to the side in question.

"Yes. There are rooms in the club people use to act out scenes while allowing viewers to watch. There are also private rooms for guests who wish to be alone, as well as the paid Dominants' own rooms."

"You have a room here?" He let his arms hang by his side. He didn't know how to act.

"I do. It's like my office." Rafael chuckled.

He wanted to ask the man to give him a tour, but that was dangerous territory. "Did you ask me over here for a reason?"

"Yes." Rafael set his jaw, and Daniel could feel the tension radiating off of him.

He raised both brows. "Are you going to tell me why?"

"I shouldn't." Raf stared him down.

"Well, do so, or I'm going back over with Ty. It's rude to ditch him."

"Those guys were circling you like sharks," Raf said through gritted teeth.

"I'm assuming it's because I'm fresh meat." He waved it off.

"It is, and you're attractive, gay, fresh meat." Rafael's tone hid the growl underneath, and it almost made Daniel laugh.

"So? They'll calm down given time. I see it at the clubs all the time." He stuck his hands into his pockets.

"I don't like it," his former lover said after a long pause.

Lips twisted up into a grin, Daniel asked. "Why not?" He thought he knew the answer, but he wanted to hear it from Rafael's lips.

"Because I don't want anyone else to have you." The words were accompanied by a piercing stare.

"But you can't have me. We agreed with Jesse." He needed to focus on the conversation he'd had with his partner. It was too much risk. He had to stop thinking with his heart.

"Well, that was before I thought there was a risk of you meeting another Dominant before the case was over." Raf took a step closer.

"I doubt that will happen." There had been quite a few attractive men talking to him and Ty, but none of them gave him the warm glow in his chest the way this man did.

Rafael lowered his voice and dipped forward. "I want to make sure it doesn't happen. I have a scene I'm being paid to do in half an hour. I want you there watching. Your eyes will only be on me. You are to sit like a good boy and wish I was beating you. When I'm finished, then you will beg to be touched, and if I see fit, we will go play in my private room." It wasn't a request.

"Yes, Sir." Daniel said without hesitation. "What should I tell Ty?" He didn't really care about what the other man thought. He would be watching Raf.

"I will speak to him for you."

"Thank you, Sir."

"Such a good boy." Rafael stroked the backs of his fingers over Daniel's cheek before walking toward the other Dom.

A little while later, they took seats in arm chairs along one wall of the semi-private room Rafael had booked. Daniel's gut rolled—a tight coil of nerves. He liked the idea of watching Raf play with someone else, but he didn't know if his jealous side would be able to handle the man he wanted being intimate with another person.

Feeling Ty watching him, he didn't look over. "What?"

"He's the one who got you interested in this, huh?" Ty asked. "Because I've known you a long time, and all I've seen from you is a 'vanilla top.' What changed?"

"Yeah, it wasn't even on purpose. He was very commanding in the bedroom, and he threw me around. I didn't have a name for it, but I wanted more." Remembering their first night made him want Rafael that much more and made it hard to stick to his decision to keep things professional.

"I guess one time's all it takes. He's a lucky guy. I've always wanted a shot with you."

Daniel knew this was the male's last ditch effort to get him into bed that night. It would be good for him to go home with someone else to take his mind off of Raf and give someone else a chance. He had never seen Ty as more than a friend. But in his current mood, any friend offering to control him might be able relieve some of the stress he needed an outlet for.

The way Rafael had just acted made him doubt he should listen to Jesse about keeping the male at arm's length. What if this was his one chance to find a life partner? He might be making a stupid mistake dismissing this for a job. If there was even a small chance Rafael would want to see him again, he wouldn't risk blowing it by spending a night with Ty.

"I guess the timing was never right, huh?" Daniel finally said.

"Guess not. He's a good Dom. I'm sure he'll train you well."

"God, I hope so."

The room grew quiet as Rafael led a submissive in by a leash attached to a collar with a D-clip. Instantly aroused, Daniel was glad he was sitting. Raf's leathers hung low on his hips, exposing the two dimples in the small of his back as well as the crack of his perfect ass. He was shirtless, displaying his broad chest and tattoos. The sight made him want to be on his knees in front of him. Rafael's boots tapped on the floor as he walked. They had chunky rubber treads with intricate lacing up the front. In his opinion, a little guy-liner would have gone well with the look.

"Stop," Rafael ordered when they reached the middle of the room. The sub obliged and stood with his head bowed. The chain on the collar went slack as Raf approached the man. "Good boy."

Daniel had to suppress a growl that built deep in his gut. Ty looked over at him, and he had to force a smile when the guy's brow creased in the center.

"Strip, boy." Rafael ordered.

The sub did as he was told, taking off his clothes in a rush. Once folded, he set them on the floor, then returned to his original position, never looking up. Rafael grabbed a crop from the table of toys, twirling it between his fingers. He snapped it out, creating a rustle in the air before it ended up pointed at the floor.

"Kneel." The tone of Rafael's command caused a shudder to pass over the room. It seemed Doms and subs alike respected him, and the thought only made Daniel crave him more.

He glanced over at Ty and quickly adjusted his seat while his friend's attention remained focused on the pair in the center of the room. Just in case he needed to hide the fact that he was aroused by another man while on a date, he needed more room. When the sub dropped to his knees, Rafael circled him, boots clicking on the patterned concrete floor. Inspecting the male's body, Rafael's eyes roamed over every inch of the attractive man. It made Daniel a little jealous, and he wished he could change places with the sub.

After making a full circle around the male, Raf spoke once more. "Good boy. Are you ready?"

The sub nodded vigorously.

One of Rafael's dark brows rose. "You don't look ready to me."

The sub swallowed hard and chewed on his lip.

In a flash, Rafael moved the crop to the man's half-hard dick. "I thought my order for you to be hard around me at all times was clear."

The submissive stammered his reply. "I'm sorry, Sir. It's just…this is my first time in public…"

Swinging the crop, it smacked down on the front of the male's thigh. "Quiet."

The sub shut his mouth and dropped his head. The leather crop traveled up the center line of the male's chest till it hit his chin, then tilted his face up.

"You will obey, or you will be dismissed." The low, growly timbre went right to Daniel's cock.

"Yes, Sir." The sub's piercing blue eyes flicked up for only a moment before he dropped them again.

Amazingly, the male's cheeks flushed bright red as his cock started to grow. Soon, it stood at full attention, jutting out from his body. A dark pit of jealousy began to grow inside Daniel because he understood the sub's reaction. He pictured himself on the floor, but he'd never done anything so bold—never had sex in public. The thought twisted his guts in knots, but it made him strangely aroused. Forcing the image out of his mind, he didn't want to give Ty the wrong idea.

"Sit in the chair facing the back." Rafael's voice broke through his concentration.

The sub scurried to do as he was told while Rafael went to the table his supplies sat on. He set down the crop and ran his fingers over the other toys. Daniel's chest ached, and a war began in his mind as Rafael returned to strap the man into leather cuffs attached to the chair. The sub faced the back of the chair, leaving his back and the top of his ass fully exposed. Next, a ball gag went into the man's mouth and hooked around the back of his head. The guy moaned around it, his eyes tracking Rafael's movements, allowing Daniel to see the male's lips stretched tightly around the gag. He wondered what it would feel like. Raf took a ball from his case of toys and shook it in front of the man's face. The sub nodded, keeping his eyes on the floor as the ball was placed in one of his hands that gripped it tightly.

"What's that for?" Daniel whispered to Ty.

"Since he can't speak, it's used instead of a safe word. When a sub is gagged, he can drop the ball if he wants things to stop." Sitting so close now, it seemed Ty took advantage of the opportunity and put his arm around Daniel's shoulder.

"Ah." Sitting back in his seat awkwardly, Daniel leaned on the armrest to gain some space, preferring more distance between him and the other man.

He was waiting for Rafael to take notice and wondered what his reaction would be. Too curious about the scene to focus on anything else, he ignored the impressively muscular arm. His eyes drifted down the line of the submissive's back to the curve of the man's ass. Was Raf attracted to the guy? Skinny, but not bad looking, the dark-haired kid looked to be about college-age. The jealousy stung, causing a hitch in Daniel's breath, and then he realized he wasn't jealous of the boy. He didn't mind what Rafael did for a living. Instead, the jealousy centered on the attention the sub received. It didn't help that the one he wanted the same attention from was off-limits.

Remembering his orders, he made himself forget about the sub. Daniel pushed everything else out of his mind, fixing his gaze on Rafael and watching his every move. The way the low-slung, leather pants hugged the man's narrow hips showed a little of his pubic hair. As soon as he saw that, the jealousy faded. He was happy to be near Raf again, excited to watch him work, to see his body in action in a way he couldn't when the man had been topping him. Arousal flared above everything else as Rafael mulled over his toys.

Returning to his sub with a different crop, Rafael's face held a sadistic smile. This one seemed to have a larger head and a shorter stick than the one he had used before. "Everyone is going to see you beaten, humiliated for their pleasure." The words were spoken as the leather traced over the submissive's shoulder blades.

The boy drew in a sharp breath as the soft leather skimmed his skin and fear radiated off of him. The sub hung his head and nodded. Rafael didn't say another word as he reared back. His tattooed muscles flexed as he landed a blow between the man's shoulder blades. The submissive moaned around the ball gag, but Rafael didn't relent, striking him again and again till a spray of light red patches started to appear across the bound male's back. Daniel was zeroed in on the way Rafael's arms tensed with each pull backward, the way his body moved. It wasn't long before the sub's and Rafael's skin glistened with sweat. Straining in his slacks, Daniel was glad to be sitting, but wished he could easily move away from Ty's grasp.

Rafael pulled the sub's head back by his hair, looking sadistically into his eyes. Was it possible something passed between the two before the tight grip loosened? Abandoning the crop on the table, Raf selected another toy Daniel couldn't see.

"You fucking dirty whore," Rafael spat, returning with a pinwheel. "Next time I give you a command, I expect you to do it."

Daniel winced but couldn't tear his eyes away as the commanding male bent down in front of the submissive and used the pinwheel on what he guessed was the guy's cock. The boy grunted around the ball, head falling back, as his hands balled into fists. Rafael licked his lips, clearly enjoying what he was doing. It made it that much hotter. Green eyes flashed up and widened with rage as they met Daniel's, and Rafael's lip curled in disapproval.

Shit. It took a moment to remember that Ty's arm was draped across his shoulder and they were sitting very close.

Daniel shifted, trying to pull away from the embrace, but the damage was already done. Rafael stalked away from the submissive, tossing the pinwheel down on the table to pick up a cat-o-nine tails. His hand twitched, and he didn't look back as he trudged back over to the bound sub. Recoiling as the boy shuttered, Daniel kept watching, eyes glued to Rafael's body. Bruises replaced the red blush, and after a few strikes, the submissive's head was pressed forward into the back of the chair. Raf pulled back, poised to strike again, but he didn't. Rafael lingered there while the submissive's labored breathing filled the room.

Tossing the whip back onto the table, Rafael hurried to uncuff the sub. He removed the ball gag, picked the boy up like he weighed nothing, and laid him out on the table. Rafael's earlier harsh behavior turned to soft touches, making goose bumps rise on Daniel's skin. He could almost feel those hands on him. The aftercare was almost better than the scene, and he loved the floating feeling he'd felt during it. He craved that release. Raf was so tender with the boy as he cleaned his wounds and applied ointment to the raw spots.

Ty's eyes were on him as if the man could sense what he was feeling. Daniel couldn't bring himself to care, though. Ty was a poor substitute for Rafael. He knew Jesse would be unhappy, but he had to follow his gut, and he couldn't blow this even if it risked his job. He didn't want to end up hating his home life and being as unhappy as his partner on a daily basis.

Over too soon, Raf donned a shirt and returned to his side. "Can I steal your friend for a few minutes?" The question was directed at Ty. Daniel assumed this was done so as not to insult his fellow Dominant or his territory.

"Sure," his date answered with a hint of grunge to his tone.

"Daniel?" Rafael offered his hand to help him stand, and they walked out of the room and down the hall.

Not caring if he was being too forward, Daniel asked, "Why did you want to steal me?"

Raf leaned into him, whispering into his ear. "You know I can smell the arousal coming off of you?"

"I figured my hard-on was a big enough clue," he responded, adjusting himself as they walked.

Rafael's eyes dropped to watch him, and Daniel couldn't help but grin. "That was my second clue. You need to get some pants that hide that better."

"Why? Maybe I like showing it off."

Rafael growled.

"Don't want anyone else to see I'm well endowed?" Daniel moved his cock so it was free to tent his pants.

Rafael gripped him by the shirt, shoving him back into an empty room. "You push my buttons on purpose." He slammed the door shut behind them.

"And you don't do the same to me?" He wasn't this man's sub, and he knew how to stand up for himself. Bumping chests with Raf, Daniel stood his ground.

"You showed up here with that hack, Ty, looking at you like he's already fucking you in his mind. I couldn't concentrate on my client." A cold stare accompanied the statement. "How did I push yours?"

It gave Daniel a stir of pleasure to know Rafael was jealous because he was here with someone else. "Ordering me to watch your scene? You don't think that counts?" he asked, fisting a hand in Rafael's shirt. "You looked like you were concentrating just fine."

"I ordered you to watch me, and I had to imagine I was beating you to get through it."

"Would you like to have me like that in public?" Daniel asked, shoving the man back toward the bed.

Moving willingly, Raf said, "Fuck yes. Did you like watching me beat someone else?"

"I would have liked it a lot better if things between us were different." Pausing, Daniel told himself he couldn't do what he wanted to do.

"Different?"

A pair of large hands closed around his biceps as he was spun about so their places were reversed. Shoved back onto the bed, Daniel barely heard Raf's next question. "

Different how?"

Bouncing a few times on the mattress before landing flat on his back, Raf was on him in an instant, straddling his hips. "If I belonged to you, it would be more fun to watch you, knowing that at the end of the night you were mine." Cursing himself for being honest, Daniel knew he was getting in over his head.

Rafael hovered over him on all fours, dipping his head and ghosting his lips over Daniel's as he spoke. "You don't mind me taking clients?"

"At first I felt a pang of jealousy, but I did as you told me and watched you. It was very arousing. Plus, I'm open-minded about sharing." He chased the retreating man's lips, wanting to kiss him again.

Rafael didn't give in to the kiss. Instead, he sat back on his hips. "We shouldn't do this."

"I know, but here we are." Daniel tugged Raf by the belt loops so he would return to his previous position and said, "Tie me up."

Rafael held his ground, not giving in. "I want you, but I want my freedom. I don't think going behind Jesse's back is the way to go." Seeming to suddenly give in, the aggressive male began kissing a path over Daniel's jaw as he whispered, "But I think staying away and losing you to that asshat Ty would kill me."

Daniel grinned and tilted his head back to give his lover's lips more access. "So let's talk to Jesse. He's reasonable…ish."

Raf climbed off of him and went to a wardrobe in the corner. He grabbed a V-neck shirt out of a stack and pulled it on over the tank top. "All right."

"Now?" Daniel felt his face fall.

"What were you expecting?" The response was issued with raised brows.

"I was expecting to break his rule, then tell him about it." Daniel slid off the bed, adjusting his angry cock. "I'm going to have blue balls."

"Keep the complaining up and you'll have blue balls for a week, boy."

"I'm going to go find Ty." Crossing his arms over his chest, he grinned at Rafael playfully.

Rafael was on him in a flash, shoving him into the wall, a large hand wrapping around his throat. "I don't want any more of this. I share, but only on my terms and never with Ty. If you want to belong to me, it will be solely to me."

Daniel nodded.

"You are going to be a handful as a sub, aren't you? You know how to push all my buttons."

"But you like it."

Rafael let him down. "Ready to go?"

Rubbing a hand over his neck, the smirk still lingering, he answered, "Yes, but my coat is with Ty's at the coat check."

"Good thing I'm in with the owner. I'll get it back for you." Raf led the way through the dark passages of the club.

"Shouldn't I say goodbye to Ty?" Daniel questioned, following at Rafael's heels.

"You do that well." Rafael gestured to the way he was walking. "I don't trust the guy. I think you should be focusing on getting your partner out of bed." He chuckled.

"I do what well?" Before he received an answer, Rafael turned to collect their coats, and Daniel dug his phone out to call his partner. "Jesse?"

Holding the phone away from his head, he allowed Raf to hear Jesse over the phone as the man helped him into his coat.

"Daniel? What time is it?" His partner muttered.

"About eleven. Are you in bed already?" He switched the phone to his other hand so he could get his arm into the other sleeve.

"My wife likes me to go to bed when she does. Otherwise, I disturb her when I come in."

"Are you kidding?"

"I wish. But you better make it fast. She's glaring at me through her sleep mask."

"How does she glare through a sleep mask?" Daniel looked puzzled and Rafael laughed hard.

"Dan, what do you need?" Daniel's tone was on edge.

"Raf and I need to talk to you."

"You need me for emergency case work?" Jesse prompted.

"Yes, the bar?"

"See you in half an hour."

Chapter Eleven

When they pulled up to the bar near the courthouse, Daniel was nervous. He let Rafael open the door for him, and they took their place at the bar to wait for Jesse.

"You guys come here a lot?" Raf asked, scanning the place.

"Yeah, it's our after work hang out when Jesse doesn't want to go home to his wife."

"Why is he married?"

"Because she wasn't crazy when I tied the knot." Jesse answered for himself as he walked up, taking a seat next to Daniel. "You know it's not very professional to be seen out with someone you're defending." He looked pointedly at their client. "I'm blaming you, Rafael, but since you got me out of early bed time, you're forgiven."

They paused to order their drinks when the barmaid came over. "Doll, you look fantastic this evening." Jesse eye-fucked her brutally, dropping his gaze down to the hem of her short skirt, then bringing it back up slowly.

"Oh, it's my favorite patron." She leaned over the counter closer to the blond man. "What brings you in this late?"

"Business, but it got me out of the house, so I'm not complaining." Jesse leered at her. "I'll take a draft of Bud please."

"Of course." She skipped off to get their drinks.

"Why are you married?" Rafael asked.

"Don't…" But the words were too late.

Jesse was already answering. "Because divorces are expensive."

"And because her daddy is the Circuit Court Judge that will ass-rape him if he divorces his baby," Daniel added, glad the attention was off him and on his partner for a moment.

"That too." Jesse drank deeply from his glass when it was set in front of him and stared at the bartender some more.

"But if he finds out you're cheating, that's okay?" Rafael looked between the two men.

"Whoa! He's not cheating," Daniel said quickly.

"No, I'm not cheating…yet." Jesse returned to his drink.

"Yet?" Raf said with wide eyes.

"Why did you guys need me? Or are we just going to sit here and drink?" He ordered a refill, then added, "Which is fine by me, by the way."

Daniel opened his mouth to speak, but Rafael cut him off. "I want to date Daniel, and I didn't think it was a good idea to do it behind your back."

Jesse sighed and pinched the bridge of his nose. "Can't you guys wait till the legal stuff is over?"

"No," Rafael said firmly. "I don't want him to meet anyone else, and it's imperative I start his training so he is satisfied."

When Jesse looked at him, Daniel felt his face flush. It was uncomfortable hearing his best friend and Dominant discussing him.

"Can you two put your cocks away for a month?" Jesse asked, then added, "Never mind, I know you can't, Dan. I've seen and heard enough about your conquests."

Rafael raised both brows.

"You make me tell you them." Daniel growled.

"True, and I'm going to make you tell me how this one beats you." Jesse nodded and grinned.

"You sure you're not gay?" Raf chimed in.

"Ish. But why can't you guys commit and hold off on the sex? Is a month really that long?" He held up his hands, cutting off replies. "As someone who hasn't had sex in six weeks, you two better not answer that because it's going to piss me off."

Rafael broke out laughing.

"He's not kidding." Daniel elbowed Rafael.

"And this is why I'm kinky. You vanilla people go without sex too much for my liking."

"Tell me about it." Jesse barked. "So a month?"

"No, we can't." He was glad Rafael answered for them both.

"Why not?" The question was asked with a glare directed at Rafael.

"Because he needs it, and he wants to be trained. Now that he's been exposed, he will crave it."

Jesse looked at Daniel, and he nodded. "That's why I was out with Ty tonight."

"Ty?" Jesse wrinkled his nose.

"See! Even your best friend hates him."

"I've never liked him before, but the idea of him…" Jesse tried to finish, but Rafael cut him off with a growl. A look of understanding passed between the two men, before his partner finished in agreement, "He's a tool. I'm with the hooker."

"I'm fucked if you two become friends aren't I?"

They both nodded, and Daniel put his head in his hands. "I thought you'd be mad. You were pissed last night."

Jesse sucked his beer and shrugged. "I was, but I got over it. I'm unhappy, and if you think this schmuck will make you happy, you've got to do it. I'll cover for you as best I can."

"You're the best friend a guy could ask for." Daniel hugged his partner.

Jesse returned the gesture with his strong arms. "But so help me God, you two better keep it on the down low. If I see you on YouTube at a pride parade during the trial, I'm going to skin you both alive and use you as rugs for my office."

Chapter Twelve

They next day, they sat on the sofa in Raf's row house, not touching, much to Daniel's disappointment.

"Can't we just fuck and figure out my limits?" he groaned. He was only ten minutes into the stupid worksheet, and his cock was so hard it felt like it was going to fall off unless Rafael touched him.

"No. I need to know and understand your limits so I can properly satisfy you as your Dominant," Raf said, his eyes glued to the worksheet.

"I hate this. It makes me feel like one of your clients." Gripping himself through his pants, the thin leather wrap-around cock ring Rafael had put on him this morning was not helping at all.

"Don't touch that. It's mine," Raf snapped, his eyes almost glowing red.

Daniel dropped his hand.

"This is what I do with clients, but with you, it's so much more important. I want to know and respect your boundaries so I don't push you to safe word during every scene," Rafael said, dropping his Dominant tone. But it only made Daniel want to touch himself again, just to push his buttons.

"Who cares if I safe word?" He was growing irritated with the whole thing. It was his only day off, and he wanted to be naked and experimenting with his demanding lover, not talking about it.

"Let's say you were burned really badly as a child, and I bring out the hot wax and give you a flash back. Not only will you panic and safe word, but you'll also lose trust in my control and ability to take you to your limits. We want to enjoy this, not get frustrated with each other."

"Fine, go on."

"Go on, Sir." Rafael said, a twinkle in his eyes.

"Yes, Sir."

Looking down at the worksheet, Raf asked, "Do you have any fantasies you want to tell me about?"

Daniel's eyes flashed wide for a moment as his mind went to the fantasies he had been having for a week. Shaking them out of his head, he got himself under control. "No." He hoped his hard-on and the flush of his cheeks wouldn't give him away. "Sir." He added as an afterthought.

"No? Why don't I believe you?" A large hand began to slide his hand up Daniel's inner thigh, fingers brushing over his leaking tip. "You're the one who pointed out how open and honest we need to be with each other."

"It's embarrassing, and I have a feeling you won't like it."

"How will you know till you ask?"

"I want to pretend like I'm soliciting you. It's always been a fantasy of mine, but I could never do it because of my job."

"But with me, it's merely pretend, and I have experience?" Rafael said in a flat voice, that made Daniel panic.

"I'm really sorry, Sir, I-I didn't mean to bring up a sore subject about your past…" he stammered as he tried to backtrack, mad at himself for even bringing it up.

"I'm not embarrassed about who I am. I have no regrets. Let's do it tonight."

A deep groan was his only response. There were some things his profession denied him, and this was one. But, with Raf, he knew he was safe…and he liked it. And tonight, he was going to like it even more.

When the evening finally rolled around, the crisp Chicago wind bit into his exposed skin. No matter how long he lived in this city, Daniel would never get used to the chill. The wind got under his clothes and iced his bones as soon as he stepped outside. His erection was the only thing the cold didn't seem to affect. It was straining against his zipper, begging to be set free. Stiff-on-command would never be an issue, and that was one of the things Rafael required of him. He pulled up the collar of his Peacoat, wishing he had remembered his scarf in his haste. His nerves were a wreck, and it seemed almost too real when he slid into his car. It wasn't normal for a public defender, but he loved his Jeep. He held a hand at a time in front of the vents while the other remained on the steering wheel as he drove to their agreed meeting spot down the street from where Rafael lived in Wrigleyville.

Turning the last corner, his eyes searched for Raf, wondering what he would be wearing. When he spotted him, he licked over his wind-chapped lips. God, he looks amazing.

Rafael wore skin-tight leather pants and a mesh shirt and nothing else. The male's nipples were hard from the bitter cold, and Daniel had to shift in his seat to try and get another inch of room in his pants. He rolled down the window as Rafael approached the car with a swagger that he could only imagine a whore having.

"Hey there, handsome, looking for some fun?" he said when their gazes met.

Daniel's voice suddenly left him, and all he could do was nod. "How much?" he finally croaked.

The prostitute's lips twisted into an amused smile. "Fifty for head, hundred for everything."

"Everything," Daniel whispered as his chest grew tight, restricting the flow of oxygen into his lungs. It felt so real, and he had never been so hard. He unlocked the car door and Rafael climbed in.

"Pull into the parking lot behind that building." They had discussed this as well. Rafael had insisted it would not be the full fantasy if they didn't play a little in the car before going up to his apartment.

He pulled forward, grateful that his grip on the wheel kept the man from seeing his shaking hands. Rafael leaned over, massaging the inside of Daniel's thigh, working his way closer to his cock. Swallowing hard, he forced all his attention onto the task of not crashing the car, but Raf didn't make it easy on him. His fingers circled the wet spot that had appeared, barely stimulating his head. Daniel slammed the car into park when he pulled into the spot, noticing the windows were already on their way to becoming opaque with steam.

Rafael held his gaze as he undid the button on his pretend customer's pants, using his other hand to massage under Daniel's sac. Expertly, he slid down the zipper, exposing his length.

"Good boy. I love when you go commando for easy access." Rafael closed his fist around his length, and Daniel couldn't hold back the deep, wanton groan that rolled out.

"Fuck, you are way too good at that, Sir."

"Good boy. You know your place, even in the car."

He gasped when Rafael got up on his knees, leaning over the stick shift to kiss his tip. He bucked up, and the man tightened his grip around the base.

"Be patient. You'll cum when I want you to. I own this." Raf pumped his hand over Daniel's shaft causing a bead of pre-cum to pearl at the slit.

Giving up all control, Daniel's head slammed back into the headrest. Rafael had made sure that he was painfully aware of who owned his orgasms. Daniel's breath hitched when Raf's tongue slid over his slit, collecting the fluid. He had to force himself to remain still. Rafael would only make him wait longer if he seemed too eager.

"Mmmm, good boy. Keep yourself in check. How bad do you want my mouth on you?" Rafael glanced up while his tongue found the underside of Daniel's cock, stroking over the overly sensitive, silky skin.

"Please, Sir," was all he could manage.

"I love the way you say Sir."

"Sir…" Daniel drew out.

"Since you asked so nicely," Rafael said, pushing his cock past his pursed lips and into his hot mouth. His voice hummed over the length, reverberating along his shaft till Daniel's eyes rolled back in his head. A hand slid into Raf's hair, urging him lower. It was everything he ever wanted from the fantasy. It became so clear why so many people paid this man to dominate them. He would pay for it.

"Fuck, yes God…" Daniel groaned, pushing his feet into the floor of the car to move his hips in and out of his lover's mouth, making him moan over his cock. "You feel so good moaning around me."

Rafael's green eyes met his, and he moaned again. Pleasure played across Rafael's face as he lifted and massaged over Daniel's balls. Tugging lightly, then pulling nearly free of cock in his mouth, Raf flicked his tongue into the slit before speaking. "Don't cum till I tell you that you can," he ordered.

"Sir," Daniel pleaded, but he was interrupted by a knock of metal against the car window.

"Shit!"

"This is the police. Please roll down your window, Sir."

"It's so not as hot when he says it," Rafael said, unable to contain his laughter.

"How are you laughing?" His eyes flashed to Raf's large jade-colored ones. "What should I do," he whispered.

"Well first, put your dick away, and then calm down. The worst thing that's going to happen is we get a ticket for indecent exposure." Rafael gave his cock a playful squeeze while Daniel tried to shove the half-hard length into his zipper.

When he had himself presentable, he lowered the window. A flashlight glared in his eyes, making him look away.

"What are you two gentlemen up to?" the cop asked with a knowing smile.

"We were talking before we go up to my boyfriend's place, Sir." Daniel toyed with his hands in his lap, not sure what to do.

"Is that so?" the cop asked skeptically.

"Yes, Sir, it is. I rent in this building." Rafael leaned forward so the cop could see him as he spoke.

"So when we saw this gentleman solicit you, that was a mistake?" the cop said, as another flashlight shined in from the passenger window.

Daniel's eyes widened and his pulse hammered in his ears. "No Sir, that was merely my boyfriend and I playing around." Shit, shit, shit. Jesse was going to kill him.

"Do you know this man is a prostitute with a record, and we have you on tape offering him money in exchange for sex?"

As soon as the cop began to corner them, Daniel's lawyer mode kicked in. "Vying for a confession before you've even read us our rights? Looks like this case is going to be thrown out."

Rafael snorted, trying to keep a straight face.

"We are going to have to ask you both to get out the vehicle with your hands in the air." The cop flicked off the clasp on his gun and stepped back, keeping his hand on the butt.

They looked at each other, then exited the car. They were forced onto the hood so that their heads almost touched. Daniel's arms were yanked behind his back and cuffed before they were both roughly searched and read their rights.

"I've had less groping from clients," Rafael growled.

"I know your rep, I'm sure you liked it," the cop said.

"Rafael, I'd advise you stay quiet till we can get a hold of Jesse."

"That's what the attorneys always tell me," Raf said to Daniel as they were carted off toward the back of the police car.

"I want it noted that we are requesting our lawyer." Daniel was shoved into the back seat, hitting his head on the roof in the process. "Police brutality? Classy guys. I'll add that to my suit against the city when I sue you for discrimination against me and my boyfriend!"

Rafael looked at him questionably. "You serious?"

Daniel winked.

"You're making me so hard right now. I love seeing you in cuffs. We're going to have to buy a pair. Would you like that, boy?"

"Yes, Sir, you can play cop with me any time you want."

"Will you two knock it off," one of the officers grunted from the front.

Raf ignored him. "Damn right. I'll do what I want, when I want. I own you."

"You're making me hard." Daniel dragged his teeth over his lips.

"Do you like when people watch?" Rafael turned toward him, a sparkle in his eyes. "You didn't say anything about that when I asked."

"I didn't know." Daniel's chest grew tight, but he liked the idea very much.

"Maybe we should play at the club, handsome."

He shrugged noncommittally.

After they were both led into the Police Station, Daniel posed for a few unflattering pictures, got covered in black ink, and was strip-searched. He thoroughly enjoyed the search because the rugged officer who performed it was well-muscled in all the right places. Being careful not to groan during it, he didn't want to look like someone who would pay for sex more than he already did.

Finding himself in a holding cell an hour later, his mind was spinning. He wondered if Rafael was okay in the other cell. They'd been kept apart since they arrived at the station, and he assumed it was to keep them off balance, or to prevent them from corroborating their stories. There was a good chance he wouldn't see Rafael again till he was released. They'd be questioned separately, and Jesse would meet with them each alone.

He hoped they wouldn't keep him long, as it might taint his perfect reputation. He had never had aspirations of becoming an elected official, but it might happen. Sitting on a bench in the corner, he avoided all the other detainees. The man sitting on the metal toilet in the opposite corner seemed to be losing part of his colon. Another man rocked in the center of the room, curled into a ball, and Daniel had seen enough addicts going through withdrawal to know one on sight. Cringing away from these men, bile rose in his throat. He could picture all the germs and viruses culturing in this room, and his breathing started to pick up. If he didn't get a hold of himself, he was going to go into a full-blown panic attack. Despite the shame he felt, he was also mad. This had all been a set up—there were clearly cops still watching Rafael's every move to the point where they had the two of them on tape during their fantasy scene. If that wasn't a violation of the court-ordered stay, he didn't know what was. A plan began to form, but he needed to talk to Jesse to see if it was plausible.

"Daniel?"

He perked up, hoping it was Jesse here to save his ass. Trying to make his walk to the front of the cell not seem like a scurry, he failed miserably. The guard led him to a questioning room he had seen so many times with clients. It looked like it was going to be a few rounds of "throw the detainee under the bus." Glancing up at the two-way mirror while he waited, it was eerie to be offered the sludge-like coffee as if it was a gift. He knew these rooms were designed to set people on edge, and it worked. Taking a seat in the metal folding chair behind the rickety folding table, anger clenched his chest. His eyes bored into the mirror as he crossed his arms.

It was at least fifteen minutes before two cops padded into the room. Daniel went to check his watch and saw his bare wrist, only to remember it had been taken from him when he was booked. He dropped his arm to his side and shifted in his seat. Anything but amused, he waited for the cops to speak first.

"Daniel, how's it going?" The thinner cop asked, dragging out one of the chairs so it screeched on the linoleum floor. He knew the cop, named Matt, from all the time he spent in the courthouse, and it was a little embarrassing to be on the other side of things.

It was clear they wanted to go a few rounds. He had no tolerance for them. "I'd like my lawyer, Jesse Goldmen, please," he spat.

"Hey." Matt held up his hands as he spoke. "We're all friends here. On the same side."

His partner, Ted, took a seat next to him. "Clearly not."

Were all cops really this bad and obvious at the game? It was sad. "You guys are terrible at the 'good cop, bad cop' thing. Maybe you should get remedial training?"

"You have a clean record, and it would be a shame to keep quiet and try to help a known criminal with a long history. You'd ruin your blank slate." Matt did his best to put on a false sympathetic face.

"Let him rot. He doesn't want to help us," Ted scoffed.

Daniel just sat there staring at them both.

"He's a known prostitute, buddy. You picked a bad one. Now I'm sure we can get things pleaded down if you help us out," Matt tried again.

"Listen, Rafael is my boyfriend, and not only that, I'm his lawyer. I can't say anything about the matter." He looked at both of them in turn. "Now, I'd advise you to get my lawyer, please, before I have the charges thrown out for you refusing me."

Ted shot to his feet and growled. The door opened, and another cop stepped in before he could get a word out. It was Lance McCoy. He had done a search on the guy as soon as Rafael had fingered him.

"Listen, let's play this straight. There's no reason for games." McCoy smoothed his tie as he sat. Nodding at the other two officers, Ted then left the room

"I have nothing to say to you," the lawyer in Daniel countered.

McCoy scooted his chair closer, leaning his elbows on the table. "You have a clean record. I don't blame you at all for exploring some kink, but this guy you were picked up with has a record, as you know." He folded his hands, and the way he was sitting made the large muscles in his arms show through his dress shirt. "This guy is into some bad stuff. I'm sure he's lied to you about it, but he and I go way back. You shouldn't have to go down with him. I'm sure we can get you a good deal with nothing on your record if you roll over and give up something to get this guy off the street. Danny…"

Daniel burst out laughing, interrupting him. When he got himself together, he nodded. "I'm sorry, I shouldn't be laughing."

"Are you high, Sir?" McCoy asked.

"No, but I do find this all very funny. Rafael is my boyfriend and my Dominant. We weren't doing anything illegal." Daniel glanced at his nails, knowing his chilly attitude was pissing the cop off. "I'm a lawyer, his lawyer. I know my rights." Suddenly, it all clicked. He had to talk to Jesse while the idea was still fresh in his mind. Where was a pen when he needed one?

"He's a known prostitute. If you think I'll believe he's your boyfriend…" McCoy's eyes were red.

"I don't care what you think he is. He's my boyfriend, and my lawyer can confirm it and so can our Dom/sub contract. I'll have a copy faxed over to you. I'm sure you're aware of what that is?" He knew it would be easy enough to fake one and predate it. He was simply pushing the guy's buttons, even though he knew he shouldn't, but he hated McCoy for what he was doing to Raf.

"Given the evidence found at the scene, I think a judge and jury will side with me. You don't want this to go to court and ruin your career." Lance's dark eyes met his.

"Are you threatening me," Daniel smiled sweetly, "As well as denying me legal counsel? My, my you must want to lose your job."

McCoy shook his head, eyes narrowing as he snarled.

"I didn't think so." Sitting back, linking his hands behind his neck, Daniel tried to give an air of confidence. "What evidence do you think you have?"

"Other than the video of you picking him up off the street?" McCoy shot back.

"Because no one has ever met their boyfriend outside of his place of residence." Daniel arched a brow.

"Condoms," McCoy said smugly.

Daniel knew how serious a known prostitute carrying condoms could be. It was like finding a junkie with a needle. They were enough evidence for an arrest under the current solicitation statute in the state. They could also be used as evidence against the prosecuted to show motive. "Good thing my boyfriend and I are practicing safe sex."

"Don't go down for him. He's on a sinking ship. You should get off." McCoy pointed at him. Obviously, the two men had more history than Rafael was letting on. There had to have been something to cause this intense anger in the cop.

"Get. My. Lawyer." He emphasized each word as he spoke it. "You're the only sinking ship here."

"Yep. We'll put a call in." McCoy got up, and Matt joined him, looking a bit confused.

The other officer whispered a few words as they walked toward the door. Lance shrugged him off and waved him out first.

When Matt had left the room and McCoy was about to follow, Daniel couldn't help calling out the taunt, "Jealous of me with him?"

"Stay out of it," McCoy ordered.

"You don't scare me. I'm going to figure you out."

"You've picked the wrong side." His hands clenched into fists.

"I have the law on my side, as well as your former Dominant." Daniel snapped. He knew he shouldn't have said some of the things he had, but the guy really got to him.

McCoy whirled around and stalked across the room to grab him by his shirt and bring their faces level, spit flying with each word. "You have a lot of nerve."

"So do you."

Daniel kept his arms at his side, remaining limp. He knew they would be taping this. If they had any evidence that he assaulted a cop and not the other way around, it would be used against him.

"And now I have police misconduct to add to my suit." He looked at the two-way glass, then grinned as he felt McCoy let him go. "I'll need a copy of that tape please."

He'd been back in the holding cell for only a short time when he heard his name being called again.

Sprinting out of the hell hole as fast as he could, he found himself face to face with Jesse. His partner barely looked awake—his hair was disheveled, and his suit was rumpled. Considering Jesse was usually better dressed than he was, Daniel knew he had been dragged out of bed.

"You have got to be fucking kidding me."

Taking a seat in the conference room, Daniel explained, "It was role-play. Rafael and I were—"

Jesse cut him off. "You and Rafael? I thought we were keeping this on the down-low for now?" His voice rose with every word he uttered.

"Yes, well, we were exploring our new…" Daniel dropped his eyes to the floor. It had been stupid. He had warned Rafael himself that the cops would still be watching. Even worse than getting himself in trouble, he'd gotten Raf in more trouble. The charges against him would be dropped, but Raf was already dealing with bigger problems. The pain hit him in the gut at the realization. How could I be so stupid?

Jesse pushed the heels of his hands into his eyes. "You think this was the best time to fucking role-play picking up a prostitute when your boyfriend has actually been charged with the crime?"

"To be honest, I didn't think about it that way at the time." Daniel shifted, knowing he had fucked up. "But I get it. I wasn't thinking."

"Christ on a cracker. Am I the only one who thinks around here?" His partner dropped his hands to the table and looked up at him, the harsh tone dropping from his voice.

"How bad is it?" Daniel got serious again. "Am I getting out tonight?"

"McCoy is pissed off, and he's trying to trump up the charges. But, I'm going to get them to release you into my custody tonight because he grabbed you like that." Jesse had a glint in his eyes.

"How do you know about that?" Daniel asked, eyes getting wide. "I was going to tell you to request the tape."

"I got friends in high places that don't like that bitch." Jesse wore a huge grin on his face. "Plus, I walked in for the end of it."

"I'm being released into your custody? How?" Daniel raised his brows.

"I'm an upstanding civil servant, something you used to be." He got up. "I'm going to go get the paperwork started."

"Raf?" he asked, his throat suddenly dry.

"He's going to have to stay the night. I'm sorry, man." The blond's face lost all the amusement it had held only moments before.

"Yeah, I figured." Daniel placed his head in his hands. It was his fault Rafael would spend the night in jail. Anger burned in his veins, but really what could he do? "But I think I have an idea how we can use it." He bit his lip. "It's a little unconventional, though."

Jesse crossed his arms and raised his brows, still acting like he was mad, but Daniel knew he wasn't.

"Did you get the tape from the interview?"

Jesse tapped his bag. "Yep, and they weren't happy about handing over a copy."

"Are you sure it's all there?" He hoped the last half hadn't been erased.

"Like I said, I was here as it was finishing up, and I snagged it before anyone could touch it. McCoy was pissed they'd called me before the interview concluded." A glint sparkled in Jesse's eyes as he spoke.

"Thank God. It will help. Did you request the tape of the alleged solicitation from the police car?" He crossed his fingers.

"You ask me these things like I'm not better at my job than the guy sitting in jail." He scoffed. "Already got a copy of it."

"Go check and see if they have the equipment off in this room." He should have waited till they were out of there, but he didn't want to forget any of the details that would make his idea work.

Jesse's brow knit, but he got up without question. When he came back, he gave Daniel two thumbs up. "No one is in the viewing room and I locked it," he said, holding up the key he had swiped.

"Nice. All right, so here is what we need to do. We need to say the whole thing was a set up—that me and my boyfriend played decoy to demonstrate to the court that the good ole detective will go to any lengths possible to get at Rafael. We can use witnesses to say we were together before I was his lawyer. Put it all out on the table for Judge Stenson. Really get him mad…" Daniel trailed off, waiting for his friend to reply.

Jesse sat, starting at him, making him wonder if his partner thought he was crazy.

"It could work. It looks pretty bad with your motion." Jesse nodded and got out a piece of lab paper to start taking notes.

Daniel started listing off all the things they would need along with the names of all the people they could get to give statements about his relationship with Raf.

When they both couldn't come up with anything else, his partner looked at him long and hard. "Tell me why?"

Daniel felt his face flush and looked down. "Um…"

"You fucking dirty bastard." Jesse shook his head and laughed. "It turned you on when you thought you had slept with a prostitute?"

Knowing his face went from red to crimson, Daniel couldn't help but join his friend in laughing. "Yeah."

Jesse smacked his forehead. "Fuck! To be young and single again."

"I knew you weren't mad at me. I got you out of the house after bedtime," he shot back.

"And for that, I thank you. I would pay every penny I own right now to have seen your face when they tapped on the car window."

Glaring at his partner, Daniel spat, "I hate you."

"I'm sure it was epic. I would have had it made into postcards." Jesse wore a dreamy smile for a moment before standing, his face serious now. "We need to go after this cop, or you're both in trouble. This needs to work."

The way he said the word 'cop,' gave Daniel's anger a focal point. "Believe me, I know. We can work on the plan Monday." He wanted McCoy's badge, and he was going to work till he got it, even if Raf had to stay in jail. That thought was like a spike in his chest. No way could he go to someone like Ty after Raf. There wasn't even a comparison. He needed Rafael. He had to get him cleared of all charges.

It was late, but if he went home and slept for a few hours, he could see Rafael first thing in the morning to reassure him.

****

"You have a visitor."

Rafael breathed easier. He hadn't slept all night and was glad that Daniel had come to see him. He had so much he wanted to say. They had been so stupid. He felt really bad, and he needed to end the relationship till they were both in a better place.

Submitting to the usual search before being escorted to the picnic tables where inmates could talk to visitors, Raf's eyes scanned the room for his sub. Instead, they landed on his boss.

Fuck. It was too late to refuse the visitor. He took a seat opposite George and nodded his head in submission. He kept his eyes on his toes. Seconds passed into minutes, and he could see George's stoic expression out of the corner of his eye.

"You missed your client this morning. You know he's only in town on business every other month, and he pays very highly for your services."

Rafael didn't say a word. He was not a sub, but everyone submitted to George. Leather boots caught his eye along with a flash of silver buckles. He looked like royalty, even in torn jeans and a polo. It was odd to see him out of his fetish clothes of period suits tailored to perfection, or leather pants and no shirt.

"Look up," came George's command.

He complied.

"Do you have anything to say for yourself?"

Doing everything he could to keep the story straight in his head, he knew he was going to get a tongue lashing. But George didn't need to know what was really going on. "I'm sorry I missed Señor Belmount. Tell him I was unwell, and his next appointment will be on the house."

"I rescheduled him with someone else."

"Why would you do that?" Rafael let a hint of anger break into his tone.

George cocked his head to the side and lifted one brow. It was a simple gesture, but Raf knew the look well. He didn't push it. "It makes me look bad when my Dominants can't keep their appointments."

"Yes, Sir, I know."

"I can't believe you're back to hooking." George folded his hands on the table.

"I'm not." Rafael thrust both hands into his hair.

George pulled open his knee-length overcoat, fishing through his inside pocket till he produced a packet of folded papers. He tossed them on the table. Neither of them went for the documents. George stared him down, and Raf relented, dropping his gaze to the papers.

"Do you know what these are?"

"No, Sir," he answered, even though he had a pretty good idea what they were.

"It's your arrest records for the past six months." George didn't move or shift in place. Rafael didn't even think the man blinked when he was this intense.

"How…" He lifted the papers and unfolded them to find his mug shots staring back at him. It was public record, and he knew George would have found out sooner or later.

"I thought the trouble was because McCoy was riding you?"

"It is. He keeps nabbing me as I leave the clubs and hotel rooms with my clients. I've lost so many of my tools in the last six months it's not funny. Evidence," he scoffed.

"This is not something we trifle with. Why weren't you honest with me from the beginning?" He didn't have to yell. He was scary enough like this. A true sadist, George was cold and calculating, but Rafael loved him like a father. He would be dead without this man.

"I thought I could handle McCoy myself." Raf dropped his eyes down to the table.

"I'm done with you." George got to his feet, his jeans tucked into knee-high boots, a hint of who he was in his realm. "I will not continue to help someone who lies to my face and spits on the opportunities I give him. I presume I'll next hear about you trading kink for drugs."

The words tore him apart. "It's not true. I'm begging you, George, please look into it." He wanted to admit what was really going on, but he didn't have the balls to disappoint the man further.

George took a handkerchief out of his pocket and wiped his hands. "When you get out of here, please return your keys." He turned his back before Rafael could get another word in edgewise.

In response, his head fell into his hands on the table.

****

Daniel scanned the room for Rafael. He had been told his client was already meeting with someone. From across the room, he saw a large, commanding presence rise from his seat across from Rafael. The man looked like he could be the King of England standing in the slums of a prison. It was quite a sight. Taking quick steps to cross the room, his curiosity got the better of him. The regal man looked over at him as he approached. They locked eyes, and the man cocked his beautiful head to the side, stepping away to make an exit.

It was the man Ty had referred to as the "King." A detainee should only be allowed to see his attorneys. When his gaze returned to Rafael, he had his head in his hands and didn't look up when Daniel sat down.

"Why was he here?"

"That was my boss." Rafael didn't lift his head.

"I thought he looked familiar." He crossed his ankle over his knee, waiting for Raf to talk.

"Bad news?" He finally said.

"They won't set bail for your hearing until Monday. It'll likely be the full bond." Daniel didn't beat around the bush—he gave it to him, then bit his tongue.

"So, I'm in here till I'm convicted or proven innocent?"

"Rafael, let me pay your bail. It's not too much for me to cover—"

Rafael cut him off with a snarl, green eyes flashing up to meet his. "No."

"This is something I can easily do for you. It's my fault you're here."

Rafael set his jaw. "It's my job to take care of you, not the other way around."

It was Daniel's turn to growl, anger flashing through him. "We are equals in this. Just because I submit to you does not mean I want to be your slave."

Raf narrowed his eyes. "Stop reading! And if you want to see what a slave really is, I'll take you to George's penthouse sometime where some of the most powerful young men in the city give up every right they have for the time they spend there. But you're right, I don't want a slave. I want a submissive and a partner."

He cracked a smile. "I'm serious. You're my Dom, but for me, for this to work, we have to be equals in everything else outside of the bedroom and Amenti."

"I'm not good at relationships. I try to use kink to work my way through them. I'm very protective of those I love." Rafael searched his face. "I want to take care of you."

"Well, I'm not good at subbing, but you're helping me. We can learn together," Daniel said confidently. "And I want to be able to take care of you, too."

"I don't want to take your money. That's something I feel very strongly about." Rafael looked away.

Knowing he couldn't force this on Rafael, Daniel's face fell before he said, "We need to get you out of here."

"It's looking like that's not going to happen, and if it doesn't, I want you to move on."

"Are you kidding me?" His hands balled into fists, and Daniel's nails bit into his palms. "We just talked about this."

"Daniel, you want to explore this world, and it could be six months or more. I don't want to hold you back…" Rafael looked like he was in pain.

Heat flashed over his face. "I don't want anyone else. I want to learn from you, and if that means I have to wait six months, so be it." He got up to leave, done with the conversation.

"Daniel…" he pleaded.

"Don't." He turned his back, fighting the waves of emotion.

"It's my job to make sure you get what you need." Raf was firm.

Does he really want me to move on? The thought made him ache all over. "Worst excuse I've ever heard." Daniel forced one foot in front of the other as he moved toward the door.

"Daniel." Rafael used his commanding voice, but he kept walking. "Boy!" This time he heard the grind of the man's teeth.

Turning around, he barely whispered, "You lost the ability to give me orders when you ended things." From the distance, he doubted Raf heard him. But he was pretty sure the set of his jaw and the hate in his gaze got the point across. He spun back around and kept his composure as he walked out of the building. When he got to his car, he gripped his chest and laid his forehead on the steering wheel. He couldn't imagine anything more painful coming from Rafael's mouth after he had risked so much.

Blowing out a breath, he couldn't take it. He would have to have Jesse deal with him for the remainder of the case. It hurt too much.

When he got home, it was to find someone waiting in front of his row house. The man stood on his porch, leaning on the door jam. Daniel walked up cautiously, recognizing him from the holding room. It was George, Rafael's boss—a man he wouldn't soon forget by the way the members of the community talked about him.

"Good morning." Because this imposing man was blocking his door, he stayed a few steps back.

"Morning, Daniel." The man spoke with a refined accent he couldn't put his finger on. "Might we step inside and have a word?"

Daniel rocked back and forth on his feet before he nodded. "Sure."

Pulling his keys from his pocket, he decided it was better to have a confrontation inside where his neighbors wouldn't see him. George stepped aside, allowing him access to the door. Heat hit them with a blast when they stepped inside, and Daniel shrugged out of his coat. George followed close behind, taking a hanger for his own coat. He set Daniel off balance.

"Have a seat," George commanded. It was not a request.

Daniel did as he was told, even before he could process why. He was in his own home. No one should tell him to sit...right? "Can I ask what this is about?"

George took a seat on the chair opposite him and placed his folded hands on his knees as he leaned forward. "I want to discuss your client."

Knowing George's type, he exhaled slowly. No doubt he was not denied often. "I can't speak about my client's case, I'm sorry." He sat back, waiting for the tongue lashing.

"But you can fuck your clients?" An amused smile took George's lips.

Daniel's mouth dropped open. "He told you?"

"No, but you just did." His smile spread, taking over his whole face. It was tough to hate him, but the grin was so charming.

They both shifted in their seats. "But you had to have had a hunch."

"There is nothing that goes on in my club that I don't know about," George's blue eyes focused intently on him, "Or rumors that I don't hear. More so when a very attractive new face comes into my club, one that turns heads, and shows up with one Dominant, only to leave with a second."

"Touché." Daniel bowed his head, conceding the point. "I still can't talk about him."

"That's a shame. I'm about to cut him off. I wanted to make sure I was just in doing so." George stood.

Shit. Daniel bit down on his lip, getting to his feet. "After all the help you've given him, you're going to turn your back on him now?" He fought hard to fight the anger he felt. Rafael didn't deserve this.

"After he went back to the very pit I dragged him out of, yes. I think it's fitting to let him go." George's voice lowered, a hint of hurt revealed by his tone, making him wonder if the two had been lovers at some point.

"I can tell you, which could get me fired, that he's not guilty of most of what he's being accused of him. He's being persecuted." Turning, Daniel rubbed a hand over the back of his neck. "I shouldn't have even said that much."

George was on him in a second flat, his larger stature menacing. Taking a step back, Daniel's heels met the couch. The assertive man grabbed his tie, preventing him from falling over when he began to wobble. George stood inches from him, peering down.

"What do you mean he's not guilty? I had his records pulled. He pleaded guilty." George's voice dropped to a sinister hiss.

"Sometimes people take a plea deal even if they aren't guilty." He kept eye contact and didn't back down, sensing it would lose him the man's respect if he did.

"Why would they do such a thing?" Neither of them moved.

"Because a fight is expensive, and there can be damning fake evidence. A plea deal can get a person off with a lesser charge or things like community service. Some lawyers push for them." Daniel had regained his balance and tried to straighten himself.

George didn't release his grip. "Sounds idiotic."

"Most legal practices are, but it can be to the benefit of a defendant. Juries are very hard to sway, and they can be a mixed bag. In most cases, it makes things easier and less expensive. But in this case, it may have screwed him. Two strikes against him looks very bad." It was getting harder for him not to lash out at the man. "I think that's what his prosecutor wanted."

"I want to know if he's lying to me." The imposing man released him and stepped back.

"I really can't share any more information on the case with you." Daniel flattened his palms over the fist-shaped wrinkle in his shirt to smooth it down. "I'd advise you to talk to Rafael if you want to know more."

"I tried that. Why do you think I'm here?" George strolled around the room, his eyes roaming the knick knacks decorating the place.

Daniel felt like George was passing judgment on his whole life. He knew what the verdict would be. Boring. "That's why you went there this morning. How did you get in?"

"I'm a very influential man with contacts all over the city."

The memory of Rafael telling him George knew he was a lawyer came to mind. "Ah, got it. But I thought you had been helping him. He said you loaned him money." Raf had made it seem like his boss knew the entire story.

"But I don't think I'm getting the whole truth. It's not adding up that a former paid sub, who should be mad at me, is holding such a grudge against Rafael. I did give him money for his legal troubles because it appeared to be my fault. I assumed McCoy was going after Rafael because I'm impossible to get to, but I was misinformed as to the details. There is more here than I'm being told. Am I right?"

Daniel's eyes went wide. "You need to talk to him. Seriously." He scrubbed a hand over his face. "There's a lot going on you should know about."

He wanted to tell George about the drugs, and how he knew how it felt to be misled by Rafael, but he knew it could hurt his case. Besides, it wasn't his place. It did, however, set in his mind what he needed to do about McCoy. He was tired of beating around the bush with that asshole.

George intertwined his fingers, cocking his head to the side a hair. "I tried. My help was rebuffed. If he comes to me with the truth, I'll see what I can do. Have a good day, Mr. Caplin." He retrieved his coat and saw himself out. Daniel locked the door behind him and returned to the leather sofa. The walls seemed to be pressing in around him with the knowledge that Rafael had misled both him and Jesse, and apparently, George, too.

LEGALLY BOUND

Chapter Thirteen

The weather was damp when Daniel woke up the next morning. He grumbled all the way to the courthouse. The rain always turned his mood sour, and he didn't want to confront Rafael about the truth. It seemed George, his supposed best friend, didn't even know the truth. He took his seat at the defendant's bench, noticing for once Jesse had beaten him in. His partner slid over a Starbucks latte, and he groaned.

"I love you." Daniel took a sip and grinned. He was still shocked that Jesse could charm anyone he wanted, and the coffee was proof.

"Ah, don't say the 'L' word. We've only been dating for three years." Jesse grabbed his chest in a mocking gesture.

Daniel rolled his eyes, slugging his friend in the shoulder. "You'd kill for a boyfriend as hot as I am."

Jesse wrinkled his nose, eyes glinting in the harsh fluorescent lighting. "You're not my type. Too small."

Unsure if he was kidding, Daniel simply stared at him. Jesse's humor was very dry, and sometimes it was hard to tell. "Really?"

"So what's up with the shiny new 'boy toy?'" Tossing Daniel a few case files, he opened up the top to see where they were for the morning.

"Turns out, he was less than honest about some of the details he shared. I don't know to what extent, but before we can set up a defense, he needs to come clean.

"That bad?" The blond arched a brow.

"Yeah. I spoke to his boss, who had no idea what was going on."

"Ouch. Lying is not a good first step to building a solid relationship. Believe me, I've been lying from the start, and my relationship is shit."

"What could you possibly have lied about from the start?" Daniel studied his best friend. He knew the man inside and out, but he had learned there were some things Jesse only talked about if he was in the right mood.

"I told her from the get-go I work late. I used to sit at the bar alone till you came along. And lots of little stuff that probably aided in the decline of our marriage."

"Will you divorce her already?" Taking another sip of his coffee, Daniel leaned back in the uncomfortable chair he was used to spending hours in.

"And risk the wrath of the circuit judge?" He shook his head vigorously. "I like my nuts, and I don't mind giving two-thirds of my paycheck to not have hell at home and on the job."

"But see, then the hell at home would vanish. It's the beauty of things." He couldn't help but laugh. Jesse was right to be scared of his father-in-law. The guy did not dick around.

"I'm at work more than I am at home. My plan is smarter than yours."

"You don't ever want to have sex again?" Daniel cocked his head to the side.

"Maybe if I meet someone, I'll divorce her." He sucked at the straw of his iced coffee, making him shiver just thinking about it. "Rafael is up first if you want to excuse yourself for the initial hearing." Jesse held up the case file.

"I should after the crap he pulled. But after gathering together all that stuff, I want to see if it works in our favor." He blew out a breath, not really wanting to see Rafael.

When everything was called to order and Arthur Brunswick set the new file on the Judge's desk, Stenson began to rail.

"Can't you control your client for the duration of this case, or do I need to hold him here before I send him to the penitentiary down state?" His large ears were red at the top, and his eyes bulged a little.

"Sir, may I approach?" Jesse asked in his suave, judge-handling tone.

"You may."

Jesse got up from his seat, smoothed a hand down his designer shirt, and buttoned his suit jacket before picking up the huge file they had compiled once Daniel had gotten out of jail. He strolled up to the Judge's bench and set it down.

"Sir, here is our case showing that the harassment we discussed before is still going on to this day. After you ordered a stop put to it. Here is a video of my partner, who has been dating our client since before we took on his case, pretending to solicit his boyfriend. No money was exchanged, and it was an act put on to show the aggressive stalking my client is dealing with. Here are stills I had printed from the video." Jesse paused to take a breath. "I also have a video and stills of my partner, Daniel Caplin, being aggressively handled by the cop in question as he threatened him for information about our client. You can also find statements in this file concerning the length of time the two gentlemen have been seeing each other. We will, of course, have more documentation about the harassment, and 'witch hunt,' this cop has been bringing against our client when we go to trial."

The Judge's mouth slowly started to fall open as he took in the file. Daniel shot a glance over to the D.A., and the man looked like he was going to murder everyone in his office when he left there. He avoided meeting Rafael's eyes, who sat on the other side of the room till it was his turn for the case to be heard, but he could see the smile on his face.

"Furthermore, the next case on your docket today is Mr. Caplin's, which I would like dropped for gross misconduct," Jesse finished.

The Judge picked up each document in the file with his sausage fingers and shook his head. "I see. Mr. Caplin's case is dismissed, and I'm about to call the Captain of the nineteenth myself and have words." He looked at the D.A. "It might save you a lot of embarrassment to look into this yourself and drop the case."

"I will carefully look into the matter, but I would like to point out that this is all hearsay, and we have no evidence of any malice on the part of the detective in question against their client. It could be anyone, or just officers doing their job keeping an eye on a known criminal." The D.A. held up his hands. "I'm not saying what they have decided to do is not misconduct at this point, but I think the case needs more proof. It's thin at the moment, and this smells like a bad set up by the defense to sway you."

"I see your side, but the mounting evidence does not look good. I will agree to set bail for the defendant, drop the charges against Mr. Caplin, and set a trial date. Something is fishy here, and I plan to get to the bottom of it."

His partner grinned all the way back to his seat.

Daniel decided to step out of the room when Rafael was brought over to talk to Jesse. Before leaving, he spotted a flicker of shock cross Rafael's face as Jesse quietly explained the situation to him while the Judge continued with the next case.

Slipping out the side door to hide in the hall like a little bitch, coffee in hand, Daniel leaned back against the plaster wall. A part of him knew Raf would be pissed about his passive-aggressive response. After a time, he pulled the cuff of his jacket back to check his watch. Twenty minutes had elapsed, so he figured it was safe to return.

The door creaked, turning heads, as he pulled it open, and he quietly tried to step back into the courtroom. He locked eyes with Jesse before the man turned back around. The Judge was scanning a file while Rafael was being led out of the room. Rafael looked over his shoulder and glared. Daniel swallowed hard, averting his eyes. He could feel the man's stare boring into him all the way to the bench.

"Perfect timing, dipshit," Jesse murmured.

They took their seats as another lawyer approached to argue for his defendant's bail.

"How did it go?" Daniel muttered out of the side of his mouth.

"Okay, he was grateful you did all that." He gave him a sympathetic look.

"But let me guess. It's not enough," he mumbled.

"He might be right, man. This could still go south. We still need a link in the police station to hang McCoy, and we may never find it. If we put this in a jury's hands, it could go either way." Jesse rubbed his temples. "I need a drink and to stab a few mother fuckers. I'm so tired of judges…"

Daniel covered his mouth to stifle the laugh. When he got himself under control, he turned to speak. "Bitter this morning about your wife's father?"

"If you think all my vendettas against judges have to do with him, then you're correct." Jesse spoke into his case file.

Daniel followed suit, picking his up to cover his face so they could mutter behind them like usual. "Things not happy on the home front?"

"The old lady wants children," Jesse said a little too loudly.

The Judge eyed them, and they both put down their files and began to write. "What?"

"I'm thirty F-ing-five, and now she decides this," Jesse grumbled.

"She is six years younger than you. Maybe it's her way of combating the big three-0?" Daniel leaned closer, barely moving his mouth as he spoke.

"Do you think she'd notice if I went and got snipped?" He cocked his head as if he had a stroke of brilliance.

"You'd need to take time off from work, and your balls would hurt like a bitch."

Jesse huffed, grabbing himself under the table and letting the day roll on.

When recess was called for lunch, all their clients had been wrapped up. "It's a miracle we got out of there before four."

"The docket gods aligned our stars." Daniel raised his hands in supplication.

"First time in six months. I swear we always have the last case." Jesse had a skip in his step that made him look like a prancing ogre.

"You're too large to skip, and you're not gay."

"That is racist! Straight guys can skip." They headed toward the adjoining temporary jail through the bridge.

"You're white. You can't claim race."

"Watch me." After scanning their paperwork and going through ID checks and metal detectors, they were heading toward the council room. "Want me to handle Rafael by myself?"

"No, I want to confront him. You didn't speak to George. It will be harder for you." Daniel stopped in the corridor that would send them toward their designated meeting room. "Can I run to the washroom?"

"Sure." Jesse looked at him strangely, but he ducked out anyway. He had someone to speak to.

****

Rafael was led down the dimly lit hall toward the meeting room. His hands were cuffed in front of him, and he smelled like a rotten prison cell. A feeling in his gut told him he would get the third degree from Jesse and Daniel would skip out, much like he had this morning. It was better that way. He would end up in jail, and Daniel would need a good Dominant to look after him.

His escort banged the door open to reveal Jesse pacing the small room, a single light flickering above his head. The scent of old women and harsh chemicals assaulted Rafael's nose. At least no one would be able to smell him over the stench.

"I see your partner ditched out again." he said to Jesse's back as the guard unlocked his cuffs. He rubbed his wrists absentmindedly while studying Jesse's profile. He was too well dressed to be a straight man. His designer suits, cufflinks, and ties all complemented each other perfectly.

His wife probably picks out his clothes.

"He'll be back."

Raf raised both brows.

"Bathroom, you nosey fuck," Jesse said with a grin.

"I get possessive." He shrugged it off.

"Yes, all people in relationships do. It's called codependency." Jesse winked.

"That why your wife dresses you?" He crossed his arms over his chest.

"I dress myself…and Daniel." Jesse's grin made him believe he wasn't joking. "You're welcome."

"Seriously?" Rafael looked him over, thinking. Jesse nodded.

"Huh…" He took a step closer to study him. "Daniel doesn't know does he?"

Jesse's eyes flashed wide before he got himself under control. Rafael noticed, and he grinned to himself. He knew he was right.

"Know what?" Daniel asked, having magically opened the door without a sound.

Both men turned to look at him. Raf couldn't hide his hint of a grin. "Do you know what happened in court this morning?"

He caught the glare Jesse shot at him a moment before they all took their seats around the rickety table.

"I'm surprised you're here." He looked Daniel in the eyes, starting the conversation.

"Someone needed to tell you to get your head out of your ass." Daniel's posture was stiff and standoffish.

"Excuse me?" Rafael growled, throwing his fist down on the table. "I was honest with you. This isn't going to end well, and you need attention while I'm in jail."

"George paid me a visit." Daniel's words were like a shot of ice water to his veins.

"You can't share case details with him." Rafael shot back, almost before Daniel was done.

"I didn't have to. Your boss was pretty clear on the subject. He seemed to think there was more going on with McCoy than you're letting on, otherwise his vendetta would be against him, not you. That means either you're lying to us about the detective, or you're lying to him."

"Shit." Rafael reached up and tore at his hair. He didn't want to come clean to any of them. It was the one blip on his conscience that he didn't want to admit to.

"You better explain it to us, or our defense won't work. I'm not going to do the research and work misconduct will require if we don't have all the facts," Jesse added.

Daniel looked over at his partner. "Don't lie. You'd rather stay in the office and do the work."

"Don't tell him that. I can go to a bar."

"Fine." Raf cut off their banter. "This has to stay privileged. If it gets back to my boss, I will get you both disbarred." He watched the two lawyers exchange a look that struck him wrong. "Understand?"

They both nodded.

"We had to boot Lance, from the club as you know. George had received too many complaints about him not respecting safe words and about him getting off on pushing things past people's limits. He had to keep peace, even if the guy was a hush-hush-top-paying customer for Dominant services. Being a police detective, he also presented a big problem. George knew he would get backlash for it, and from what I understand, there was a little blackmail to be had. George took the risk. Everything was quiet for about a month, which surprised everyone involved."

Rafael sighed and continued. "I guess it began a couple of weeks after George booted him from the club. I was driving home after closing up at Amenti because of a late client that ran long. Thunder storms were rolling through like crazy, making the night thick with steam. I hadn't noticed the lights in the rearview mirror. I was too zoned out in my own world thinking about the scene I had just done. When I realized I had a cop on my tail, I was instantly nervous. I'd popped some pills before getting into the car. I pulled over to the shoulder. The streets were dead but loaded with parked cars, so I couldn't move the car over far enough. I waited for the cop to approach, not sure what he had me on."

Ignoring the look from them when he mentioned the pills, he went on. "When I rolled down my window, I saw it was McCoy, and I felt sick. I knew he would be pissed at me about dumping him as a client. But I wasn't sure how much he knew about my involvement in his getting booted from Amenti. Lance never much liked anyone knowing about his submissive side. I kept it cool and said my usual "Hey, whats up?" He didn't say anything, so I asked him if I had been speeding or what, telling him that I must have been zoned out on a control high from my last scene."

He looked up to catch Daniel's eyes, to gage his reaction, but couldn't read it.

"Then what did he do?" Jesse asked.

"He asked me to step out of the car. Acting like he didn't know me, he was real cold about it, like a typical cop. So I got out and tried something different. I talked down to him, asking him why he pulled me over. He seemed to respond to that better as he stepped into me and told me he'd missed that tone from me. I talked down to him some more, asking him if he'd been too busy crossing lines with subs to find someone new to punish him. I got him all worked up." Rafael looked at his lap.

"What do you mean?" Jesse asked.

"Turned on. He loves being degraded. Well…then he made some comments back about them liking the abuse."

"The subs he abused?" Daniel visibly stiffened as he spoke.

Rafael nodded, and he could see the pain in Daniel's eyes. "So I called him on the reason he pulled me over. He was beating around the bush, so I asked him again and got in his face. He admitted he had no other way to get a hold of me, that he wanted me as his Dom again. He offered to pay me three times my normal rate, but I still turned him down. I told him it was against the club rules. George was like a father to me, he'd taken me off the streets and under his wing. I couldn't do that to him."

"I was turning to go back to my car when the cop grabbed me and kissed me. I flipped him around and slammed him into the hood of his patrol car. He smiled at me over his shoulder and told me that he'd just caught that on tape. I was so fucking pissed, and I knew I had fucked up, so I agreed to play his Dom till he could find a new one. Plus, the money would help with my pill habit." Rafael shrugged, not making eye contact. Daniel was surely going to be ashamed of him. He had made some stupid choices that he wasn't proud of. How did he ever think he deserved happiness, or Daniel, at all?

****

Daniel didn't know if he should be turned on or upset by Rafael's admission. It made him feel better, though, that the dick cop had submitted.

"If you told your boss what he was doing, couldn't he have done something?" Jesse asked the question he wanted to.

"I doubt it, and I'd have lost his trust." Raf's body tensed.

"At this point, he thinks you're back to hooking and drugs. Can it get worse?" Daniel threw his hands in the air. "I feel like you're determined to turn down any and all help that's offered."

"This is worse." Raf sounded defeated as he tugged at his hair. "George works on trust, I lied to him, and I went behind his back to keep playing with someone he banned from the club. On top of that, it was someone I helped him ban."

"I really don't want to sit here for this lover's spat when I could be eating a Chicago dog and getting rid of my fantastic abs the wife loves," Jesse cut in, getting up. "We need evidence and reasonable doubt. If you have any more text messages, emails, or anything that would be helpful, now would be a good time to tell us. The connection to the cop via a sexual relationship can make a big difference."

Daniel checked his watch as they got up to leave. The guard in the hall was called, and they waited.

"You're free to go Mr. Argon," the guard said when she came back into the room.

"Huh?" Jesse and Rafael said together.

"Your bail has been paid. Let's go finish the paperwork." The guard led Rafael out, and he shot a puzzled look back at them.

"Bathroom, huh?" Jesse rolled his eyes. "I need to take a note out of George's book on how to deal with liars."

"You see right through me anyways. I don't know why I bother." Daniel shrugged, holding the door open before following his partner toward the parking garage. "He shouldn't have to stay here during the trial."

"You think with your cock on this one too much. Dinner?" Jesse was sarcastic, but he still seemed to be in a great mood.

"Yeah, I don't want to go home. You never know who I'll find."

After dinner with Jesse, Daniel didn't go home. He couldn't. He'd made up his mind the night before, and it had festered all day. Driving toward the south side of the city, he followed the directions his contact had given him. It was a good thing that McCoy wasn't the arresting officer in his case, or his actions could be seen as harassment.

No wonder the detective doesn't want to be outed. The south side of Chicago was religious and blue collar, and Daniel knew the atmosphere was very homophobic. If McCoy had the kind of big family that was common there...he saw the full picture now. Pulling up in front of the small ranch in Oak Lawn, he parked on the street. Already after dusk, most people were home from work and the road was lined with cars. Large trees shaded the length of the avenue, casting shadows over the road and making it appear darker than it was.

Getting out of his car, he locked it behind him. On edge, he told himself to calm down. He didn't know why he was there. If he was looking for a confession, it would be hearsay at best, and it was against Illinois law to record someone without their express permission. Ringing the bell, he dragged his teeth over his lip as he waited. When five minutes in the breezy night air had passed, he began to think that maybe the guy wasn't even home. Just then, the door opened, and a gun was pointed in his face. Eyes flashing wider, Daniel resisted the urge to run back to his car.

"What the hell do you want?" McCoy kept the gun trained on him.

"Is that how you answer the door for everyone? I never realized the neighborhood was that bad." Not knowing how else to ease the tension, he needed to be asked inside so no one else would see what he was about to do.

McCoy lowered the gun a little. "What do you want?"

"To talk." Holding his ground, Daniel noticed the gun was conveniently pointed at his dick. He really hoped McCoy wouldn't shoot him to get back at Rafael. "It's better if we take this inside. You don't want your neighbors to think I'm your lover, do you?" He cracked a smile. It was something Jesse would have said, and he was thankful, for once, for his partner's brand of humor.

"Get the fuck in here." McCoy stepped aside, allowing him access.

Daniel ducked in to find himself in a nicely furnished living room. It had the original wood floors and it was obvious it had been taken care of. He felt like an ass. "Nice place," he blurted out. What the fuck am I doing? It was not like him to confront a jaded ex-lover. Then he remembered everything the shit bag had done to both him and Raf, and he found his resolve.

"Get to your point." McCoy faced him, pushing the gun back into its holster on his belt while shifting his weight. "Are you here to hand Rafael over?"

McCoy was still in his suit, and the dress shirt he wore hugged his chest, showing off how well-toned he was. Daniel could see what Raf saw in him. The guy had longer hair that curled at the overgrown ends, a strong jaw that was dusted with scruff, and broad shoulders.

"I'm here to tell you to back off." Clenching his hands into fists at his side, he stood in the middle of the room. Sweat broke out on the back of his neck.

"I don't know what you're referring to." McCoy smirked as he said the words.

Daniel could tell how much the jerk liked the game, how much he got off on fucking with people, and he barely kept the edge of anger out of his tone. "You do too. You're trying to ruin him."

"Isn't it against the law or something for a lawyer to confront a possible witness in a case he's working on?" McCoy licked his lips. "Like, witness intimidation?"

"Are you suggesting you have something to do with the case against my client?" Daniel crossed his arms over his chest. Two could play at this game.

"I did question you. Maybe you're here for revenge. I could call this in, or I could just shoot you." He placed his hand on his hip, exposing his gun again.

Daniel growled under his breath. "So when your neighbors say they saw you let me in, you'll what—be suspended? Works for me."

"I'm an upstanding member of society, and you're a lawyer who picks up prostitutes." McCoy dropped his hand and laughed.

"And you're a bad bottom who wants someone to make you their bitch." As soon as the words left his mouth, he could see the anger flair in Lance's eyes, but he went on anyways. "Is that why you ignore your submissive's safe words, hmm? Because that's how you want a Dom to treat you, isn't it?"

McCoy stalked toward him. "You don't know what you're talking about, boy, and you better shut your mouth before someone teaches you a lesson."

Daniel held his ground as the aggressive dick got in his face. The cop had a few inches on him. "I don't know what I'm talking about? You're a bad sub and a worse Dominant. I think you're just mad because Rafael wants me over you, so you're pushing this to separate us."

McCoy looked down at him. "You think I give a shit about you? You don't even register. You're a pretty face he'll use, but you're not what he wants. He'll toss you like the rest. I've always been what he wants."

His mind whirled. What does he mean by the rest? "That's why he's training me and ignoring you, right?" Daniel leaned forward. "You have to arrest him just to see him."

McCoy's dark eyes focused in on him. "I had him arrested…" A wave of emotions washed over the man's face. "I see what you're trying to do. You want a confession out of me? How about an illegal search?"

"You admitted it. I've always known he was innocent and that you're just jealous."

"I'm not jealous," he scoffed.

"Really? Is that why you stalk him?" Daniel tried to control his emotions, but he wanted so badly to punch the bastard in his smug face.

McCoy's lips turned into a scowl. "He's getting what was coming to him. He's no Dominant, but I'll admit, he even had me fooled. He's nothing better than a druggy whore. That fool George dresses him up to make him who he is."

"Maybe you're jealous of just how many people want him." Daniel was grasping at straws. He wanted the guy to admit it, just for his own peace of mind. "Even George wants him…and no one wants you."

McCoy's hand shot out and fisted in his shirt. "George should have preferred me. Rafael is a decent Dom, but I do both. The self- proclaimed King of the underground called me dangerous, but what about the addict he has under his wing? Huh? You're right. When The King," he said, spitting out the word with disdain, "kicked me out of the club, all I had was Rafael. I thought he was my friend, but he turned his back on me for that man he worships."

Daniel leaned in closer and spoke softly, "So you ruined him for turning his back on you, and through him, you hurt George?"

"Yeah, and George's face when he turned his back on his prized pupil was priceless. Jail for my former Dominant is icing on the cake." McCoy licked his lips. "Your involvement gave me a bit of a woody, though."

Daniel shoved him off. "I should kick your ass, but you'd enjoy it too much. I got what I came for." He turned his back on the cop and headed for the door. "Plus, I'm going to get him off, and I'll get to fuck him every day. So you lose."

And then, everything went black.

LEGALLY BOUND

Chapter Fourteen

Daniel woke with an aching head and a pulsing in his ears. Stars danced over his vision, and it took him a few moments to remember where he was. He panicked for a moment as he tried to piece it all together and figure out what Lance had done to him.

"Your breathing changed. I can tell you're awake." McCoy's voice came from somewhere behind him.

He tried to move and found his arms were pulled straight above his head. His eyes shot open wider, and he realized he was naked, dangling by his wrists. "What the fuck?" He looked down and found his footing, the soles of his feet barely reaching the floor.

McCoy only laughed.

Daniel's shoulders ached, leading him to believe he had been hanging there for a long time. He was in a room with dark wood floors and warm, brown walls. There was a mini fridge in one corner and a St. Andrew's cross pushed to one side.

He craned his neck back to try and catch a glimpse of McCoy. He could see a figure with his back turned. Panic gripped his chest, and he found it hard to keep his breathing even. Rafael's words echoed in his mind—He ignored safe words and some subs got really hurt. Looking up to see how bad it was, he saw his wrists were tied with rope in elaborate knots. He reached with his fingers to see if he could push them undone, but it was impossible. His eyes followed the rope to the top where it was attached to a D clip on a pulley system from the ceiling.

Trying to make his voice calm, Daniel spoke softly. "Very funny. You've had your fun. You've scared me." He shifted his weight, trying to get more relief for his shoulders, but found he couldn't push off his toes high enough. Soon, his calves began to cramp.

"You really are a bad sub, aren't you?" McCoy came into view with what he could only guess was a cane.

"Let me down. This is bordering on assault," Daniel demanded, but the quiver in his voice gave him away.

"Not bordering, son, but who are they going to believe? A detective with an outstanding record, or a lawyer who was just arrested for soliciting?" The bastard wore a smug grin.

Searching for words, he had none. The dirty cop walked around him, and he squeezed his eyes shut, waiting for the first blow. But it never came.

Opening his eyes, McCoy was nowhere in sight. He knew what the man was doing. It was all a big head game, but that didn't stop him from mentally freaking out.

"I see why he likes you. Your skin is perfect." McCoy's warm fingers trailed down his spine.

Daniel had never felt so helpless in his life. His heart pounded in his ears.

"Have you gone silent on me?" His lips were next to his ear, and his hot breath fanned over Daniel's cheek. "I can taste your fear. It's dripping from your pores, and it's never been so addicting."

Feeling like he was going to vomit, an idea struck him. Whipping his head back with all the force he could muster, a sickening crack made the pain in the back of his head worth it. He heard McCoy stumble back, cursing. When McCoy turned around to face him, there was blood trickling from his nose, and his eyes were already starting to blacken.

"You're going to pay for that." Wheeling back, McCoy threw a right hook to Daniel's left eye.

His head smacked to the side with the force of the blow. A throbbing ache set in instantly, and he could feel his face begin to swell till his eye couldn't open all the way. But it was worth it. He wouldn't go down without a fight.

McCoy walked behind him again, and Daniel braced himself. Digging deep to find a way to survive this, he didn't think McCoy would kill him. He would deal with everything else later. Fear bubbled up inside him, but he tried his best to push it down, not giving the jerk what he wanted.

"Mmmm…good boy." McCoy's voice was patronizing, not like Rafael's had been when he said the same thing.

"I'm a very good boy for Rafael, and he loves fucking me."

He heard the hiss of the cane flying through the air a second before it struck. Thwack! His ass seared. He had never in his life felt pain so intensely concentrated on one small area, and he couldn't help the scream that left his lips. Lance didn't stop. The crazed man landed blow after blow in quick succession. Gasping for breath when McCoy finally paused, Daniel's throat hurt from his cries. He didn't know if it had been four, like McCoy had said, or fifty hits. All he knew was the sharp, white pain. Coarse fingers skimmed the wounds, and Daniel withdrew inside himself, holding his breath.

"God, I love fresh welts." McCoy pressed what felt like a fingernail into his very raw skin. "Now for the fun part."

He tried not to show McCoy anything, to keep the pain masked behind a blank stare.

"I'm going to bar the gate." McCoy licked the blood off his lips that dripped from his nose. "That, if your terrible Dominant hasn't told you, is a British term for the pattern the cane makes on your skin. It's a five bar gate pattern, and it's the most painful of all because it crosses diagonally over the other four lashes."

Daniel sucked in a breath and winced involuntarily. He didn't mean to give in to the fear, but he couldn't help the reaction.

Fire broke out across his ass as the cane struck over all his previous strikes. It was like no pain he had ever experienced, and his whole body stiffened as he tried not to cry out. He felt ashamed and taken advantage of, but he didn't want to give the asshole the satisfaction.

"A virgin to the cane, huh?" McCoy's vile laugh echoed around the room. "I love it."

Daniel could tell he was getting off on this. He tried to dig for any reserve of strength he had to stifle the reactions that were feeding his tormentor.

McCoy stepped back in front of him with a set of nasty-looking barbed clips in his hand, and he had a feeling he knew where they were going. The guy pinched one of his nipples, twisting it before placing the clamp on it. The sharp teeth bit into his sensitive flesh. Had Rafael done this to him, he would have liked it. He couldn't believe how little he knew about this world he was now trapped in with the wrong man. But he knew he only had himself to blame for being in this position. Daniel hated that he hadn't listened to Raf about how dangerous Lance was. This all could have been prevented had he used better judgment. It was almost like he deserved it for his poor choices made in anger.

"While you were unconscious, I debated if I should show you this, but fear is my thing. Even if you're prepared for it, no one will believe a user." McCoy picked up something from one of the tables along the wall. Pictures. His captor brought them into view, and Daniel could barely make out what looked like an orange pharmacy pill bottle through his pain-laced gaze.

"I don't get it?" he admitted when he looked up into the McCoy's eyes.

"Filled with Vicodin that Raf doesn't have a script for, and the bottle's covered in his fingerprints."

"You could have faked that." Daniel's voice was dry and cracked, and his heart sank. It seemed like Rafael was constantly lying. His tongue stuck to the roof of his mouth, but he wasn't going to give in and show how upset he felt.

"Not when his prints are on the pills." McCoy licked his lips, shaking the bottle.

He swallowed as McCoy walked out of sight. They had Rafael, and Daniel would be lucky to get enough people to corroborate his story to get the charges dropped. Cops stuck together, and it was a long shot, even before the pills could be introduced. He mentally kicked himself. All this suffering on his part would now be for nothing.

McCoy came into view again, twirling a flogger in his fingers. Over and over the black leather tails whirled in front of his face. It was almost hypnotizing against the fading light from the window over his shoulder.

"Know what this is?" McCoy stopped the handle and held it in his hand.

Daniel nodded. He didn't trust his voice after the caning.

"What?" The prick had a look, he couldn't place it.

"A flogger," he forced out.

McCoy's smirk widened. "Close. It's a cat-o-nine tails." He held it out so Daniel could see the tiny, rough rosettes on the ends of the leather strips.

"Okay." He didn't have the energy to ask. It was going to hurt, whatever it was. "Going to pull my fingernails off next?" he shot back, starting to feel the overwhelming wave of despair.

"Not my thing, but maybe if you beg." McCoy flexed his arm and pulled the implement back.

When it landed, Daniel felt the difference as the tiny knots tore at his skin. He cried out, and his head slumped forward, limp. Again, the specially-tipped leather landed. He kept telling himself that he would enjoy this under Rafael's hand, but the fear and depression that had sunk in magnified everything that happened. Coming here had caused this. He was the idiot who deserved what he got. The spray of marks covered his chest and abs. Blood welled up in tiny flecks at some of the points that had been stuck repeatedly. He began to wonder if he had been wrong. Did McCoy have it in him to kill? Panic gripped his chest, making bile rise in his throat.

Minutes ticked by and nothing happened, so he agonizingly picked his head up and looked around, but the cop was nowhere in sight. His legs were weak, and he didn't think he could take anymore without them collapsing beneath him. He tried to turn his hands. Except for a ring of fire that circled his wrists, they had gone numb at some point. Darkness crept into his mind, and he wished the cop would just kill him. He couldn't endure anymore.

The crazed Dom used every tool he had to paint bruises and welts all over Daniel's body until he was hoarse from screaming. By the time the dirty cop had had his fill of the toys, sweat was dripping off Daniel's nose and down his brow, into his eyes. One moment he was completely lucid, and the next, he had lost himself to blackness.

LEGALLY BOUND

Chapter Fifteen

Daniel jolted awake. Jerking his limbs closer to his body, he found he was shaking. It was so cold he could see his breath. It took him a moment to orient himself, and he realized he was in his car. Fully clothed, when he glanced at the clock, he saw it was after eleven. It had been at least three hours since he had stepped foot in McCoy's home. Looking around, he expected to be in the same neighborhood, but his car had been moved. He wasn't in front of McCoy's house. Instead, he was in front of his office building. If he called the cops, he would have no proof he was ever at Lance's. Shivering harder, he felt around for his keys and found them in his pocket. He shoved them into the ignition and started the car as he began to wonder if it had all been a dream. But when he moved his arm, the pain shooting through it reminded him that it had all been real. His shirt stuck to the raw, oozing patches of skin on his chest. Every movement chafed, causing excruciating agony. The bruises on his body were all he had, and he knew the cop was smart. There would be no physical evidence at McCoy's house that he could use against him. With just the marks, it would be his word against McCoy's.

How could I have been so stupid? He looked in the rearview mirror and stretched out a hand to hold in front of the vent. Still blowing cool air, his joints screamed at him. He watched the traffic go by out the partially fogged window. Time was moving in slow motion. If he went to the hospital, he would feel like even more of a failure, and having a rape kit done would be a low moment in his life that he didn't think he could deal with. It hadn't gone that far, though, it was pretty easy to tell. Since he didn't bottom often with his lovers, he knew his ass would hurt if he'd been sodomized. But because he lost consciousness during the assault, he knew they'd push for it.

Gray clouds rolled across the sky, and it was long dark. Street lights and headlamps illuminated the empty roadway. He put the car in gear and shifted in his seat so he could reach the pedals. His ass cheeks burned, and it took everything he had not to scream. Daniel had to slant his body and rest on his hip as he drove. Flashes of memory filled his mind as he drove—the cane, the clamps, and the whip. He didn't want to know what the marks on his ass looked like.

Every part of his body hurt as he drove, even the patches of skin McCoy had missed. His shoulder joints ached. The front and back of his dress shirt was flecked with blood and stuck to the leather seat. He wanted to take a bottle of painkillers, clean himself up, and pass out. How was he going to explain the two black eyes to Jesse? They were so swollen it was hard to drive. It was a good thing he knew the city like the back of his hand, because he had to squint just to see the road. When Daniel pulled back up to his row house, there was a figure waiting at his door. Truly ashamed and embarrassed, he hoped it wasn't Rafael. But as he got closer, he saw it was.

Parked in his driveway, he took the front stairs to his place slowly, not wanting the confrontation he knew was coming. Each step was painful, and the back of his legs burned from the caning. As he got closer, Raf's face swam into view. The look the man gave him made him wince. He pushed his tongue into the side of his cheek and crossed his arms over his chest as best he could with his sore joints. When they were face to face, he knew Rafael would have to move because he blocked the doorway. The only good thing about his black eyes was that Raf wouldn't be able see the red in his cheeks. Both men stood for a minute, their stances similarly defensive. The cold nipped at his neck, and he pulled his scarf up to his ears, hoping to hide some more of the marks around his neck. Daniel studied him, waiting for him to move, then noticed Rafael's lips were tinged blue, making him wonder how long he had been waiting.

"What the fuck happened to you?" Rafael reached out to him, and he took a step back.

"Don't touch me. You told me to move on." He made no move to open the door, but instead, kicked at the leaves that had piled on the small stone porch. Trying to lean against one of the pillars to hide his unsteadiness, it was hard to find a spot on his body that wasn't bruised. "I don't have anything to say to you."

"Why did you pay my bail?" Anger was written in Rafael's expression, and his posture was tense.

So lightheaded, Daniel knew he would be on the ground if he didn't sit soon. "Because I wanted to. Deal with it. I'll see you at our next meeting." Finally shoving past him, Daniel bit his lip to stifle the groan of pain before jamming his key into the door lock.

"Daniel…" Raf had the commanding tone back to his voice. "You're hurt."

"Which, of course, is not your concern. You told me to move on and find another Dom." He regretted the words as soon as he said them.

"Another Dominant did this to you?" Rage flashed over Rafael's face. "Who? That Ty fuck?"

"No, and it's really none of your business." He was in and slammed the door in Rafael's face before he could say another word. Slumping back into the door, Daniel cried out in agony as pain lanced over his raw skin. He pressed his eyes closed and knocked his head back into the unyielding wood. The pain was too much, and he was too tired to process this all now. Gripping the railing to his hardwood stairs, he took them one at a time. At the top, he groaned, realizing he would have to go back down for ice. He stumbled toward the master bath, contemplating his next move. Standing in a hot shower while banging his head against the tile for about an hour sounded appealing. But he knew his wounds were too raw to tolerate the hot water. Instead, he ran the large walk in shower that sat next to the tub to steam the room. He needed the warmth while he cleaned his wounds.

Perched on the edge of his large Jacuzzi tub, he closed his eyes, telling himself he had to undress. It was going to be painful—every movement made him wince. Plus, he was willing to bet the blood had mostly dried, the shirt sticking to him by now. He took a deep breath, wishing he could remain still for a few more minutes. He'd give himself sixty seconds, then he would bear the pain. A creak brought his mind out of the haze, and his eyes snapped open to see a smiling face watching him through the now-fogged glass shower door that stood wide open between him and the bathroom door.

Daniel's mind whirled, and he tried to grasp for anything he could use as a weapon, but he knew he couldn't move far. A toothbrush wouldn't get the job done. He got to his feet, shakily stepping around the glass door to clear his view. "How the fuck did you get in here?"

"In the murder capital of the country, why do you have a fake rock with a key in it in a fuckin' flower pot next to your door?" Rafael held up the rock in his palm, giving it a little shake, jingling the key inside.

"A whore would know that." It was a low blow, but he was too pissed and hurting to rein in his temper.

"No, anyone would know that. It's what most people who have never had to think about their safety do." Rafael set the rock on the counter as he crossed the room.

"Leave. You don't want me." It was hard to say the words. Daniel turned around to assess the damage to his face in the mirror.

Raf's fingers were on him, brushing up his back. Daniel winced, his face contorting.

"You've been beaten." There was pain in the man's words. "Don't lie to me."

He nodded, too tired to fight. "Please leave. I need to clean up and lie down."

"Why didn't you use your safe word?" Rafael grabbed his coat by the collar, ignoring his request, and eased it off his shoulders. "This is why you need to be trained. No one should do this to you."

"That wasn't an option." He clamped his mouth shut, cutting off the confession he wanted to make. "I'll be okay in a few days."

"It's always an option. It doesn't make you less of a man." He saw Rafael's eyes drop down his back in the mirror, and he frowned when the man growled. "Where the fuck did you meet a sadist? I can't imagine anyone else doing this to a newbie." The words caught in his throat as he spoke.

"I didn't. Please drop it. It's over." Daniel lifted a hand to undo the buttons on his shirt, spotting the marks on his wrist a second too late to cover them up.

Rafael's hand shot out, grabbing him by the cuff and pushing it up to expose the full rope burns around his wrist. "Bullshit. I know the signs." Dropping the hand softly, he thrust his own into his hair and moved around to rest his butt against the sink. "Who?"

"Just go." Daniel swallowed past the lump in his throat, finishing with the buttons on his shirt. He staggered forward to get a washcloth out of a drawer.

With an unsteady hand, he held it under the warm shower water.

Rafael pushed off the counter, taking the cloth from him. He set it aside and helped him ease out of his shirt. "I'm so mad, I'll go to George if you don't spill."

"He's not even talking to you." He knew he should tell all, but he also knew he'd been stupid.

Rafael kissed the back of his neck—one of the only areas without a mark. "Okay." He picked up the cloth again and started dabbing at his wounds. "He should be taking care of you if he did this."

Daniel sucked in a sharp breath, but he bit his tongue to hide the pain. He knew he deserved what he got for confronting McCoy. "It wasn't like that."

"I don't understand." Rafael looked at him through the mirror. "Is there more?"

He knew what the man meant and nodded.

"Let's get your pants off so I can get you all cleaned." Rafael reached around him to undo his belt and ease him out of his slacks. A sharp hiss filled the room when his thighs were exposed. "I'm not going to give up till I find out who did this, and then I'm going to kill him." Raf made a fist, clenching his fingers so tightly his knuckles turned white.

Daniel caught his hand as it went for his briefs. "You can't," he said, holding Raf gaze. "Promise me you won't." Ashamed of how bad the scars would look, he felt ruined. He would have to live with it.

"Not unless you tell me why and who?" Rafael pulled away from his grasp and slid his briefs down, gasping again. "Fucking hell. How long did this go on?"

"A few hours. I'm not sure. I wasn't lucid the whole time." Daniel closed his eyes briefly. He didn't want to see the horror written on Raf's face.

"You passed out?" Rafael's hands clenched into fists again.

He shrugged one shoulder and looked away.

Rafael's expression changed, and he couldn't read it. "That is so fucking dangerous. This guy needs to be stopped."

"I know." Daniel licked his dry, cracked lips. He turned to try and catch his reflection in the mirror, but his caretaker was in the way. Maybe it was for the best, though. He didn't need to add to the pain he was already in. It could wait.

"I'm going to call the police if you won't tell me." Rafael's voice had dropped to a gritty command as he rinsed the rag.

Flinching away from the newly warmed cloth, Daniel said, "You will not call the police to my house without my permission. I'll say it was consensual BDSM."

"Stop fucking reading!" The exasperated male took a few slow breaths. "I am going to call Jesse."

"You wouldn't dare." His hazel eyes flashed up to meet Raf's green ones, anger showing in them as Rafael pulled out his phone.

"It was McCoy," he blurted out.

He saw the rage flash across Rafael's face. Then a parade of emotions as the man's eyes went back to his ass.

Anger flared through Daniel, but he knew he couldn't be mad if Rafael didn't want him anymore. "Stop. I went to confront him. It's my fault." Pressing his eyes closed, Raf resumed cleaning the blood off his ass. Not wanting to look, he knew he was ruined and what Rafael must be thinking. The seething anger in his face let Daniel know how stupid he must look. It was a wonder that the man didn't just leave.

"Did you volunteer for this, Daniel?" Rafael said at last as he knelt down and pressed his cheek against a hip while he cleaned. The gesture was confusing. It was too—loving?

The actions were so gentle, and Daniel knew he should feel bad for thinking that Raf didn't want him. He laid his palm over the Rafael's cheek. "No. We fought, then he gave me a taste of what a real Dom is like." He shook off the horrid memories. "I don't want to talk about it, please."

"Did he give you a safe word?" Raf's voice shook.

Why did he have to go there? Daniel was already so ashamed of the decision. It was embarrassing enough. It would be much easier if he could wallow in private. He wanted to forget. "Please, can we just move on?"

He finally lost his cool and screamed, "Daniel! Did he give you a fucking safe word?"

"No, okay? It wasn't like that." He put his hands on the counter and leaned forward. "I just want to forget it happened."

"I want to kill him." Rafael stared him down in the mirror, then grabbed the aloe and vitamin ointment from the medicine chest. "You are mine."

Daniel's eyes grew wide, his chest getting tight. Had he heard correctly?

"Say that again." It was what he needed to hear most in the world right now—what he needed to heal. The words fixed more than Rafael could possibly imagine.

Raf held his gaze in the mirror, emphasizing each word. "You. Are. Mine."

Daniel smiled a little. "Okay. Then this was worth it." He could breathe. The pain he'd gone through didn't matter now. He was wanted, no matter what he looked like.

"You were mine before you went to him. Why the fuck do you think I was waiting at your house?" Raf kissed a line across his shoulder blades, avoiding the worst of the injuries with his lips as he massaged the cream into the wounds on his chest.

"He admitted what he was doing. If I'm off your case, I can testify."

"Baby, you need to sue him for assault." He put some gauze over the open wounds. "This should help so you can sleep on your stomach."

Daniel shook his head. "He'll get me for assault, and we need to focus on you. He has a bottle of pills with your fingerprints. Did you lose one?"

"Oh, shit." Rafael hung his head. "I threw it away after our first meeting. He must have been watching and taken it out of the trash."

"We have to get him at his own game." Daniel clenched his hands into fists. The action hurt, but he was too angry to care.

"I'm calling Jesse." Raf looked defeated, and he hated it.

Grabbing the phone from Rafael's hand, his words came out a bit angrily. "Like hell you are. He's going to be so pissed. Jesse can yell at me tomorrow, not tonight."

"Fine." Rafael rinsed the towel and went to work on Daniel's back.

"Okay." His reply was weak as he lowered his head, too drained to fight any more.

When he lifted his head, he was met by Rafael's lips. The kiss made the ache in his body ease. When the man pulled back, he gasped and chased his lips, aching for more. "Don't stop."

"Baby, no. You're raw. Anything I do will hurt." Raf's brow knit in the center, and he stepped back. "Let's get you in bed so I can coat you with more ointment and ice down some of the bruises."

Disappointed, Daniel let the other man lead him to his bed. His room had dark hardwood floors and soft colors. There was no overhead fixture. Instead the dim lights radiated out of the crown molding that lined the ceiling. The king-sized bed was antique hand-carved wood, in old French style. It was the center piece of the room. On it were fancy decorative pillows and a white down comforter with a burnt orange duvet folded across the bottom that matched the pillows. Rafael turned down the covers, and he gingerly rested on his stomach, the soft sheets scraping at his welts.

"Do you have any ice packs?" Rafael stood at the edge of the bed, his eyes never leaving him.

"I have one or two in the freezer in the kitchen. There might be some bags of frozen veggies in the one in the garage."

When Rafael turned and left the room, Daniel pressed his face into the bed sheets, muffling his scream. So fucking stupid. Why did you go to confront McCoy? What the hell were you thinking? The ache in his chest hurt worse than the agony his body was in.

Rafael's fingers on the sole of his foot brought him out of his self-condemnation. "Why are you face-down like that?"

"I'm trying to suffocate myself, to no avail." Rafael growled

"How should I feel?" The words were muttered into the sheets. "I'm…fuck, Rafael. I'm an idiot." He felt the man sit on the edge of the bed.

"You are not. I want you. I hate that his marks are on you, but you have to heal inside and out before I can replace them with mine." Raf moved, and the burning in Daniel's wrists intensified when the cold packs were placed over them. His ankles got the same treatment along with the welts on his ass. He was breathing hard, working through the pain like Rafael had shown him. He laughed bitterly to himself at the fact that sub training was good for other things and not just play.

When he turned his head to breathe, Rafael pressed the ice gently to his blackened eyes. The pressure on the bruises hurt, but he hardly noticed, he was too wrapped up in the mental pain that had taken over.

"How's that?" Rafael bent down to kiss the back of his arm.

"Hurts worse, to be honest." He laid his cheek against the pillow so he could look at the man he wanted.

"I can imagine. Maybe we should take you to the hospital just so they can check you out." As he spoke, he began to spread more salve on the cuts.

Daniel tried not to gasp, but some of the wounds were still extremely tender. "No. They'll ask what happened. I think it's clear this was not consensual, even if I claim it was." His cheeks flushed. He didn't want to feel like a battered woman tonight on top of everything else.

"Tell them it was me." Rafael's tone was firm.

He looked up at the man, mouth gaping. "No! I can't believe you would even suggest that." He stopped talking and smashed his face back into the pillow when Raf lifted the ice off his ass. The man's coarse lips skimmed his skin followed by the warm ointment, making Daniel grit his teeth against the pain. "Fuck."

"That was the worst of it." Replacing the ice, the man kissed his lower back. "I'm glad I'm here to take care of you."

"Me too, even if I'm pissed at you."

"I would bite you for that comment, but you're in enough pain." Rafael set the supplies aside and stretched out next to him so that their bodies were barely touching.

Breaking the silence, Daniel asked, "You like to hurt me?"

"Yes." Rafael looked at him skeptically. "Why?"

"I'm hurt. You fucking me into the mattress will hurt," he stated matter-of-factly.

"Yes, badly, but it wouldn't be me hurting you. It would be residual pain left over from him. Plus, you need to heal."

"But it's so much more than that. I don't want to go to sleep thinking about how much he hurt me. I want to go to sleep happily sore and satisfied by you." His swollen eyes pleaded. It couldn't be put into words how much he needed to forget, if even for an hour.

"I think you need to mentally heal and deal with what he did to you before we play again." Rafael placed a hand on his cheek.

"I don't want him to be the last thing that hurt me. Then he wins." Daniel looked down at the burns on his wrists and rubbed over them before meeting Raf's eyes again. "If I give up this lifestyle when I've barely started, he'll have a double win." He licked his cracked lips.

Rafael leaned in to kiss him, then tilted his head to the side to deepen it. "Daniel…" the words softly chastised, but he could tell by the look the male gave him that he was winning this discussion. "You're not giving up. You're just giving yourself time."

"I want this, I want it with you." He nudged his nose over Rafael's. "If I let him take you away, he succeeds. He doesn't want us to be together."

Raf kissed the corners of his lips as he pleaded his case.

Daniel pressed his forehead to the other man's. "I'm going to live my life and remember it as a bad experience. One bad experience, but I won't allow it to jade my future with you." He carefully rolled to his side and pushed the man's shirt up, placing a kiss over his chest. "Help me make it better?"

"You know, I'm really attracted to how logical you are." Rafael raised his arms, letting Daniel strip him of his shirt. Their mouths met again and Rafael sighed into his lips.

"Good. At least I still have some clout with you." Nimble fingers went to work on stripping Raf's jeans from him.

He kissed a path down Daniel's neck, lifting his hips off the bed at the same time, then kicking his jeans to the floor. "You have more than a little."

Strong fingers traced around the marks on Daniel's body, the gesture so loving, he could only press his face into the man's chest. He scooted closer, even though each movement was painful. "I need you." He didn't try and hide the desperation in his voice.

Rafael wrapped an arm around his back, holding their bodies flush, and Daniel groaned in pain. "See? I'm hurting you."

"Yes. Use it. Your hands are your weapons." He carefully hitched his leg over Raf's hip, sending their cocks gliding over each other. "Make me feel you and only you."

"I'll try." His hand ghosted over the welts on his ass.

Moaning, Daniel willed himself to stay hard and enjoy the pain, forgetting where it came from and only focusing on the fact that it was for Rafael's pleasure. "More, Sir."

It didn't take long before he was floating, his mind hazy and the pain dull. Rafael reached between them to grip them both in one hand while he pumped his hips, causing his cock to press into Daniel's. He could feel every vein in the pulsing dick, and it brought him so close.

"Sir…" he panted against Rafael's lips.

"Hold it. I want it to hurt." He bit down on Daniel's lower lip, sucking it back with him.

Realizing for the first time that he could touch Rafael, he used it to his advantage, exploring the contours of the male's body with the tips of his fingers. While Rafael seemed focused on stroking them, Daniel leaned down to flick his tongue over his nipples. Raf gasped and pushed his chest into Daniel's mouth.

"Maybe I should leave you untied more often," he moaned.

"I think untied sometimes would be good." Biting down on Rafael's nipple, it pebbled in his mouth as he reached around to trace his fingers down the inviting seam between the two taut cheeks. "I'd like my tongue here."

Rafael retaliated by squeezing his shaft with a grunt. "If you keep teasing me, I'm going to need to be inside you."

Daniel bit down on the same nipple again, then licked down the center line of his chest. "What's stopping you?" He let a moan of pain pass his lips, every movement on the soft sheets reopening some of his wounds.

He hissed. "The knowledge that you're clearly in pain."

He cupped Rafael's cheek and kissed him slowly and thoroughly. "Trust me."

Their gaze met as he moved in for another kiss. "Okay. How?"

"Are you the Dominant, or am I?" Daniel asked defiantly.

"On your hands and knees." The command was snapped in a familiar tone.

Shoulders screaming he was stiff and it was hard to move, but he did as he'd been told. When he had taken his place, his body settled into a dull ache he could live with. Raf had gotten off the bed to rummage in the nightstand. He'd found a condom and had the lube in his hand when he climbed back on the bed. Daniel let his head fall slack, looking between his legs as he watched. He heard his lover rip the condom open with his teeth, then toss the wrapper aside, giving him a good view of Rafael pushed the latex over his swollen head and rolled it down to the base.

Resisting the sudden urge to ask him to go without, Daniel bit his tongue. They had discussed his training, but nothing relationship wise, so it was possible Rafael would think it was too much. Rafael took his dick in his hand and drizzled lube down its length. When Daniel felt the rounded head press against him, he sucked in a breath and pushed back against it. He needed this man's mark on him, not McCoy's. It was the only way he would feel better.

Rafael pushed hard against him, and he gripped the sheets, bracing for the pain of his welted ass, but it never came. The intense pressure was replaced by the full feeling of Rafael fully-seated cock inside him.

"God, you feel good." Daniel winced as Raf pushed his last inch in, hips meeting his ass.

"Doing okay?" Rafael gripped him by the hinge of his hips, working himself slowly in and out, stretching his ass wide open.

"Fuck you, just fuck me." Frustrated with the coddling, the growl just slipped out. He panted, breathless from the pain, but he wanted more…more of Rafael. Every time he, with good intentions, tried to be careful, the more helpless Daniel felt. He'd never be helpless again. This needed to be his choice, and he needed Raf to understand that.

"Excuse me?" Rafael's thrusts faltered as he spoke. "I'm inclined to forbid you from coming for a remark like that."

Daniel pressed his head into the sheets and clenched his hands till his knuckles were white. He would pay for this later and take the consequences, but he needed this now. "Quit being a bitch and take me."

Rafael's hips hit the welted flesh of his ass, causing him to cry out. This seemed to spur his lover on, and he could feel the man growing impossibly harder inside him.

"If I were mean, I would force you to suppress your release," Raf threatened, his cock twitching and pulsing within its tight grip.

With each thrust, Daniel's head jarred closer to the headboard. His own dick seeping at the slit as the idea of Rafael controlling him brought him so close to the elusive high he was chasing he could taste it. "That's the problem with you," he growled. "You're not being yourself. You're holding back." He howled in pain as the man's palm came down on his already bruised ass. "You're not dominating me. This is a rough fuck. I could get this at a bar in town. Only I'm already beat up so it hurts more."

Rafael's voice hitched as he spoke. "Grab onto the headboard like you're tied to it."

Doing as he was told, Daniel edged closer to the freeness he craved.

"Don't let go or you will be punished." The male slowed his movements while speaking.

Daniel focused on gripping the headboard, his wrists, hands, and shoulders aching.

"Where the fuck is my 'Yes, Sir?'" Raf ground out, shoving himself home to make his point.

"Sorry, Sir." If Rafael kept up what he was doing, it was going to be very hard for him not to lose it.

"Good boy." His ran fingers down Daniel's bruised back.

The touch hurt, but stimulated him deeper than the physical pleasure. The stroke a sign that Rafael's dominant side was coming back. Rafael's thrusts jolted Daniel till his shoulders throbbed incessantly. Sweat burned his open wounds, but he let go and began to float, detaching from everything. And for the first time since the beating, he could take a full breath.

"Good boy," he panted. "I can feel you letting go, letting me use you."

His pleasure creeping up on him, he closed his eyes, the mumbled "Yes, Sir" sounding more like a purr.

"Are you getting close, boy?" Rafael's fingers dug into his hips, pulling him back to meet each thrust.

"Yes, I don't even need to be touched at this point, Sir." Daniel could feel the tightness in his gut building, like a dam threatening to break.

"Then cum for me." Rafael slowed his pace a little.

Things felt as if they moved in slow motion, Rafael's tip kept stroking over his prostate while his ring clenched tightly around his dick.

"But Sir, I was disobedient..." It was hard trying to hold off.

"Are you questioning me?" Raf barked.

"No Sir." Daniel gasped as his balls drew up.

He let go of the building tension and gave into his Master. Wave after wave of release overtook him—lightning shot up his spine and lit every nerve in his body on fire. His release spilled out over the sheets as he felt Rafael's cock pulse inside him. He was warmed from the inside out by his partner's release, and it only intensified his own—his body clenched around the dick buried deep as Rafael panted in the throes of his own orgasm. His body fell over Daniel's so that they were chest to back, writhing together, using each other in that moment for their own pleasure.

At some point, Daniel collapsed, losing track of time. When he came to, his hands were still gripping the bed frame and Rafael was on top of him. Everything hurt. But he knew he was wanted, and that went a long way toward fixing the mess in his head.

****

When Rafael regained himself, he rolled quickly off Daniel, his eyes scanning the damage he had done.

"No, come back." Daniel's tone begged, but he didn't move.

Remembering his instructions to his lover to hold onto the headboard, he gruffly said, "You can release your hands. Shit, are you hurt?" Raf sat up, cursing himself out in his mind for letting things get out of control. There was something about this man that pushed him past his own lines, letting him free.

"Stop babying me, please." Daniel pried his fingers off the bed frame, flexing them.

"This is my job. I'm going to go get supplies to clean you up again." Rafael got off the bed and returned with fresh gauze.

The sight of Daniel's set jaw and buried face in the pillows made him exhale as he took a seat next to him. He knew that what happened with McCoy must be bothering Daniel, and he didn't know how to help. He went to work applying the cream and gauze, staying silent. He figured fucking had been a bad idea, but Daniel had pushed for it. Wishing he could talk to George about this, he knew his mentor would have better advice on how to treat someone after they'd been abused. Rafael had never dealt with something of this nature. At least nothing more had happened, something that this man might never be able to get over. Exhausted after the night's events, both men finally passed out.

The rays of sunlight that filtered through the open windows woke Raf. He opened one eye to find himself in a strange room. It was soft, compared to his more modern one. The colors were warm. The surfaces clean of any clutter. There were books on the shelves as well as knickknacks from the type of childhood he had never had—photo's of family events, awards, things that had never even crossed his mind to put on display. Not that he had any, anyway. He rolled over to reach instinctively for Daniel, to check on him, but he found the space next to him on the bed empty. Panic gripped him until he heard the sound of the running shower. He winced a little, thinking of the damage he'd seen on Daniel's body and how the water must feel on his raw skin. He was out of bed and stumbling to the bathroom, his vision darkening a little, and he knew he had gotten up too fast. When he pushed open the bathroom door, his eyes landed on the very naked Daniel. Raf raised his arms over his head to stretch, twisting his back and getting the bones to pop when he did.

Growling under his breath when he realized the marks on Daniel looked worse in the morning light, he took in the body covered in bruises that were more barbaric than any he had ever seen as a result of consensual play. The urge to kill McCoy came anew, and Rafael had to fight himself not to turn on his heels and find a gun, or better yet, kill the cop with his bare hands. He took a step closer to Daniel, who didn't know he was there yet. Knowing he might be jumpy after what happened, Rafael didn't know how to alert him to his presence without scaring him.

"Daniel," he said softly.

He jumped and spun around, his arms coming up in a defensive position. "Fuck. I'm sorry."

"Don't be sorry." Rafael crossed the room and kissed him lightly. "I didn't mean to sneak up on you. I'm sure you'll be skittish for awhile."

Once the unstable Daniel got his breathing under control, he nodded. "Yeah, looks pretty bad, doesn't it?"

"Jesse is going to freak." Raf's eyes did another once-over of his lover. "Think you can sit today?"

"I don't plan on telling him." Daniel turned on him and opened the door to the shower. Sticking his hand under the water, Daniel winced when the spray hit the marks on his wrist.

"That's too hot for your burns." Rafael kicked off his shorts and moved to adjust the water, then helped Daniel. "And are you fucking kidding me? You don't think he'll notice?"

Daniel used his hand to steady himself as he stepped over the lip of the shower and stayed out of the spray. "I'll tell him the whole thing was consensual."

His lover's expression was hard to make out with the steam already wafting up around them. "No. You will not let him believe I hurt you like that." Raf stepped under the water, his face twisted in disgust at the thought that Daniel would let anyone think he had done that.

"Since when do you get to dictate what I tell my friends?" Rafael saw Daniel flinch when the spray coming off his body hit the injured male. "You didn't care if the cops thought you did this to me."

"Because I don't care what the cops think of me. I care what Jesse thinks of me. He is your best friend." Hurt filled him when the other man didn't seem to understand that.

Daniel's expression changed.

"Let me turn it down." Rafael readjusted the water, then changed the controls on the shower head so the trickle of water was lighter. "Let me wash you." Trying to choose his words carefully, he felt his anger at the situation building, and the dam would soon break.

Daniel tried the water again and remained, wavering close. "It's like acid rain."

Rafael felt his muscles tense as he tried to keep his hot temper under control. "I'm really trying to be patient here, but I can't let you do this to me. No, you are not my slave, and no, I cannot dictate what you tell your friends." He took a deep, long breath. "But letting Jesse of all people believe I hurt you is something I would consider a deal-breaker for me. I'll help you get ready for work, and then I'm going to go." It hurt to say the words, and he knew he was being stupid.

"What are you saying?"

"I'm done."

****

Daniel drew in a harsh breath. He felt like he had been stabbed in the heart. "Raf…" His brows knit in the center. "I didn't know it would make you feel that way."

"I understand," Rafael said coldly.

"If Jesse asks, I'll explain that it wasn't you." He closed the distance between them. "I can't lose you. I'm sorry. I didn't realize it was that big of a deal." Holding his breath, he waited for Rafael to speak. It was like a void had been opened into a black hole that threatened to suck him in. "Raf…" His hands shook, he was going to lose it right here in the shower if the other man didn't say something.

"It does. I take my job, and your well-being and safety, very seriously." Raf's eyes were cold.

"I'm sorry," Daniel muttered. Turning his back, he laid his forehead against the icy wall.

Rafael's body pressed against his back.

Flinching, Daniel knew Rafael had to know the movement hurt, but he didn't move.

"Let me take care of you."

"I can do it. We're going to be late. You should go get dressed." The ache in Daniel's chest went with Rafael as he stepped out of the shower.

The water hammered down on his back and he pinched his eyes shut, letting the sound envelop him as he waited for it to warm his cold body. He stood there, each drop burning his cuts as he waited for that relaxed feeling a shower usually gave him. It never came. Half-hoping Rafael was on his way home, he knew the man would be waiting. The car ride to the office would be painful. He had to stop floundering. Even pissed, he was still worried about Rafael's well-being. Tilting his head forward, he let the spray hit the back of his neck, and his body started to unwind at long last. The tension dripped off him like the beads of water from his fingertips. A thought crossed his mind, and he reached up to detach the shower head from its wall mount.

Leaning back to brace himself against his shoulder blades in the corner of the large shower, he aimed the water at the least injured part of his body—his abs. Wrapping his hand around his thick base, he drew in a long breath as he began stroking himself to images of Rafael behind his closed eyes. He imagined Rafael coming back in and catching him. Scraping his teeth over his lower lip, he moaned under his breath. Pressure built deep within his gut, and he knew he wasn't going to last long. Head falling back, he started to fuck his hand, ignoring the pain of his raw skin with each jerk.

Looking up when he caught movement through the steamed glass, his eyes grew wide with guilt. A part of him was turned on, and another part felt foolish for all the hurt he had caused Rafael.

"Don't let me stop you," Raf called over the roar of the water. "I'll watch, and we can finish fighting when you're done." He leaned his ass back into the granite counter, ankles crossed.

Daniel clenched his jaw, and his nostrils flared while he opened his grip one finger at a time, letting his thick erection fall and smack into his thigh. He shoved open the shower door and took one step out onto the mat to grab a towel.

Rafael flew across the room to grab his wrist. "I told you to finish," he growled.

"Make me," he spit the words out.

Rafael had just told him they were done.

Raf, fully clothed, shoved him back into the water, using his larger size to force him back into the corner he had been in. The long-sleeve, skin-tight thermal tee clung to Rafael, and his leather pants sagged low on his hips as they absorbed the water. Still hard, Daniel's cock pointed straight out from his body like a red flag, begging for attention. Rafael twisted his arm, raising it above his head. The cool tile burned his heated, raw skin, making him twist against the male's hold.

"Remember your safe word?" The question was asked in a gravelly voice.

He moved, still fighting, trying to free himself, then nodded. "Yes."

"Now would be the time to say it." Intense green eyes searched his.

The word Rafael had given him was on the tip of his tongue, but he wouldn't give him the satisfaction.

Rafael's large hand wrapped around his throat just under his jaw. It seemed he was going to add bruises to the only clean spot of flesh. Rafael waited, and when Daniel said nothing, calloused fingers flexed and closed in.

"You won't be able to speak shortly. Say the word, Daniel."

Lips pulled back to expose his teeth, his hand came up to slug Raf in the shoulder. It was all he could manage in the confined space. Tired of feeling helpless, and not in the submissive way, he wanted control of his life back.

Rafael flipped his hand away, pushing his head back into the corner. "Say it."

Struggling and trying to inhale past Rafael's hand, Daniel found enough air in his lungs to utter the word. But he remained silent, not saying the safe word. He knew if he made any sound at all that Raf would release him.

"I want to watch you get yourself off." The words were repeated.

Daniel didn't move to comply. Holding eye contact with Rafael, he focused on sucking air past the large palm pressing down on his windpipe.

"Now."

Daniel lifted his hand to his cock. Subspace was already near. He could almost taste it coming on. He drew in a few wisps of oxygen while flexing and straining his neck against the restriction. Steam engulfed the room, and it would have been hard to breathe without a hand around his neck. The first roll of his hand over his cock brought him right back to where he had been when Rafael found him. It wouldn't take long for him to let go.

"You look so perfect like that." The voice was low and thick with his Brazilian accent.

The phrase pushed Daniel into euphoric bliss as his nerves began to fire. Body tensing, his abs tightened as he started to thrust his hips into his fist. His brain seemed to be on overload, causing him to edge. He couldn't bring himself the release he needed. The pleasure was so intense he could feel his body hurtling toward the finish as his lungs burned.

But the closer he got, the further the line moved back. His body would clench in the beginning stages of orgasm, only to misfire. He moved his hand faster, gasping, his throat burning, his lungs begging for mercy, but nothing happened. Shaking uncontrollably, the darkness ate at the corners of his vision. It suddenly felt as if he was dying, but the pleasure, too intense, let him know otherwise. He never wanted it to end.

"Cum for me."

The words were magic. Daniel's release slammed into him, jolting his body as his muscles spasmed and his balls drew up to spill long ropes of his hot seed into his hand. The pleasure was other-worldly, like he had left his body behind and entered some alternate universe where every nerve in his body was being stimulated simultaneously. He started to lose himself to the shadows, but he wasn't scared. Strangely, he was alert and too far gone in sensation to care. The tight grip of Rafael's nails biting into his wrist, and the man's weight on his body kept him grounded. His body convulsed as he panted and bathed his chest with spurts of fluid over and over until it was too painful to keep touching himself. The grip on his neck had vanished.

Daniel's knees went weak and he couldn't catch himself. He was sliding to the floor when Raf's strong hands caught him. Rafael picked him up, being careful of his wounds and carried them both out of the shower toward the large bed that was the centerpiece of the bedroom. Tossing one of the two towels he'd grabbed on the edge of the bed, Rafael sat, dripping wet, and started to dry him. Doing a half-assed job on himself, he then climbed into the bed enveloping Daniel in his arms.

Still floating, Daniel curled into his Dom's embrace.

****

Because of Daniel's injuries and their morning activities, the possibility that his reaction time might be slower than normal became an issue Rafael couldn't ignore. Insisting that he do the driving, he tried to explain his concerns to Daniel. When they finally walked into the office, they were forty-five minutes late.

"How do I look?" Daniel asked when they stepped into the elevator.

Raf rubbed a hand over the back of his neck. "Want me to be honest?"

Daniel scowled and narrowed his eyes.

"You look like you lost a bar fight…" he said, then muttered the rest, "To a bad BDSM gang."

"Thanks." Daniel straightened his tie and barreled into the office, blowing past the receptionist.

Given no time for a response, Rafael trailed after him into Jesse's office. He didn't know which was funnier: Daniel's fuming look or his partner's gaping expression. Jesse blinked a few more times, looking between them both. Jesse got to his feet, eyes locked on him.

"Are you fucking kidding me?" Jesse stormed toward him.

Usually not scared of anyone, the look in Jesse's eyes told Raf the guy planned on killing him.

"That's right. You better get the fuck out of here and never see him again." The irate man pushed up the sleeves of his button-down shirt.

Daniel's arm shot out and stopped his partner from advancing further. "It wasn't him."

Turning on the injured man, Jesse's ears were bright red. "Who?" he spat.

"Sit down and I'll explain." Daniel didn't let his friend go.

Rafael stayed in the hall for safety, not trusting the situation.

Still obviously angered, Jesse looked between the two of them, then took a seat behind his desk. "Get your ass back in here Raf," he instructed, his flush still showing on his fair skin.

Rafael took a reluctant step back into the office.

"Close the door." The irate male barked. "And if I don't believe him," he hitched a thumb at Daniel, "then we're off your case."

Rafael swallowed, staring Daniel down.

"It wasn't him. I made a mistake that I'm embarrassed about." Daniel chewed his lip before going on. "Can we please not talk about it?" The words were released like a balloon of hope only to be shot down by Jesse.

"Nope. Explain, or I'm ditching your boyfriend. No one gets away with turning my best friend's eyes black." Jesse crossed his arms over his chest.

When Daniel recounted the same story that had been told to him the night before, Raf felt better knowing that it was definitely the whole truth.

"Tell my wife I never really loved her." Jesse stood up, digging around in his desk drawer.

Daniel met Raf's eyes and mouthed, "What the hell?"

Rafael shrugged a shoulder.

Jesse straightened back up with a .45 caliber automatic pistol in one hand and a clip in the other which he slammed home. "If at all possible, blame the cop and get him fired." He shoved the gun into his pocket and made his way around the desk.

They both scrambled around the desk to block the door.

"Outta the way." Jesse had rage in his eyes, which made the dominant in him see the man with greater respect.

"Hell no! You're not going to jail for me. We just need to get others to join our side and help us take him down." Daniel stood right in front of his friend.

Rafael stepped to the side to let them work it out. If he was honest with himself, he had to admit he was with Jesse on this one. McCoy needed to be shot in the head.

Before long, Jesse had his breathing under control and his gun stashed back in his desk. Raf wanted to find a way to get it away from the man, but he didn't know if that was going to be possible.

"I swear, if we don't get him, I'm going to go Dexter on his ass." Jesse slumped back in his chair.

"Maybe it's best if I leave you two for a bit. I have some errands to run." Rafael got to his feet and was already edging toward the door.

Daniel turned to him and crossed his arms over his chest. "If it's drugs or going to take care of McCoy yourself, I forbid you."

"It's not, I swear to you." He didn't want to admit where he was headed. Just the thought was a blow to his pride already. Both lawyers stared at him. "Can't you two just trust me?"

"No," they said in unison and then started laughing.

"Need my car?" Daniel held up his keys.

"Got a tracker in there or something?" Raf chuckled.

"No, but maybe I should." He grinned.

"I can just take a cab. It's not a big deal."

"I don't mind." Daniel dropped the keys into his hand. The weight of Daniel's trust felt good, and it made him smile.

"Thank you. I'll be back."

"Bring lunch," Jesse shouted after him.

LEGALLY BOUND

Chapter Sixteen

Rafael bypassed George's doorman, going around to the back entrance he used when he wanted to see the man alone. Worried that after their last conversation, he would be denied, he hoped the man had not changed the codes to the freight elevator. Taking a deep breath, he punched the numbers into the keypad and waited for the light to flash green or red. It went to green, and he smiled. Maybe it meant George was willing to listen to him. Riding the large elevator up to the penthouse, he lingered in the middle till it opened into the man's utility room. The large steel doors closed behind him once he took a step inside. Cocking his head to the side, he listened. Not a sound. A few steps later, and he had the door to the rest of the penthouse open.

It was still early, so George would probably be up playing with one of his slaves or working. Rafael decided to check the playroom first. The room had a picturesque view of the Chicago skyline and Lake Michigan, but when he looked in, he saw one of George's pets still in his cage. The man was gagged so he wouldn't be much help in locating George. The club owner's office door was across the hall, and it was closed. Raf rapped his knuckles on the solid door, waiting for a reply before he entered. He might not be a sub, but everyone was submissive to The King.

"Come in," came the even, lightly-accented voice. His boss didn't even sound startled that someone other than his slave was present.

He opened the heavy door and stepped inside the room. Furnished with floor-to-ceiling bookshelves on three walls, the fourth wall was all glass with an equally spectacular view of the skyline facing away from the

Great Lake. The wood in the room was stained a rich, dark color, and the armchairs were upholstered in complementing leather. Rafael stood after closing the door, waiting for an invitation to sit.

"Can I inquire as to the reason for your intrusion into my home? I thought I made it clear at our last meeting that I wished to discontinue our acquaintance." The imposing man's booted feet were kicked up on the desk, and he held an espresso cup in one hand. Instead of one of his signature Victorian era suits, George wore a silk robe.

"Boots and a robe?" He eyed the feet on the desk.

"I like how the leather feels on my feet," George said, bringing his cup to his lips.

"It's a wonder more people don't call you snobbish." Rafael remained where he was.

Pinky up, the older man saluted him with his cup, which he read as "fuck you." "They're too frightened of my dark side."

The invitation to sit still had not come, so he lingered by the door, knowing his place. "We need to talk."

George's dark eyes met his. "On your knees." The tone of his voice never rose, but Rafael complied immediately, kneeling on the dark hardwood floor. His head bowed, he sneaked a glance up through his eyelashes.

George pursed his lips. "What in the world would compel me to forgive a liar?"

Rafael remained silent.

"Speak." The shot-sized espresso cup was obviously made of hand-painted bone china, and paired with what the commanding individual wore, it was hard not to laugh at him.

But Raf didn't dare. "I want to beg your forgiveness, King."

George set his coffee on the hand-carved, rosewood desk and sat up. "Give it to me quickly. I have a slave who needs to be sent to work."

"I can talk while you punish your boy." Rafael's knees ached, reminding him of why he hated submitting.

"Or perhaps you can help and leave me to sip my coffee while you take care of his beating." A smile curled over George's lips. "Up on your feet."

He climbed off his knees. "You know I don't mind." Actually, he was itching to take the pent up aggression of the past few days out on someone since his own sub was hurt so badly.

George got to his feet. "Lead the way." Picking up his small cup, he rang a bell on the way out.

"How many slaves are you keeping nowadays?" Knowing the penthouse well, Raf knew where he'd have to go to get to the room the man played in.

"I just took this one on, so I have four now." A young man wearing an apron met them at the door to the playroom. "Another espresso, slave." George held out his cup, and the boy took it, never meeting his eyes. When George waved him off, the boy hurried to do as he was told.

"He's young." Rafael tried not to stare at the boy's ass as he walked off.

"Elliot just turned twenty." His blue eyes twinkled. "Have you not seen him before?"

"Has he been to the club with you?" Pausing so his mentor could fill him in, they entered the home dungeon.

George shook his head. "When it hits you who he is, you'll know why."

Rafael shot him a questioning look, but refrained from asking any more questions. He knew he wouldn't get an answer. "I knew you liked 'em young, but damn."

"He's good at what he does, and he looks younger than he is." George walked straight over to the caged man Raf had seen when he came in. "This one needs a lot of training. He came into the lifestyle a few months ago, and I snatched him up. I'm sure he'll get someone to take him on full-time when our contract is up. But he's working on his law degree and interning at a top firm in the city." He turned to the confined male. "Good boy."

"Impressive at his age." Rafael followed at his heel. "What are his limits?"

The robed man tugged at the thirty-something male's dark hair, and the slave purred. "Pretty standard. He doesn't like any edge, but we don't have the time for that. He likes light beatings, but he needs to be able to sit at work and can't have any bruises that would show when he wears a suit."

"Easy enough." Raf turned to gaze at George's extensive collection of weapons.

"I can't be bothered to punish you today, you worthless, stupid slut." George spoke as he removed his hand from the slave's hair. "I've arranged for this man to come take care of you for the morning. Nod if you understand."

The gagged sub nodded and didn't look up at either of them. George left the cage, moving to take one of the black leather armchairs in front of the window. Rafael bet that if he had a black light, the things would be spotless. George's slaves were well known for keeping the room scrubbed and in perfect order after playtime. He unhitched the latch on the cage and stood back.

"Out. Kneel at my feet."

The man did as ordered, and Raf let the ball gag loose when he came near.

"To your feet and over to the table." he ordered, his tone taking on the dominant one that was second nature to him.

George didn't turn around. He picked up the paper from the coffee table, no doubt delivered by one of his other house boys. "Earmuff him if you wish to speak, and hurry up. He needs to be released to shower in thirty." George unfolded the paper and started reading.

"Lay down face up on the table."

The pet did as he was instructed, and Rafael trailed his fingers up the thin man's abs. "If you're a very good boy, I will let you fuck your hand before we are done."

The slave's reaction was instant and his length went from semi-hard to fully erect, standing straight up between his legs. Raf adjusted himself. The boy was perfect.

"You're going to spoil him," George scoffed, flipping the page of his newspaper.

"Want to take care of him?"

His mentor waved him off. "I can't be bothered."

He took the boy's wrists, binding them to the cuffs at the top of the table. Then he moved around to the foot to fasten the sub's legs. He looked at the wall of toys again, walking over to select a strip of leather to wrap around the man's hard dick and balls that would function like a cock ring. It would also make sure the pet wouldn't cum while being played with. The slave didn't make a sound.

"You may be vocal if you wish, slave. Rafael likes to hear his boys," George commented.

"Yes, King," the man said.

Next, Raf grabbed spiked nipple clamps, pinching the boy's tips to place them correctly and earning him a nice moan from the slave.

"You sure make erotic sounds. No wonder your King keeps you around." He flicked the nipple clamp hard just to hear the man again.

"Thank you, Sir," the man gasped.

When Rafael placed the muffs over the slave's ears, he turned to his boss. "I came to apologize, King, and explain why I haven't told you what's been going on."

"I'm listening." George kept his eyes on the paper in his hands and his back to Raf.

The move typically made to humiliate, Rafael had done it himself to subs many times, but he hated it from his mentor. Of course, that was why George did it. "I got involved with McCoy after you kicked him out of the club."

That got George's attention. He swiveled the chair around, boots tapping on the floor as he did so. He had one ankle crossed over his knee, opening the robe up at the bottom and putting his cock on full display. Rafael swallowed at the sight of the well-endowed man.

"You helped me revoke his membership. He was your submissive. You knew how unstable he was." Electric blue eyes drilled him as George lowered his chin.

"Yes, and he was my submissive for a reason. As you already know, no one else could handle him." Rafael looked at his feet.

"What possible reason would you have for playing with fire?" George growled, tossing his paper to the table beside him.

"He offered me three times your rate." He didn't want to admit the other reason he had done it. But maybe it was time to come clean and tell his mentor everything—reveal the personal connection he'd found with McCoy and explain that it wasn't the money alone that led him to accept the offer.

"If you needed more money, we could have upped your fee and gotten you more clients." George curled the hair at the back of his head around one finger. Rafael had seen him do it on more than one occasion and knew it meant he was annoyed.

Raf swallowed loudly as he gave his pride to George. "I've always been attracted to him. I missed his submission, even if I thought he was dangerous when switching and playing as a Dom."

"You let your attachment to people make you weak." George laced his fingers together. "A quality I cannot condemn you for."

Rafael turned away to grab a medium-weight crop off the wall. He whipped it around to test it before he struck the slave on one pec. The man cried out in shock and pain that muffled the thwack. Then he laid into the sub, painting his chest with a spray of tiny, painful red kisses.

He turned back to George breathing hard. "I'm sorry. It was poor judgment, and I thought I could handle him on my own." He exhaled a long breath. "Once I felt guilty, I tried to handle it myself so I wouldn't disappoint you."

"I guess I've done the same in the past and let my weakness for you rule my judgment. You are no more at fault than I am." George eyed his pet and licked his lips with a hungry look.

Raf held the crop out to him.

George shook his head. "Carry on."

Elliot interrupted with a knock before bringing in his Master's breakfast along with two cups of espresso on a silver tray. Rafael kept his eyes on the young man and his fantastic ass. The savory aroma of the food made his stomach rumble.

He turned back, tracing around the slave's girth with the soft leather before landing a blow on the man's sac. The guy pulled at his restraints, which only dug into his wrists. He'd have lines there if he was not careful. Rafael moved around to the head of the table, nimble fingers working to uncuff the sub's right hand.

He lifted one of the ear covers before speaking. "Stroke yourself, put on a good show for me and your King." He left the man to touch himself and took the seat next to George.

The soft, yet firm, leather of the chair underneath his ass was good for all sorts of play. Raf took the second cup of coffee and sat back to watch as the male arched his back off the table and violently worked his hand over his length. The man didn't spare any time. It was easy to see he was well-trained. The sound of skin smacking skin filled the room, and Rafael fought back his own arousal. He needed George's forgiveness. "Please forgive me. I should have never gone behind your back or lied to you. You've been like a father to me, and I can't lose that."

George turned on him with stone cold eyes, and Raf lost all hope.

"Untie the boy," George directed.

Rafael set down his coffee and complied, removing the cock ring, the nipple clamps, and then the earmuffs from the boy.

"Go shower. I will see you tomorrow night, slave."

The man half bowed and excused himself into the adjoining bathroom. Raf returned to his seat, looking out over the lake for a long while before he spoke again. "I want to kill him." It was the most honest he'd been with anyone in a long time.

George looked up at him over his poached eggs. "He is taking your freedom, but that is a little harsh."

"No." He sucked in a breath. "McCoy beat Daniel, badly. There is hardly an inch of him without a mark. He could barely walk when I saw him afterward."

His mentor put down his fork. "Did your submissive go to him?"

"Not for that. He went to confront him about me. He wanted the guy to back off." It began to hurt the more he talked about it. "Daniel is mine. Knowing that, McCoy drugged him."

"I would ask if he gave him a safe word, but I know the answer."

He covered his face with his hands. "This one is different to me. I want to kill that bastard."

"At this juncture, I do too." George took a bite, chewed, swallowed, and dabbed his lips with the linen napkin before speaking again. "Did Daniel go to the police?"

Rafael shook his head. "No. He knows McCoy is a cop. No one would believe him if he accused the man of doing the damage and then dumping him."

George sipped his espresso. "I think that was a wise choice."

A silent look passed between them before Raf said, "I'm sorry I've been such a disappointment."

George held up a hand, cutting him off. "I've forgiven you, but this won't be forgotten. You will have to serve your penance for it."

Rafael nodded. "Yes, Sir."

****

After mulling over the situation while playing with Elliot, George made a snap decision and called the police department dispatch while he stood at the expansive windows that viewed Lake Michigan. He had the call transferred to one of his friends inside the department. After a few minutes, he knew McCoy was on duty as well as his location. Because the slave didn't have any college classes till later in the day, he decided to give the young man, still gagged and chained to his table, something to do. He leaned over, unlocking the chains. It was a shame. The boy looked so pretty all stretched out on display.

"Want to stretch your legs since you've been such a quiet slave since my earlier guest left?" George unhooked the ball gag, letting it fall to the floor.

The slave kept his eyes downcast as he rolled off the table, and stayed on all fours. "Yes, Sir."

"Get dressed in something simple. I was thinking those jeans I like you in and that button-down shirt that matches your eyes. Then you can help me dress."

"Yes Sir." He went toward the back bedroom where he was allowed to hang his street clothes while in his King's presence.

George watched the young man's perfect ass as he walked away. A student during the day, the pet spent his nights and weekends begging for the privilege to be bound and tied. Nothing pleased him more.

When they were both dressed, they headed down to his Mercedes, where he allowed his slave to open the door so he could slip inside. Elliot navigated the city's traffic heading toward the south end of the Loop. Eyes scanning for McCoy's undercover car he knew well, he barely kept the anger he felt in check. He knew he'd have to spend the evening welting his slave's pretty skin after this encounter. Scouring the twenty block radius for forty minutes, he finally found McCoy parked at a doughnut shop. George stopped his slave when the young man made a move to get out of the car and open his door.

"Stay where you are. Keep the engine running and make sure to record the whole thing." He handed Elliot a tiny camera. The young man took it, and he exited the car.

He rapped the knuckles of one well-manicured hand on McCoy's passenger window and waited. The man jumped, but didn't make a move. The doors clicked as they were unlocked, which was all the invitation George needed.

McCoy waited until the door slammed closed before he spoke. "To what does a mere peasant like me owe for the pleasure of a visit from his Majesty?"

"Amusing. As you know, I prefer to go by George."

"What do you want?" McCoy barked.

George shot him a look, and he cowered back. "Better. Know your place," he said, stroking over his graying goatee. He knew making McCoy wait would put him on edge, which was exactly what he wanted.

"I'm waiting."

"Yes, and not patiently."

McCoy met his eyes and sneered.

He grinned, his eyes twinkling with amusement. "You and I have an issue, and you're going to back off."

McCoy's low forehead wrinkled as his brows shot up. "I'm impressed. I really thought Rafael would serve time before he disappointed dear old Dad."

"He told me what you've been doing, and I plan on making sure you never play in this city again. I'm also going to put your balls in a vise if you don't back off." His voice stayed even and his tone normal. The inflections got the point across.

"I don't need to do anything else but laugh when he goes to jail. He's buried and so is that new lawyer friend of his." Lance's grin was smug.

George straightened his perfect tie. "Your foul treatment of Daniel is disturbing, and it will have consequences of its own."

McCoy's smiled wide and chuckled. "I have no idea what you could be referring to."

The smug smile awoke the sadist inside him. He kept his demons at bay, day in and day out, but people like this prick were so good at bringing out the worst in him. "Nonetheless, don't expect me to forget it."

"Don't. I'm not scared of you. I think that's why you don't like me," McCoy said.

"I have my reasons, most of which involve submissives being pushed past their limits." As he spoke, George adjusted his body position in the seat. The car smelled of old fast food and sweat, which only repulsed him further. "You need to fix it." Each word carried a demand, and he saw the man recoil.

"What are you going to do to me? You've already taken everything from me. Rafael was the only thing I had left, and in the end, he chose you over me." He turned down his police radio as it started to squawk.

George was not an easy man to surprise, but McCoy had certainly done that with his last words. Raf had not told him that he had stopped with the dirty cop because of him. "I let you play with the subs that would still have you, but that is no more."

"Do your worst. Maybe you'll enjoy being behind bars yourself." The prick leaned forward. "I think I'm going to tell that lawyer kid that if he rolls over on you, he and Rafael can walk."

George growled deep in his throat, his vision tinting red. "You're not only a bad Dominant, but also a terrible sub. You're a disgrace to our kind, a coward."

McCoy moved to hit him, but he saw it coming, deflecting the blow and grabbing McCoy by his shirt. He moved their faces inches apart and hissed. "Do your worst, but I have many people on my side. It's better than bullet proof glass, and what do you have to hide behind? Your little badge? I think that will be the first thing I take." George inhaled deeply, smelling his fear. It was his favorite smell. He rarely indulged in his favorite game, but this made him crave it.

McCoy didn't move. "Assaulting an officer will be the first on a long list."

George's lips curled into a smile. "Good thing my boy was taping our entire conversation for YouTube." He released the McCoy and climbed out of the car. His palms ran over his suit, straightening the non-existent wrinkles as he walked back to his Benz. Even if he hadn't wanted to bury the bastard before this, he sure as shit wanted to now.

After he got back in the car and told Elliot to take them home, he put in a call for another favor. Between the agonizing drive back to his penthouse in the traffic that had no rhyme or reason in this city and the discussion with McCoy, George was on edge by the time he made it back. He spent the next two hours instilling fear into Elliot, one of their shared interests, while he waited for the favor to be performed.

Finished for the time being with his slave, George walked into his office to find just the person he had wanted to see kneeling on his floor.

"You wanted to see me, Sir?"

He didn't respond at first. Instead, he stripped off his suit jacket and hung it on the back of his chair before acknowledging the man with downcast eyes.

"Theo, it's good to see you again. I don't think I've had the pleasure of seeing you kneeling in years." He inspected the man as he spoke.

A very good looking man, Theo Wells had flawless dark skin that made his perfect white teeth stand out at a distance. He was tall and thin with a shaved head. The purple shirt he wore under his dark suit accentuated his dark coloring. Why this man had become an attorney when he could have been a model, George would never know. Even in his late forties, the male looked amazing.

"You may speak." George crossed his arms behind his back.

"Not since I've been married, King." There was a hint of a smile on Theo's lips.

"How is your Mistress?" He smiled, loving the sight of long lasting Dominant/submissive relationships, even if he never hoped to find that kind of love for himself.

"She is pregnant and makes me kiss and rub her swollen feet nightly. I am in heaven." Theo's smile turned into a broad grin, showing off all his teeth.

"Keep spoiling her. She deserves it." George chuckled. "I need a favor, and I think you'll find the evidence warrants it. Plus, it will help you piss off your boss and possibly undermine him." He waited.

Theo looked up with raised brows. "Permission to sit, Sir?"

"I should whip you for looking me in the eyes, but I need your help first." George strolled around to take his own seat at the desk and pushed the file over so Theo could read it.

"Yes, Sir." Theo groaned as he got up but remained silent as he took the file.

"I don't want anyone to know about this, is that understood?" He sat back and leveled his gaze at the man. "We did not have this conversation."

Theo looked up at him. "Yes, Sir."

LEGALLY BOUND

Chapter Seventeen

The next day Daniel pulled up at Jesse's house. He didn't want to drive his partner to the meeting this morning. He wanted to stay in bed with Rafael. But Jesse had called bright and early to say his car was in the shop.

The crisp morning temperature had left frost on the grass. Gray clouds rolled across the sky, a warning of the impending winter. Jesse's place was in the northern suburbs, and they would have to backtrack past his own house in order to get to the office. What he couldn't figure out was why Rafael was so giddy.

Digging his phone out of his pocket, he pushed the speed dial for his partner. "I'm calling Jesse to tell him to be waiting in the driveway, so we don't have to wait on his prissy ass."

Rafael grabbed it out of his hand, hanging it up. "Are you kidding? We didn't get up at the ass crack of dawn to miss this opportunity." Rafael's eyes glinted with mischief.

"Raf..."

"We came all the way up here, so I want to meet the Mrs. Jesse." Raf pulled open the door and stepped out onto the icy drive as soon as they arrived.

"She's nothing to write home about." He followed Rafael as they walked up the brick path to the massive white house.

"Did he marry her for her money?"

"They both had money going in." He took his time, walking gingerly up the front steps while Rafael hovered at his elbow, but he did it on his own. He needed to.

"Then why did he marry her?" he asked as he rang the bell.

Not a moment later, a toothpick blonde with her hair in a high ponytail and designer sweats pulled open the door. She wore a pound and a half of makeup, and her face was pulled up a little around the eyes. Daniel thought it looked like she'd had plastic surgery. Her hands were perfectly manicured, and she cocked her head to the side when she looked at him.

"That's why," he muttered out of the corner of his mouth before turning his gaze to the woman at the door. "Jesse ready to go?"

Rafael shot him a side glance.

"Who are you again?" Priscilla Goldmen asked in her high-pitched, sing-song voice.

"Daniel Caplin, Jesse's partner," he said exacerbated. "And this is my, um…boyfriend, Rafael."

"Oh, right. We met once before at that thing he dragged me to." She turned her head away and yelled, "Jesse!"

Her voice echoed through the large foyer. Picking at her nails, she waited, huffing impatiently, clearly perturbed. When her husband didn't answer, she turned back around to address them. "I'm sorry. It's a miracle he's ever on time."

When she turned her back on them again, Raf leaned over to speak to him. "Damn. She's hot, even in sweats. No wonder he's enamored."

Both Daniel's brows shot up into his forehead. "Are you bi?"

Priscilla walked up two of the stairs on the elaborate, dark wood grand staircase, the focal point of the room. "Jesse!" she hollered again, this time at the top of her high voice.

Rafael plugged his ears mockingly behind her back, avoiding Daniel's eyes.

"Raf?" he whispered.

"Okay, fine. Maybe I'm attracted to women, a little. That's why being a paid Dominant worked so well for me," he murmured, still not meeting his eyes.

"You scene with women?" He wasn't mad, he was intrigued, but Rafael seemed embarrassed.

Priscilla brought her attention back to them and sauntered over, sighing. "I don't know where he is, and I'm going to be late for my charity planning committee if I don't start on my Pilates."

"We're talking about this later," Daniel whispered to Raf while the blonde bombshell was talking.

"You wouldn't want to miss your meeting, bela dama," Rafael purred, turning the charm way up so that Daniel couldn't help but laugh.

Priscilla did a double-take and rubbed her lips together, dabbing her lipstick. It was like she was looking at the man in a different light. "I've got to keep my body looking perfect. Do you know how much pressure is on a trophy wife? Can't get traded in."

Daniel couldn't figure out what was going on.

Raf had moved from his side to stand near her, mimicking her body language. "Senhora, I understand. But you are gorgeous, and a man would be stupid to think he could do better."

She let out a long exasperated breath again. "I know, and Jesse never would. Between us, I have him wrapped around my pinky. But, I have other women to show up. These suburban soccer moms can be real caddy bitches."

"That, bela dama, is important." Rafael was smiling so wide it made Daniel wonder if his cheeks hurt.

Priscilla shrugged. "I try," she said coyly. "Where is that man?" She rolled her eyes and hollered up the stairs again.

So amazed, Daniel was speechless.

"What?" Jesse's voice bellowed from somewhere upstairs.

Rafael turned to him. "This was so worth getting up early for."

He could only roll his eyes in response.

"What could possibly be taking you so long?" She walked up a few of the stairs again and straightened a giant portrait of them on the wall. Jesse wore a horrid, bored expression in the photo, making him chuckle.

"I got a new shirt, and I was trying on different ties with it. Daniel's always late anyway."

"Daniel has been here for ten minutes! I swear you take longer than I do to get ready."

"Like that's even possible," came the grumbled reply.

"You look fine. Get over yourself. You're married," she shrieked, her tiny voice cracking.

Jesse appeared at the top of the staircase without a tie and his shirt open, revealing his well-muscled chest. "Invite them in, woman. What the hell is wrong with you? It's freezing outside." he lowered his voice and sighed. "You're going to run our heating bill through the roof." He took a visible deep breath before finishing. "I'll be down in a few. I'm having trouble picking out a tie."

"Baby, have Dan help you. I think you said he was gay. He's got to be fantastic at that." She closed the door behind them once he and Rafael had stepped inside.

Rafael had to fake a yawn and turn around so he wouldn't be caught laughing. When he got it together, he cleared his throat. "Want help, Jesse?"

"Anything to get me out the door." Jesse turned and walked back in the direction he came from as Raf walked up the stairs to follow him.

"I guess I'll get coffee or something." Priscilla turned around, walking out of the room, seeming to lose interest in Daniel now that Rafael had left. "I'm missing my talk show and Pilates time." She flitted out of the room, leaving him standing in the foyer.

Remembering where the kitchen was, Daniel shuffled his way there and poured himself a mug of coffee. The kitchen was bigger than his living room in his town house and was done in rich colors and dark woods. Everything was perfect, right down to the slate floor and granite countertops. He went to the large walk-in pantry to get the sugar and cream. When he walked back out of the kitchen, the two men were coming back down the stairs.

"I have bagels and assorted pastries in the fridge," Jesse offered, moving into the kitchen and filling a travel mug with coffee.

Raf rummaged through the fridge, coming back out with a flaky, red-filled something.

"I'm good." Daniel knew he needed to get back to the gym if he was going to keep up with Rafael. The man had muscles he didn't even know existed. He forced the images of how Rafael looked sweaty and shirtless after beating him, every muscle defined from the exercise, out of his mind. Still covered in bruises and marks, he knew he would not be beat again until he was fully healed.

"I'm in awe." Rafael went to the sink to wash his hands. "She is worse than I could've ever imagined. So worth it."

"I told you." Jesse did some sort of hip-thrust-jack-off gesture that made Daniel ashamed to call him a friend.

"I don't think she's that bad. Aren't all women like that?" He took the travel mug Jesse offered him and dumped the contents of his mug into it. "Thanks."

Jesse looked at Rafael.

"Not in my experience, but I deal with fetish women." He side-eyed the fridge.

"I've got no idea really. I met her during my first year of college, and she's had her hooks in me ever since."

The three of them went out the back door into the brisk morning and climbed into the car.

"There wasn't a thumbtack out of place in your house, man." Rafael chuckled. He kept his space much the same, so Daniel wasn't surprised that his man would bring it up.

"I can't function if the house is a mess. Cill leaves shit all over the place, so I hired someone." Jesse sat with his knees almost to his chest, sipping his coffee.

Raf turned around in his seat to look at Jesse. "You're a natural submissive, did you know that?"

Daniel almost spit his coffee on the steering wheel. "Not everyone fits into your world."

"Our world, baby." Rafael flashed him a smile, then reached out to rub his thigh.

He felt his cheeks redden a little at the term of endearment.

"Wait, I wanna hear this," Jesse said before he could change the subject.

Rafael turned back to him and nodded. "Okay, you submit to your wife beautifully and you don't even love her. You let her sit at home like a queen, doing nothing around the house or helping you in any way. And she gets away with it all without the reward of sex. That tells me that you like it, at least a little. I don't think she got like this overnight."

"I used to get sex…" Jesse grumbled.

"In my world, you would do all that, but you would be praised and rewarded for it instead of getting the down talk you get from her." Rafael cocked his body so he could face Jesse comfortably.

"The first issue is Cill's daddy, and the second is, I don't know how I feel about being fucked by a man."

Daniel's mouth dropped open.

"There are female Dominants."

"Oh, well, you learn something new every day."

He kept glancing at Rafael, and his partner went back to staring out the window like nothing had just happened.

Finally arriving at the office building, they all shuffled into the cramped, little office the D.A. had requested they meet in. Daniel had been blown away when Raf told him that his boss was going to help them with the case by using his contacts. The Assistant District Attorney was one of George's many associates, and he and Jesse had discussed it and thought the idea was worth a shot.

"So, George is King of your world," Jesse scoffed, making air quotes as he said the royal title.

"Yep." Rafael looked over at him. "What about it?"

"What does someone have to do to be elevated to the status of 'King?'" Jesse's eyes were wide and playful. Daniel knew he was mocking the position, but he didn't point it out to his Dom.

Before Rafael could even answer Jesse, the door opened and in walked the elegant man as if on cue. He wore another handmade suit, this one in dark gray, complete with an overcoat slung over his arm. He had a cane in the other hand, knee-high boots adorned his legs, and the outfit was topped off with an elaborately knotted ascot around his throat that looked freshly pressed. George looked around the room as if he was appraising everyone where they sat.

Jesse stared at the man, and Rafael looked over and whispered, "That's what."

Daniel finally looked up at the regal male. "Please, have a seat. We're still waiting for the A.D.A."

He was surprised when George didn't pause to stare at him since he still looked pretty beat up.

"I spoke to Theo Wells on my way over here," George began, but abruptly hesitated when he laid eyes on Jesse. His head cocked to the side, and his gaze dropped down the equally well-dressed man. Stepping up, he stuck out his hand toward Jesse, ignoring everyone else in the room. "I am George. I do not believe we have had the pleasure of being previously introduced."

Daniel looked over to meet Rafael's eyes, but didn't receive a return look. It was obvious his lover was staring at their friends.

"Jesse Goldmen, Daniel's partner" he said, taking George's hand. "The more competent of the two of us, I assure you." His lips spread into a wide grin. As they kept shaking hands, it appeared as if neither one wanted to let go.

An uncomfortable knot formed in Daniel's gut, making him feel like he was witnessing a private, stolen moment between the two men. He tore his gaze away, staring at Rafael till his lover finally looked back. Raf made eyes at the two, then motioned back, clearly trying to communicate something without words. Catching the gist of the expression, he wondered about Jesse and George as well.

When the two men finally broke apart, Daniel opened his mouth to speak but was cut off by his overzealous partner.

"That's a fantastic suit. You have exquisite taste."

He caught Jesse's eyes lingering below George's belt and did a double-take. But just as quickly as his eyes had wandered, the gaze was torn away and Jesse began shuffling the papers on the desk as he sat down. Watching Jesse shift awkwardly a few times, Daniel began to wonder if he had woken up in a different universe.

"Thank you," George said in his unusual, smooth accent. "I have a tailor who hand makes them at my request."

"They're also very flattering on you." Jesse stole another look.

Daniel sat with his mouth agape. Rafael leaned close and popped his mouth shut with one finger. "It's rude to have your mouth open, baby."

He turned to snarl at Raf, but his smile made it impossible to stay mad. "Do you see this?" He side-eyed their friends as he spoke.

Eyes twinkling, Rafael nodded.

"These two dipshits piss you off as much as they do me?" Jesse asked George.

"I had hoped an attorney would mellow Rafael out." George sat in the chair like it was a throne, and if he had said he owned the city upon their first meeting, Daniel would have believed it.

"Good luck with that. I think they feed off each other, and neither one of them listens," Jesse shot back.

George pressed two fingers to his temples, the hair there flecked with gray. "Fantastic. The only redeeming factor in all of this is the attractive man I can complain about them to."

Daniel could have sworn he saw Jesse's face flush, and he couldn't tear his eyes away.

"I agree, and I wouldn't mind picking your brain for fashion tips." Jesse's retorts were smooth, just as he was with the barmaids that so often hit on him.

George's eyes blatantly dropped down Jesse's form before he spoke again. "I don't think you need any help."

Daniel leaned over to whisper to Rafael. "He's gay?"

Raf nodded, not taking his eyes off the two men. "I thought you said Jesse was straight?"

"He is. He must just be playing around," he muttered.

"We can hear you two," Jesse said lazily, like it didn't really bother him.

"Yes. Not very covert," George agreed. "I suspect that's why you keep getting caught, Rafael."

"Even worse, they decided now was the best time to role play a scene where Daniel solicited him," Jesse snorted.

"It seems your new sub is exacerbating the issue." George's eyes remained glued to his Jesse as he spoke, neither of them looking at him or Rafael.

This time, they were all interrupted by the A.D.A. as he barged into the room. A stunning African-American man in a crisp suit, he was tall and thin as a rail, with skin so dark it looked like polished slate.

"Keep your seats," he bellowed in a deep, rich voice, even though no one had made a move to get to their feet. Taking a deep breath, he seated himself in one of the chairs, with his ankle over his knee. "Now, what can I do for you that my assistant couldn't help you with?"

Jesse kept his eyes on George, looking much like a dog drooling over a piece of meat he had been forbidden to devour.

"Theo, we have more of an issue with someone neither of us likes, and I figured things would be better if they were explained to you in person," George said, taking point. "Like we talked about."

The A.D.A. steepled his fingers and leaned forward, putting his elbows on the table. "I'm listening."

"Remember that scum bag McCoy?" Distaste was evident in his words.

"How could I not? You know how small the community is. Subs talk worse than bored housewives."

Daniel blinked a few times, but no one else had any visible reaction. He was amazed to find out one of the most powerful attorneys in the city was a submissive. The thought made him grin.

"I figured as much. Well, if you remember, about nine months ago, I revoked his membership to all my clubs for ignoring safe words."

Theo was shaking his bald head from side to side as George spoke. "I heard about what he did to Paul. Poor kid. He needed stitches, and then his parents found out."

Daniel tilted his head to the side and frowned. He hadn't gotten details on why McCoy had been booted from the club. Rafael saw his look and leaned over to whisper in his ear, "Paul was eighteen and new to subbing. McCoy snatched him up. Didn't end well. His parents found out after he was sent to the hospital. They threatened to cut him off if he went back to the club. George has been trying to help, but his parents seem to be unyielding. Since he's still living at home, no one can get to him. He's been very depressed and out of contact for months. We are worried as hell."

Growling under his breath, Daniel had enough reasons to want to strangle McCoy, and this added to that list in a big way. He knew how the kid felt. If Rafael had been taken away with the new world he begun to love, he would have lost it.

"Even worse now, he is drugging people who didn't volunteer in the first place and subjecting them to his type of play."

Theo raised his brows, and George nodded at him. Daniel sighed as the A.D.A. really looked at him for the first time.

"Damn, boy."

"Yes, it is bad." George drew the man's attention away, and Daniel nodded in thanks.

"Now, I'm a smart man, and I'm guessing that Lance and Rafael tie in, am I right?" It seemed Mr. Wells was not the type to beat around the bush.

"Bingo." Jesse pointed his forefinger at the other attorney.

"How does this involve me then, boys?" He adjusted himself on the seat. "I'm a busy man with places to be."

Jesse opened his mouth, but George held up a hand. "Please, allow me." He looked him in the eyes when he spoke and offered him a smile. Jesse nodded, and George continued. "You're my friend and a respected member of the community. Rafael made poor choices after we excused Lance from the club, which he will be reprimanded for, but now we have a mess to clean up."

"I'm listening." Theo crossed his arms over his chest, and they almost didn't fit.

"Rafael agreed to be McCoy's paid Dom outside of the club's jurisdiction, and when he quit, McCoy started a witch hunt." Daniel noticed George grip the metal head of his walking stick under the table.

No one spoke for a long moment.

"Let me look at his file." Theo held out his long fingers for it.

Jesse placed the manila folder in his palm.

The A.D.A. thumbed through the papers, his eyes scanning the documents. "Why am I just hearing about this now? The first case was almost seven months ago."

George growled, his piercing blue eyes narrowing, and Daniel could see the sadist behind them. "If I had heard about it, you would have been my first call. I apologize for bringing this to you so late in the game."

Theo's eyes moved to Raf. "You'd better to listen to George. Don't think those of us who dragged you out of the hole the first time have forgotten."

Daniel turned his attention back to Rafael as the man hung his head a little. As ashamed as Rafael might be, he was glad someone had stuck up for him. Addicted to drugs and soliciting at such a young age was a bad path to be on. It made him even happier when George stood to come around and stand by Raf, despite all he'd done to fuck up their trust.

Theo turned his attention back to George and pursed his lips. "Don't you think it would serve him right to spend some of this time in jail?"

Daniel held his breath and clenched his fists as Rafael put a hand on his arm that he immediately shrugged off. "Are you kidding me?" Barely able to control himself, his tone rose by the second. "He may have lied, but he didn't do anything to warrant this." He knew he was letting his own experience with McCoy color his opinion, but he didn't care. "That cop is a monster, he needs to be handled."

"Silence!" George slammed the tip of his cane into the cheap linoleum, making the room go silent. "Rafael, get your submissive under control before I do," he commanded, his eyes boring into Daniel. The look held thinly-veiled power, making him scared of the male.

This was a side of George he had not seen in their previous brief encounters.

Raf's eyes locked with his, and his lover swallowed hard. George's eyes passed from person to person in the room, almost like he was daring them to say something.

The grip the commanding male had on his cane loosened. "I personally believe he has learned his lesson. McCoy now needs to be taught one." His tone had returned to normal.

"Okay, I'll look into it. Do you have any evidence?" the Assistant District Attorney asked, shifting and clearing his throat.

"I was hoping to shake down one of the cops who have been helping the detective, tying them together. Maybe we can scare them and get Internal Affairs involved?" Jesse offered. He was the only one in the room who seemed unfazed by George.

"It can't hurt. I'll lean on my people and see what I can do about his files. Rafael is in a pile of shit, depending on who the judge is—" Theo began to reply.

George raised a hand, cutting him off, and Theo instantly fell silent. "I know, it's an election year. You have to look good in the murder capital of the world."

Chapter Eighteen

Daniel stood, for the first time in his life, behind the glass. It was unusual to be watching things from an officer's perspective. He knew what they were about to do was not strictly legal, but he had put his neck on the line, as had Jesse, to try and help. Pinching the cuff of his shirt and pulling his sleeve down, he then did the same to the other arm. Internal Affairs had gotten involved at Theo's request, and the D.A. had also pushed back Rafael's trial, pending the results of the investigation. It was the most they could hope for, and it left his lover free for a few more weeks, which made it easier for him to breathe. He paced the small room. There was a long list of people they had to question and at the beginning was the arresting office on Raf's first pick up.

"Is he always like this?" George seemed at ease with his butt leaning on the lip of the window that looked into the interrogation room.

"He's a nervous wreck, but when the pressure is on, he's good." Jesse sat across from George, his eyes at cock level.

It made Daniel wonder if it was a coincidence. The door on the other side of the glass opened, and in walked the I.A. officer along with the cop. Rafael stiffened, and he placed his hand on his lover's thigh. "Doing okay?" he whispered.

"Have you tried any of your contacts, Jesse?" George asked, keeping his back to the interrogation room. Because it was wired for sound, and everything was being recorded, he didn't have to watch.

"I've been pounding them pretty hard. Nothing yet." Jesse grabbed the pen from behind his ear and turned to pick up his notebook.

In the process of taking off his suit jacket and laying it carefully over his forearm, George questioned, "You write on graph paper?"

Jesse's head cocked to the side before he spoke. "I like to keep my notes neat. This helps."

"Curious." George closed the space between them with two steps, then leaned over to read. Jesse let the man, which surprised Daniel because he rarely let him read over his shoulder.

The two voices in the room on the other side of the glass started speaking, and everyone fell silent, focusing on the meeting.

"I am Detective Simon Bold with the Internal Affairs Bureau." The man didn't sit, but simply placed his hands on the flimsy table, leaning over it.

"Did he really just say his name is Bold?" Jesse drew his attention away from the interview.

"He did." George stepped away from Jesse and turned to watch the proceedings.

"Do you think that's why he got stuck with Internal Affairs, because he's Bold?" Jesse did a version of jazz hands that had him wincing.

"Please don't ever do that again." George kept his eyes on the other room as he spoke.

Jesse huffed and Daniel returned his attention to the glass.

The vice cop's eyes went to the window they all stood behind and then back to McCoy. "I've done nothin'. What's this about?"

"We are here because it has been brought to our attention that a detective in this department has been using his fellow officers to stalk and intimidate a former boyfriend." Bold was reading from his notes, not looking up.

The cop kept shifting in his seat and looking up at the glass. "I didn't know he was seeing anyone, let alone a guy. I swear."

Bold cleared his throat. "Detective McCoy's sexual orientation has nothing to do with this investigation. The reason you are here is because of an accusation that the detective is having his fellow officers harass the man."

The officer kept shifting his gaze to the left and would not look Bold in the eyes. "I don't know nothin' 'bout that, man."

"There is strong evidence that suggests otherwise." The I.A. detective was a step ahead of him at every turn.

"What kinda evidence?"

Ignoring the stall tactic, Bold continued. "I need to know if Lance McCoy," the detective held up a picture of Rafael, "asked you or anyone else in your division to pick this guy up on erroneous charges." His tone was stern, like he was scolding a child.

"I think I need to talk to my union rep man. I don't wanna get involved in any of this shit." The vice officer kept looking up at the glass as if he knew Daniel was standing behind it.

Bold closed the file and crossed his arms over his broad chest. "If you think that's wise, but union reps are not going to make this go away, and I'm going to advise you to get on the right side of this immediately."

"Snitches don't last long in this business," the cop snapped.

"And men who hide things from I.A. to save friends' asses don't last long, either." Bold fixed his gray eyes on the cop. "The first guy to flip always gets the best deal. Remember that."

"I…I…I'm going to talk to the union rep and get back to you." The officer got to his feet and shoved his hands into his pockets.

"You do that. We'll be speaking again. I'm just going down the list today, but if someone else talks, and you miss your opportunity, it could be bad for you."

Daniel almost laughed. The guy was good at his job.

"Thanks man, can I get back to work now?"

Bold nodded and the young detective bolted out of the room like he'd been shot from a cannon.

The Internal Affairs detective waltzed into the viewing room like he owned it. "Sorry boys, I'm going to keep hitting 'em, but if they don't talk, there is nothing I can do about McCoy."

George held out his hand to the man. "We understand, Simon. Thank you. Please give your lovely wife my best."

The detective took his hand. "Why don't you give her your best this weekend?" A sly twinkle in the man's eyes made Daniel raise a brow.

"She is one of my favorite playthings. I would very much enjoy assisting you however you need." George sounded as if he was being genuine.

"You two going to stick around for the rest of these?" Bold directed his question at him and Jesse.

"No, I think we are going to go speak to some other people, and keep trying to build our case." His partner stuck his notes back in his messenger bag and turned to him.

"Mind if I stay?" Daniel asked, noticing the look the Internal Affairs man and his partner shared.

"Err…sorry, Dan, you can't. The detective is going to be bringing in the cops that brought you and Raf in," Jesse interceded before anyone else could talk.

"It's cool." He rubbed over the back of his neck. "It happened. Let's move past it."

"Go home. Enjoy the time with Raf," George commanded.

Rafael got to his feet. "Yes, Sir."

"Sure you don't want me to go with you?" Daniel asked once more.

The blond glanced at George, then back to him. "No, go. I got it handled."

His brow knit as he shrugged and said, "Okay."

****

George followed Jesse to his car, studying the man as he walked. Jesse was very sure of himself, and he found his witty sense of humor immensely enjoyable. The stressful task of shaking down possible witnesses would definitely be more tolerable this way.

"Thank you for coming with me." Jesse slipped into the driver's side of his Jaguar XF and started the icy car.

"This is not what I would have pictured you driving."

Jesse shrugged. "The wife won't let me get an Audi."

George joined him, declining to buckle his seatbelt. "I think it will be best if we double-team our contacts." He raised his leather, fingerless-gloved hands to warm them over the vents.

Jesse groaned as he pulled out of the parking lot and into traffic. "You people and your sexual innuendoes. Have pity on a guy who hasn't been laid in a month."

Jesse had a few friends on the force, and he had a few people who frequented the club who also were on the force. Even though none were in vice, it was worth a try.

"Surely you're exaggerating things?" George turned in the seat to look at the man driving.

"In all honesty, it's been thirty-two days." Jesse didn't return his stare.

"Take ninety-four north. It will be faster this time of day." George picked a piece of lint off - his jacket. "I don't recall the last time I've been with someone."

Keeping his eyes focused on the road, Jesse took the exit before he looked over. "What?"

"I need the dominance, the rest I reserve for those I feel strongly for. I have abstained for a long time." Used to defending his non-typical position, he sincerely wondered what the guy beside him thought of it.

"Why not indulge while looking for the 'rest?'" Jesse laid on the horn as they hit a wave of traffic, and he whipped around the car ahead of them that suddenly slammed on its breaks. "Asshole," he shouted at the guy as he passed.

"Please refrain from killing us in a fiery crash." George hid a smile. The well-dressed male's driving amused him.

Jesse flashed him a grin as he spoke. "I'm a good driver. My road rage is more likely to get us shot."

"Thank the gods we are heading to a good part of town." George clasped his hands together and raised them toward the heavens. "I will not be taking any trips to the south side with you."

"Suit yourself. I'm a kick-ass chauffeur." Jesse looked at him again as the traffic slowed to a crawl. Already staring at the beautiful man, he didn't look away.

"Why are you choosing to abstain?" He turned down the radio.

Jesse narrowed his eyes. "No choice in the matter. The wife doesn't think it's necessary anymore."

"She doesn't enjoy it?" He looked over Jesse again. The man was well-built, in very good shape for his mid-thirties, and it looked like he went to the gym daily.

"I thought she did." It was obviously a sore subject if the way he clenched his jaw was any indication.

"Foreplay?" George wondered if the other man was still attracted to his wife.

"I love foreplay." Jesse looked out the window. "I am a giver in bed, plus, at this point, I would do anything to get some action."

"Strange. Not small below the belt?" He dropped his eyes to Jesse's bulge.

He growled. "I am very well endowed, thank you."

Used to couples coming to him to spice up their relationships, he continued, "She get off?"

"Many times. And always first." Jesse smiled again. "Now, quit dodging. Why don't you sleep with people?"

George studied the man behind the wheel with an intense stare for a long moment. "Because to me, sex is more. It's giving myself over to another person. I don't take it lightly. I can't live without inflicting pain. In fact, I can't get aroused without it. Sex connects two people." He smoothed a hand down his tie. "I'm also a tad possessive, and I don't like to share," he finished, shrugging one shoulder.

Jesse's eyes stayed on him longer than they should have while he was driving. "I respect that. It's much better than being a whore."

Adjusting his seat, George smoothed the nonexistent wrinkles from his pants. "What is your acquaintance to this woman we are going to see? I do not believe I inquired before?"

Jesse cursed at the light. "She's an old girlfriend of mine. I'm not allowed to talk to her. If the wife finds out, she'll go straight to Daddy."

"I see. Well, your secret is safe with me." He got out of the car as soon as it was parked in the driveway of the suburban home.

Flanking Jesse, they climbed the stairs, and he stood back as the other man rapped on the door. "She's a good chick, and we don't have anything going on anymore, but I respect my wife's jealousy issues."

A petite woman, with dark hair styled in a pixie cut, wearing a SWAT uniform with the shirt unbuttoned and a white tank showing underneath opened the door. George raised both brows and looked between the two of them. She was stunning, and it made him wonder what Jesse's wife looked like. Going straight to Jesse, the woman wrapped him up in a big hug and pressed her face into his chest.

"Good to see you, babe," she said, lingering longer than she should have.

He pressed his face into her hair. "Thanks for doing this."

Pulling back, she stared George down like she was daring him to say something. When he didn't, she offered him her hand. "Kennedy."

He took the woman's hand as she offered it. "George and it's a pleasure."

"I just got home from a double, so sorry for the mess, Jesse." She took her hand back and led them into a fairly clean townhouse, taking a seat on the sofa. "How's Cill?"

"About the same." Jesse rolled his eyes and took a seat on the chair.

"Still a raging bitch?" She picked up her beer and took a sip. "Can I get you two anything?"

"No, thank you." George remained standing, his overcoat over his arm. His eyes were glued on Kennedy.

"Please don't, Kennedy." He let out a long breath.

"Jesse, you're too good for her. I've been telling you this for years." Setting the beer back on the coffee table, she toed off her boots.

"Since the day I started dating her." Jesse chuckled. "Thanks for agreeing to talk to us."

"You know I'd do anything for you." She smiled for the first time.

George tilted his head, watching their interaction, and felt as if there was something not finished between them. She did, however, look familiar. "Have you been to Amenti?"

She flushed and looked down at her dark blue fatigues. "A few times. A guy I dated for awhile was a submissive."

"I thought I had the pleasure of gazing on you before." He took a seat next to her.

"I saw you there, too. The suit is hard to miss." As she spoke, her eyes raked down his form.

"If you ever wish to be fully trained as a Dominant," he took a card from his breast pocket and held it out to her, "please give me a call."

"I think I'll take you up on that."

Pursing his lips, Jesse interrupted. "Can we talk about McCoy?"

"Sure, what did you want to ask about him?" When Kennedy turned her attention back to Jesse, he didn't mind.

Kennedy was probably trying to make her ex jealous. "He is causing problems for a close friend of mine."

"We have I.A. looking into it, but they are having issues getting anyone to talk," Jesse added. "Have you heard anything about him asking the other boys in Vice to arrest someone as a favor?"

"He's a real asshole, and there has been gossip about this guy he has a grudge against who apparently fucked his sister or something. He's laying it on hard. From what I've heard, he's called in all his favors."

When George looked at Jesse, the man was grinning, a very cat-that-ate-the-canary grin. "Have you ever heard him asking for these favors?"

"Yeah, I was there the night he recruited a couple of my drinking buddies." Kennedy picked up her beer again and took a long pull. "Want me to talk to I.A. for you?"

"It would mean so much to me."

"I don't mind being a snitch. That guy needs to be caned anyways." She leaned closer to him and narrowed her eyes. "But you owe me."

"I know. What's that, five now?"

"Six," she said with a smirk. "Now get the fuck out so I can sleep."

When they got back in the car, Jesse broke the silence. "I know I.A. won't be able to use Kennedy's statement to take McCoy down. It will only be considered hearsay, but maybe Bold can get someone to flip who was directly involved with it?"

George nodded. "It's possible, but what I really want to know is what do you owe Kennedy six of?" The man looked away and muttered something he couldn't make out. "What was that?"

"If the wife and I ever get divorced, I owe her six fucks. It's a little joke we have going since she knows I would never cheat." Jesse's eyes never met his as he spoke.

"You've used her five times before this?" George's brows rose.

Jesse shrugged coyly. "Don't tease a sex-starved man. Speaking of, do you think Raf and Daniel are enjoying their free time?"

"They better be. Part of me wants to throw him in jail for the headache he's caused me with all of this." His blue eyes glinted as he looked over at the other man. "Maybe I should put him in a cage for a few days as a lesson."

"Can I be involved in that?"

George's lips twisted into a smile. "Curious are you?"

LEGALLY BOUND

Chapter Nineteen

Back at home, Daniel stretched out naked on the bed. They had the rest of the day alone, and he wanted more training.

"Are you sure?" Rafael ran fingers over his body as he climbed onto the bed next to him.

"My bruises are healing. I don't want him to win by taking this away from me," he said again as if telling his lover often enough would finally make him believe it. Looking up at Rafael, he pleaded with his eyes.

Rafael dipped his head to lick over a nipple. "Okay, but if you need to, use your safe word, or if you need to slow down say—"

Daniel moaned, arching his chest up into the other man's warm mouth. "What's the word for slow in Portuguese?"

Raf bit down on his nipple before saying, "Vagaroso."

When he repeated the word, it sounded throaty as Rafael moved to the other nipple.

"I'm going to take it slow, and no pain till your marks are fully healed." Raf's hot breath blew over his body as he spoke.

Unable to concentrate on the words, he was too caught up in the feelings overwhelming him. "Anything you want, Sir."

"Anything is a dangerous word, boy." Raf dragged Daniel's briefs down, springing his cock free.

Lifting his hands to brush his fingertips over Rafael's skin, his lover snapped, grabbing both wrists and forcing them into the mattress. Although his chest tightened, he kept his eyes open, but when he looked into a set of intense jade eyes, he could breathe again.

Roughly shoving a jean-clad knee between his legs, the tattooed Dom pried them wide open, slipping himself into the middle. Their bare chests pressed together, Rafael's jeans chafed at Daniel's cock, making him moan wantonly while pushing his hips up in invitation.

"You're so beautiful, Daniel." The words were whispered into his neck as teeth lightly bit his skin.

He was glad his man's face was buried in his neck. This way Rafael wouldn't be able to see his brows knit with worry. He hadn't admitted it yet, but he felt scarred and ugly after what McCoy had done to him. Dealing with the pain and the restraints was easy to work through, but he no longer felt desirable anymore.

Rafael kissed over the hollow of his throat. "What's wrong?"

"Nothing." Daniel forced his breathing to even out.

"If you think I can't read your body, you're wrong." Strong hands pushed their way down his form. "You're stiff. You need to be honest with me."

"I'm okay. Please don't stop." Writhing under Rafael's touch, he tried to get him to continue.

Rafael moved to sit back on his haunches, licking a hot trail down Daniel's abs. "If you don't talk, I won't continue." This time Raf's wicked tongue rolled over the rim of the head of his cock. "But if you share, I will use my tongue while you do."

"Fuck…" Pushing up on his forearms, Daniel tried to watch.

"Well?" Rafael straightened back up, flipping open the button on his jeans, exposing the close-cropped patch of dark hair.

"What do you want to know?" Daniel put one arm over his face.

Rafael's fingers encircled his cock and stroked. "I want to know what made you stiffen up and pull back."

It took him a few moments to reply because as soon as his lover was done speaking, his mouth was on him again. "You called me beautiful."

His lover's eyes met his. He didn't speak, just crawled up his body and kissed him. He could taste himself on the lips that sealed over his and smell the sex on him. It made his cock press upward as he lost himself to the sensations.

"You are beautiful. You're the most perfect man I've ever laid eyes on," Rafael said when he broke the kiss.

Daniel sighed. "How can you say that? I know what I look like. I'm all messed up..." He couldn't finish the words as his voice broke, and he pressed his face into Raf's neck.

"You're wrong." Rafael's hands slid down his body. "You'll have a few scars on your ass, and that's sexy. It's proof that you stood up for me, and you took everything McCoy had to give and still told him to fuck off." Rafael kissed him again. "You're my brave sub, and that's so fucking hot."

Lying back on the bed again, a smile tugged at the corners of Daniel's mouth. "I love you."

"I love you, too."

LEGALLY BOUND

Chapter Twenty

The next morning, Rafael sat at the conference table in his lawyers' small office. He had made a resolution not to let the case fester in his mind anymore.

Jesse ran in like a lunatic. "I got it!"

"What?" Daniel asked, taking another gulp of the coffee he was pouring down his throat. "Why are you late?"

"Because I was hunting down this…" Jesse waved a piece of paper in front of the two of them.

"And?" Rafael stared at the sheet of paper at the same time his lover cocked his head to the side, attempting to read it.

"Did you get a statement notarized?" Daniel asked.

"Damn right I did. This is from a cop friend of mine. You remember Kennedy? Well, she heard your butt buddy talking smack. It's enough to get I.A. to press harder and hopefully roll a guy or two our way." Jesse moon-walked across the boardroom. "Who's the man?"

"What is he doing?"

"That, right there, is how I know he's straight. It's his 'touchdown dance.'" Daniel made air quotes as he said the words.

"It's scary," Raf whispered.

Daniel nodded emphatically.

"Don't be mocking my touchdown dance." Jesse now broke down into something that resembled air guitar with a booty shake. "I am a sexy beast."

"Why didn't you call us last night?"

"I wanted to get it all finalized and talk to I.A. before I said anything," Jesse said. "George and I went to dinner to celebrate as well."

Daniel raised a brow, fixing Jesse with a curious stare. "Will you focus, please?" He got up and ripped the paper from his partner's hands to read the statement himself.

"Well?" Raf asked. Chest tight, he wished someone would spit it out already.

"It's very good." A smile spread over his lover's lips as he leaned in to kiss him. "It looks like a 'get out of jail free card,' baby."

"Are you sure?" he spoke into Daniel's lips. "Don't get my hopes up for a maybe. After I.A., I can't take any more disappointments."

Daniel stroked a hand through his hair. "Nothing is for sure, but this should get more cops on our side."

Jesse stopped dancing and put his hands on his knees, bending at the waist as he huffed and puffed. "I.A. will be up McCoy's ass, and not in a good way, when they see this."

"I'd like to ask what you know about up the ass in a good way, but I'm scared," Rafael said with a grin.

"Doesn't everyone experiment in college?" Jesse shot back as his partner's mouth fell open. "We need to get this to George." His breath was starting to return to him, and he took a seat in one of the chairs.

"Don't you have the contact info for the I.A. guy?" Daniel asked.

"I…misplaced it." Jesse avoided both their gazes, and Rafael had a feeling the man wanted to get to know his boss a little better.

George was called, and he agreed to meet them at the Internal Affairs office.

"Whose car are we going in?" With all of them in the elevator, Daniel punched the button for the parking garage.

"Either mine or yours. I'm still working on getting Raf's out of impound." Jesse slid both hands into his pockets. "Let me drive. I like my car better anyways." Leading the way to his Jaguar, he unlocked the doors with his key fob.

Deciding it would be easier to slip into the back, so Daniel could sit in the front, he was surprised when his man shuffled in next to him. "I like being close to you, Sir."

Rafael slanted his body so that his head could rest on his sub's shoulder, allowing them to whisper to each other without drawing too much attention from Jesse. "The little ways you submit to me in public really make me hard, boy."

"If you two start necking, I'm separating you," Jesse grumbled from front seat as he looked over his shoulder and put the car in reverse.

"Can we make out just to irritate him?"

"Sure, darling." He captured Daniel's lips in a deep kiss.

"Who is the one that's been defending you?" The question came from the front seat.

"You were the one who forbid us from seeing each other in the beginning." Breathless when they broke apart, Rafael saw Jesse grip the steering wheel with both hands and mumble to himself. Shrugging it off, he returned to Daniel's lips while grabbing his ass.

Daniel shoved him off. "I'm going to be hard for the meeting if you don't stop."

Rafael winked as he brushed his fingers up the inside of Daniel's thigh. "You better not show off what's mine in there."

"Yes, Sir." When the man closed his eyes, he knew Daniel was calming himself down by the deep breaths he began to take.

"I should be taking notes. I always wondered about the mechanics of such things." Jesse took a hard left, throwing Raf into the door.

"Ass," he grunted, his shoulder hitting the handle hard.

"Seat belts." Jesse grinned in the rearview mirror.

Both men in the backseat hurried to buckle themselves in, forcing their bodies apart.

"When do you need to take notes?" Daniel looked at his partner.

"We're here." Jesse swung the car into a spot, crooked his finger at them both, and jumped out.

****

They took their seats in the police station to wait for the detective to be brought up. McCoy started ranting as soon as the door was closed. "I told you, investigate me. You have no proof! There's not a judge in this county who's going to believe a whore over an upstanding officer of the law!" He crossed his arms over his chest and refused the seat that was offered to him.

"Detective McCoy, I need you to speak out loud for the record that you refused your right to have a union rep here with you," Bold said calmly.

The prick turned toward the window. "I know I'm entitled to a union rep. I'm innocent, so I don't need one."

"Great. Now, can we all have a seat?" The Internal Affairs detective took a seat on the edge of his chair.

"I ain't sitting till I know why there are criminals here." McCoy glared at Daniel and Rafael in turn. "Plus, real cops never sit in the presence of a narc."

Bold looked at the ceiling like he was counting back from ten.

"They are here because they plan on suing the city, and you, if you don't drop this campaign against my client," Jesse snapped. "So unless you want us to file all our evidence with the court instead of just I.A., you better sit your ass down."

"Which, of course, we don't want happening." Bold recaptured the conversation. "Any lawsuit is going to get you a suspension, and my department already has good reason to look into you."

"They've got shit or I would already be suspended." McCoy took a seat, arms crossed over his chest.

Jesse dropped a copy of the notarized statement on the table in front of the bastard. "Too bad someone overheard you spouting off. We've already got two of the arresting detectives to roll over on you." He added two more notarized witness statements to the stack.

"And you're being suspended as we speak. The captain is letting them talk to you first because of the threat of a suit being filed." Bold checked his nails as if this whole process bored him.

McCoy made no outward sign of guilt except for the split second opening of his eyes a hair wider. If Daniel had not been looking at him, he would have missed it. McCoy's eyes scanned the papers on the desk. "I still don't think this makes a case against me," he said after staring at the statements for a few minutes more. He looked at Detective Bold. "I plan on fighting this."

Daniel had seen enough guilty defendants to know they had him.

"You do that, and we will continue our own investigation." Bold scrubbed a hand over his face.

McCoy scoffed. "I don't have to do shit."

The Internal Affairs detective cleared his throat. "You better make this go away. I'm already going to bring hell down on your head, and you'll be lucky to keep your job after the suspension. If the city pays out millions in damages to these people, you'll be sure to lose it. Hell, when I'm done, McCoy, a rent-a-cop job will be impossible for you to get."

"What do they want?" McCoy snarled. His question was directed at Jesse.

Jesse's whole mouth turned up into a huge, smug grin. "Everything."

****

Rafael would never admit it, but he was enjoying the look on McCoy's face more than he should.

"Out with it then." McCoy went back to his corner, glowering at everyone in the room.

"First off, you need to appear before a judge and recant your statements so that all the cases against my client get thrown out," Jesse started. "Your friends already are."

"Fuck that! That will make I.A.'s case," Lance snapped.

"Then we will see you in court." Daniel's partner got to his feet and beckoned both of them.

"Detective…" Bold started, "we are already investigating this case. You're already suspended. Don't make this harder than it has to be."

"Fine." Lance threw up his hands. "What else."

Jesse checked his notes. "A public apology and a restraining order."

"For what?" McCoy gasped.

"My partner's job is in the public eye, and getting arrested does not look good." Jesse was firm.

"He deserved it." He crossed his ankles. "But, whatever."

The door opened and all the heads present looked up. "You could cut the tension in here with a knife, gentlemen." George strolled in. "I have something that needs to be added. McCoy, if I see your face around any Dominant or sub in my area again, I guarantee I will ruin you."

The man's eyes flashed with rage. "You are a…"

"Find another town to torment. We've had quite enough." His boss' blue eyes focused in on McCoy. "I have been pushed to my limit, and at this point, I will make sure everyone, and I mean everyone, who knows you, will see a copy of your file."

"I agree."

Raf recognized the man who suddenly stuck his head in the door as Theo Wells from Amenti.

"You're not getting off quite so easily. The only way the D.A. can see to save face is to slaughter you in front of the public, so he will."

McCoy's eyes flashed red and his face contorted with anger. He started yelling, but no one was listening. The A.D.A. then grabbed two officers to escort him out of the room. McCoy got up and paused to whisper to Daniel. "I will get you and your partner back for this."

The policemen called in jerked the bastard up, and he was forced out of the room.

"Why did that all seem staged?" Rafael looked around.

"It was." George yawned and turned to Jesse. "Coffee?"

"Sure." Jesse started to gather his things.

"No, you can't leave without explaining." He narrowed his eyes at his boss.

"Do I need to punish you for speaking to me like that?" George asked.

"No, Sir."

"It was staged. As you know Rafael, Mr. Wells, the Assistant District Attorney, and I go way back. We had a meeting before he came here in which I solicited his help with McCoy. Then, after Jesse's friend, Officer Kennedy, helped us out, Theo agreed to go after Lance and everyone that helped him." George said like it was nothing.

"So is he going to give me a hard time?" Rafael's eyes widened in anger.

"You needed to be set straight, and I'm not convinced you shouldn't serve time for the drugs," George snapped.

He bit his lip. "I understand. If you think that's best."

"I don't. I need my best Dominant to keep my clients happy, but it was close." George pointed a finger at him.

"Yes, Sir."

"But Theo did get most of the charges thrown out. And the other ones he set up a plea deal for. You better keep your nose clean this time, because I had him add mandatory drug tests for the next five years into the deal."

Rafael swallowed hard.

"Now, I want coffee, then Jesse and I are going to calm down the D.A. who is going to be ranting all over for the way I just handled his case." George gestured for Jesse to come with him and left the room.

Raf stared at Daniel.

"Did you know about this?" he asked.

****

Outside, George got into the back of his car, taking the seat that backed up against the driver and letting Jesse and the Assistant District Attorney slide into the seat facing forward.

"Where are we going?" Jesse asked once he and Theo were seated.

"To calm down the D.A." The A.D.A. looked out the window.

"You haven't told him yet?"

He told his driver to go, then poured himself a glass of scotch. "No, we wanted to make sure McCoy gave himself away to I.A. It will help soothe his feelings."

"I doubt he'll be D.A. this time next year." Jesse laughed, taking the glass from George's hand to take a sip.

"Hey, you're on the clock." George grinned and took the glass back. "I'm hoping this time next year, Theo will be the D.A." He winked at him as he spoke.

Jesse narrowed his eyes. "There is something going on here I shouldn't ask about, isn't there?"

George nodded. "Just city politics. Nothing that would draw your interest."

Jesse laughed. "I'm going to pretend I know nothing about this."

"Good."

LEGALLY BOUND

Chapter Twenty-One

It was Saturday and Daniel sat back with a beer, channel surfing while Rafael finished up some work on his computer in his home office. It was good to be at Rafael's place with the weight of everything that had transpired off his mind. All the drama had finally been put behind them. Now, at last, they could begin his training and their life together. Shifting positions, he rested his head on one of the decorative pillows, his eyes getting heavy. Raf had said they would celebrate, but it was getting late, and he was tired. It took everything he had to keep himself focused on the TV.

Suddenly awakening, he knew he had nodded off when footfalls on the wooden floor startled him. Daniel opened one eye to see Rafael coming toward him. Still groggy, he rubbed his eyes and tried to sit up. A stack of papers were dropped on the large trunk his lover used as a coffee table, causing him to jump. With a questioning look, he glanced down at the quarter inch thick white heap, then back up at Raf.

"It's a contract. I want you collared."

His heart stopped in his chest. "You want me as your submissive?" He wasn't sure Rafael was saying what he thought he was.

A grin spread over Rafael's face. "I don't want anyone else to snatch you up. I'm never going to want anyone else."

"But...But..." His mind was too foggy from the sleep to process what was being said. "I thought you were only going to train me? I only expected an extended contract."

Raf sat down next to him and cupped his face with his hands. "I'm going to do that, too. But I want more."

Daniel turned his head to kiss the man's palm. "More?"

Rafael closed the distance between them, kissing him thoroughly. "A lot more."

"I like the sound of that," he admitted and stole another kiss. Scooting his body forward, he got as close as he could comfortably get to Rafael.

"Mine."

"Yours."

Epilogue

"Have things returned to normal?" George kicked back in the oversized chair in his formal living room. Elliot brought in the coffee they had ordered on a tray.

Jesse raised a brow as he took the mug. "I thought Daniel or Rafael mentioned your slaves serve naked?"

George smiled slightly. "I didn't want to make you uncomfortable." He picked up his tiny mug of straight espresso and brought it to his lips. Out of all his slaves, Elliot made the best coffee.

"Maybe I came hoping for the full experience."

George was shocked by the openness his new friend expressed toward his world. It gave him hope that he wasn't reading into the subtle flirting that had been going on while they worked the case.

"You can stay for dinner and get the full experience." George looked over the rim of his mug at him.

Jesse checked his watch and dragged his teeth over his lip. George thought he seemed hesitant.

"Sure, why not."

"Have somewhere else you need to be?" He set his mug on the arm of the stiff-backed chair he sat on.

"Yes, but I don't want to go. I'll make an excuse. I do it all the time." Jesse's eyes twinkled, and he laughed.

"That poor wife of yours." George shook his head, but he enjoyed Jesse's company too much to encourage the man to be a good husband.

"If you met her, you'd be singing a different tune." Jesse set his coffee down on the table and dug in his pocket for his phone. He dialed, then held a finger to his lips. "Hey, Cill. Daniel and I got this big case thrust on us, and it goes to trial tomorrow. I can't bail on him. We have so much research to do. I'm going to miss the benefit tonight." He paused.

George could hear a yappy voice on the other end.

"I know, I know. Tell your father I'm sorry." Making eye contact with him, Jesse rolled his eyes.

He chuckled softly.

"I'll make it up to you, I promise." Jesse hung up the phone.

"Tell me, why don't you divorce her if you're so unhappy?" George asked after the man tossed his phone down on the coffee table.

Jesse sighed and picked up his drink. "Because her father is the circuit court judge over our district. Any case I would need to appeal the ruling on, for my clients, goes to the Appeals Court which is his boy's club. If I piss off his daughter, he's going to blackball me."

He suppressed a growl, hating when people were forced to stay in relationships they were unhappy with. "It would be hard to be an attorney in this city if you left her."

Jesse nodded, sadly. "So, unless I plan on moving out of state or picking a new profession, I'm screwed up the ass."

"Without lube."

"What's for dinner?" the blond asked, seeming to push away the bad topic.

"I'll have to ask Elliot what he had in mind. I think I have a few steaks he can toss on the flat iron for us." George checked his watch. "He should be prepping things now. Want me to see what he's getting ready?"

"No, don't call him away from his work. I can't believe they cook for you." Jesse chuckled, and George loved to see the smile on his lips.

"It's part of the application process." He grinned coyly.

"Was Rafael ever one of your slaves?"

George laughed for a solid minute before he answered. "No, there is not a submissive bone in Rafael's body. He does it from time to time, and did to learn, but he doesn't enjoy it like, say, your friend Daniel does."

"Your world is fascinating." Jesse took another sip of his drink.

"There is no need to pacify me. I know it's not for everyone." George fixed a hard stare at the man.

He didn't blink. "You should know me better than that by now. I don't bullshit about that. I'm genuinely curious."

"Can I ask you something personal? Feel free not to answer if it makes you uncomfortable."

Jesse nodded.

"Are you even remotely bisexual?" He knew it wasn't his business, and this was a married man he was talking to so it shouldn't matter, but it did. Maybe, if the attractive blond told him that he had no interest in men at all, it would put the feelings inside him to bed.

Jesse looked over at him and opened his mouth just as his phone began to ring. He pulled it out of his pocket. "Hold on, it might be Dan." He checked the caller ID and frowned. "It's Cill. Hello?"

"Get your ass home. Daniel told me you weren't with him, which means you're cheating. Are you with Kennedy?"

His wife was yelling so loud, George could hear her from across the room. Anger stirred within him. His rational side told him that Jesse had lied to her, and he deserved the accusation. But the primal part of himself that had feelings for the kind, funny man argued that there were reasons to lie to her. A mess of conflicting emotions, he hated feeling this way.

"I'm sorry. I am having an impromptu dinner with a friend," Jesse muttered.

"You can call her a friend if you want, but it's not okay. We have a benefit to go to that my father is hosting." The woman's voice shrieked out of the phone.

"It's not a girl…" He pinched the bridge of his nose. "Plus, you know I hate going to those things."

"Says the man who already lied to me. I have no reason to believe anything you say is true."

George began to get angrier with every word the woman said.

"I'm not fucking cheating! I'm getting out of a boring dinner and doing something I like, which you'd never understand."

"You can do stuff you want to do on your own time," she barked.

"Which you give me none of!" Jesse sounded defeated.

"You're married! Your time is mine."

Jesse covered his face with one hand. George got up and crossed the room to take a seat on the arm of the chair the man sat in. He usually had himself so poised and under control. That all went away when Jesse was near. He stroked his long fingers down the attractive male's broad back.

He leaned in to whisper in the man's free ear, "Want me to leave?"

He shook his head. "I'm on my way home." Flipping his phone shut, he side armed it like a fast ball at the wall. It hit and exploded into a thousand pieces. With his elbows on his knees, Jesse put his face in his hands.

"You can't live like this," George said softly when the defeated male didn't make a move to go.

"What choice do I have?" Jesse looked up at him with red eyes.

His chest clenched. The reason he liked Jesse so much was because of his light spirit and sense of humor. It hurt to see this side of him. He had a very protective nature, and George hated feeling powerless. His hand clenched into a fist. Being helpless brought up so many dark memories he'd rather not remember. "You have a choice."

Jesse shook his head. "I don't. I love my job too much to give it up. It's the only good thing I have." Scrubbing a hand over his face, the crushed man got up.

George got to his feet as well and retrieved his coat. "Jesse, listen to me."

The blond looked at him as he pulled on his coat.

"You've done nothing wrong, save for the lying. Don't take this from her. You do owe her an apology for lying. That is unacceptable, but as I think I saw, you have good reason to do it. She can't make your life miserable if you don't want to go to all her charity functions with her." Pausing momentarily, he was starting to put the pieces together in his mind. He realized the man had a very submissive personality, and the thought went straight to his cock. He cleared his throat and went on. "Do not allow her to accuse you of cheating. You're too honorable, from what Rafael tells me."

Jesse nodded. "I get what you're saying, but what can I do? I have no leverage."

"Yes, you do."

"What? Threaten divorce? She'll go crying to daddy." He zipped his jacket and turned for the door. "Rain check on dinner, although I doubt I'll be allowed out for a long time."

George walked out the door with him and they both fell silent in the elevator.

"Are you happy?" George asked as they hit the ground floor.

Jesse glanced at his feet and blew out a breath before he met George's blue eyes. "As happy as I can expect."

"If you need a place to come cool down, come here." They stopped at Jesse's car once they'd reached the driveway. Jesse lingered near him, and George held his tongue. He wanted to say so much more, but it wasn't his life to lead.

"I will. Thanks." He slid into his Jag without a backward glance.

Two hours later as George was finishing dinner in his playroom, the bell rang. He looked up. "Elliot go answer the door." He wasn't expecting anyone.

"Yes, King." The slave got off the floor and swayed his naked hips as he left the room.

Putting another bite of tender steak into his mouth, he thought that it was too bad Jesse had missed dinner. It had turned out so well.

"Shit," he muttered as he got to his feet. Jesse had smashed his phone before he left. He set his plate aside and trudged toward the front door.

As he came around the corner, he saw Elliot had already opened the door. The blond man he'd just been thinking about stood with a garment bag over his shoulder, staring wide-eyed and red-cheeked at the young slave. George burst out laughing, and Jesse scowled at him.

"Serves you right for smashing your phone and asking for naked dinner service."

"It caught me off guard. Who answers the door naked?" Jesse stammered.

"I'm the King of the underground. Would you expect less?" George asked.

"Good point." Jesse's shoulders were rounded, and he looked defeated.

"Are you hungry? Can I get you a plate?" George took the garment bag from him and handed it to Elliot. "Take this to the guest room."

Elliot bowed and sauntered off. The blond stared at the young man's ass, and George had to stifle a laugh.

"No, I grabbed shit fast food on the way home. I could use a drink, though." Handing over his coat, George took it and hung it in the closet.

George led them into the formal living room where the fire was already going. He liked to retire into this room after the slaves were caged for the night to read, so he always had the boys build up a big fire. He went right to the bar and retrieved two crystal tumblers and a bottle of Johnny Walker Blue. After putting two cubes of ice in each glass, he then poured two fingers into them. As he handed Jesse one, the man whistled.

"Nice." Taking the glass, Jesse sipped it. "But you should get out something cheaper. I plan on drinking my feelings away tonight."

"Don't worry about it. I can afford it." George carried the bottle over to the sofa and set it between them on the coffee table.

He kept Jesse's drink refilled as they sat and talked. Listening as the man rambled on drunkenly, he smiled as he examined everything filtering through his head. After feeling nothing for anyone for so long, the feelings he had for Jesse came out of nowhere. It wasn't just the blond's looks. He was an attractive man, but George was surrounded by attractive men day in and day out. He always took on the best looking young men as slaves.

Sex meant more to him. It always had, with his strict upbringing. There hadn't been anyone in a very long time. If he had to pinpoint it, he thought it was Jesse's wit and 'no fucks given' attitude that caught his attention. Most in his circle were scared of him, but Jesse didn't seem to be frightened at all. And that evening when he realized Jesse was submissive by nature, it had sealed the deal for him.

As he watched Jesse in the glow of the firelight, George decided that he would find a way to get the male out of his marriage. He was in love with him, and even if Jesse never loved him back, he wanted the man happy. Married to the harpy he'd heard over the phone, Jesse was definitely not happy.

"Thanks again for letting me stay." Jesse commented, leaning close as he said it.

Surprised by the movement, he welcomed it, even if it was due to the influence of the alcohol. "It is my pleasure, for as long as you need."

The End

www.jrgraybooks.com

Evernight Publishing

www.evernightpublishing.com